PRAISE FOR LILJA SIGURDARDOTTIR

Shortlisted for the GLASS KEY AWARD for BEST NORDIC CRIME NOVEL

'A masterful tale of political intrigue, deception, betrayal ... and death. Who knew politics in such a cold and pleasant land like Iceland could be so dark? Gripping' Michael Ridpath

'This is a fine piece of storytelling that touches on a number of important issues, from the personal to the social and global, while never getting bogged down. A very good read' Craig Sisterson

'What a tangled web of intrigue this was! Lilja has a whiplash writing style, and merges her culture and country with the plot with ease. Hang on tight!' The Book Trail

'The cutthroat world of politics is laid bare in a fast-paced novel that doesn't hesitate to show the craven nature of political wheeling and dealing, where power is everything and women in particular are expendable' Live and Deadly

'With great characters, an intriguing story and an injustice from the past that seemed destined to be corrected, the book kept me completely enthralled from start to finish. Whether you love the author's work or are looking for your first taste of Icelandic fiction, this book is definitely recommended' Jen Med's Book Reviews

'Interesting social and governmental politics ... a dramatic twist too ... and betrayal on various levels' Goodreads

'Tough, uncompromising and unsettling' Val McDermid

'An emotional suspense rollercoaster on a par with *The Firm*, as desperate, resourceful, profoundly lovable characters scheme against impossible odds' Alexandra Sokoloff

'A smart, ambitious and hugely satisfying th~·''
originality and written with all the
Lilja is destined for Scandi supersta

'Clear your diary. As soon as you begin reading *Snare*, you won't be able to stop until the final page' Michael Wood

'Zips along, with tension building and building ... thoroughly recommend' James Oswald

'Crisp, assured and nail-bitingly tense ... an exceptional read, cementing Lilja's place as one of Iceland's most outstanding crime writers' Yrsa Sigurðardóttir

'Tackling topical issues, the book will tell you a great deal about why the world's in the state it is, while never neglecting its duty to entertain' *S Magazine*

'Written in a clean, understated style, the author letting the reader put together the emotional beats and plot developments. Smart writing with a strongly beating heart' *Big Issue*

'Tense, edgy and delivering more than a few unexpected twists and turns' *The Times* Crime Club Star Pick

'A tense thriller with a highly unusual plot and interesting characters' *The Times*

'The intricate plot is breathtakingly original, with many twists and turns you never see coming. Thriller of the year'
New York Journal of Books

'This rattlingly good read could only be improved if this were the first in a trilogy. And it is!' Strong Words

'Terrific and original stuff, with some keen-sighted and depressing reflections on Iceland's place in the world' European Literature Network

'A sparkling firework of a novel, tightly plotted, fast paced, and crackling with tension, surprises and vibrancy' Crime Review

'A taut, gritty, thoroughly absorbing journey into Reykjavík's underworld' Booklist

ABOUT THE AUTHOR

Icelandic crime-writer Lilja Sigurðardóttir was born in the town of Akranes in 1972 and raised in Mexico, Sweden, Spain and Iceland. An award-winning playwright, Lilja has written seven crime novels, with *Snare*, the first in the Reykjavík Noir series, hitting bestseller lists worldwide. *Trap* was published in 2018, and was a *Guardian* Book of the Year, and *Cage*, winner of Icelandic Crime Novel of the Year, followed in 2019. The film rights for the series have been bought by Palomar Pictures in California. In 2020 *Betrayal* was shortlisted for the Glass Key Award for best Nordic crime novel. Lilja lives in Reykjavík with her partner. Follow Lilja:

Twitter: *@lilja1972*
Instagram: *www.instagram.com/sigurdardottirlilja/*
Facebook: *www.facebook.com/sigurdardottir.lilja*
Website: *www.liljawriter.com*

ABOUT THE TRANSLATOR

Quentin Bates escaped English suburbia as a teenager, jumping at the chance of a gap year working in Iceland. For a variety of reasons, the gap year stretched to a gap decade, during which time he went native in the north of Iceland, acquiring a new language, a new profession as a seaman, and a family, before they decamped en masse to England. He worked as a truck driver, teacher, net-maker and trawlerman at various times before falling into journalism, largely by accident. He is the author of a series of crime novels set in present-day Iceland (*Frozen Out, Cold Steal, Chilled to the Bone, Winterlude, Cold Comfort, Thin Ice* and *Cold Breath*) which have been published worldwide. He has translated Ragnar Jónasson's Dark Iceland series for Orenda Books. Visit him on Twitter *@graskeggur* or on his website: *graskeggur.com*

Betrayal

Lilja Sigurðardóttir

Translated by Quentin Bates

**ORENDA
BOOKS**

Orenda Books
16 Carson Road
West Dulwich
London SE21 8HU
www.orendabooks.co.uk

First published in Icelandic as *Svik* by Forlagið in 2018
First published in English by Orenda Books in 2020
Copyright © Lilja Sigurðardóttir, 2018
English translation copyright © Quentin Bates, 2020

A catalogue record for this book is available from the British Library.
ISBN 978-1-913193-40-9
eISBN 978-1-913193-41-6

The publication of this translation has been made possible
through the financial support of

 ICELANDIC LITERATURE CENTER

Typeset in Garamond by typesetter.org.uk

Printed and bound by CPI Group (UK) Ltd, Croydon CR0 4YY

*For sales and distribution, please contact info@orendabooks.co.uk or visit
www.orendabooks.co.uk.*

PRONUNCIATION GUIDE

Icelandic has a couple of letters that don't exist in other European languages and which are not always easy to replicate. The letter ð is generally replaced with a d in English, but we have decided to use the Icelandic letter to remain closer to the original names. Its sound is closest to the hard th in English, as found in *thus* and *bathe*.

The letter r is generally rolled hard with the tongue against the roof of the mouth.

In pronouncing Icelandic personal and place names, the emphasis is placed on the first syllable.

Úrsúla – Oors-oola

Óðinn – Oe-thinn

Rúnar – Roo-nar

Gunnar – Gunn-nar

Kátur – Kow-tuur

Eva – Ey-va

Gréta – Grye-ta

Freyja – Frey-ya

Herdís – Her-dees

Ingimar Magnússon – Ingi-mar Mag-noos-son

Thorbjörn – Thor-byortn

Katrín Eva – Kat-reen Ey-va

Jónatan – Yo-natan

Pétur – Pye-tuur

Guðmundur – Guth-mund-uur

With the benefit of hindsight, it was clear that Úrsúla's promise, made on her very first day in office, was her downfall. At the same time it cracked open the armour that had encased her heart for far too long.

The night after accepting the keys in front of the press, she had dreamed terrible things. Her dreams were of fevered bodies, open sores, despair in the eyes of those bringing sick relatives to the camps, and then explosion after explosion, as if her former roles in Liberia and Syria had merged into one seamless nightmare.

The next morning she was still dazed and exhilarated after the previous evening's reception at the ministry, and the cards bearing messages of goodwill and the flowers that had been presented to her were still piled high in her office. But the dream had left her feeling raw, so she was ill-prepared for the heartfelt rage of the woman who sat opposite her, begging her to help bring to justice the police officer who had raped her fifteen-year-old daughter back home in Selfoss.

The girl had hardly spoken a word since, didn't want to leave the house. She had lost herself completely, the woman said as the tears flowed down her face. She wiped them away, whimpering with frustrated fury, and asked where the case had got to. She had asked the police, the state prosecutor's office and her lawyer, but nobody seemed to know anything. So Úrsúla made a promise. She promised to make it her business to find out. She took the woman's hand, who clasped it in her own, looked into Úrsúla's eyes and thanked God that the minister of the interior was a woman.

Friday

1

He was still full after the hot porridge at the Community Aid canteen, and the snow was deep, reaching halfway up his calves, so he ambled rather than walked. The snow was still coming down hard, so he decided to shorten his usual walk today. He wouldn't go all the way down to Kvos as coming back again would be heavy going.

He started at Hlemmur, always at Hlemmur. There was a kind lady there at the bakery who always pushed a pastry his way. He'd usually keep it in his pocket so he had something for later on, when he'd feel the need of it. Sometimes he was hungry and would eat it the same day, and at other times he'd save it and have it a day or two later. Danish pastries kept well. Normally they were just as good after a couple of days. He left this time with both a twisted doughnut and some kind of fancy, nutty pastry in his pocket. It was a comfort to know that he had something to fall back on, in case he couldn't make it to the Community Aid canteen but was still hungry, just like that summer when he had broken his leg. He had been properly in the shit then, living on his own in the bushes up at Öskjuhlíð, unable to walk and find himself anything to eat. It would have been great to have had something in his pocket then.

The next place was the kiosk. Sometimes he'd get coffee there, and sometimes small change, depending on who was behind the counter.

'Good day, and may it bring you joy,' he said as he pushed open the door. The cheerful response to his greeting told him that today there would be a handful of coins, so he may well be going all the way to Kvos, where he could visit the booze shop and buy beer.

'G'day, old fella,' said the pleasant young man who was there a couple of days a week. 'What do gentlemen of the road have to say today?'

'It's snowing,' he replied.

'Proper snow,' the lad added.

'A proper winter,' he said, and winked roguishly. 'Any chance you could slip me a few coins, my friend?'

There was a *ker-ching* as the boy opened the till and scooped a palmful of hundred-krónur coins from the drawer.

'There you go, old fella,' he said. 'Go and get yourself a bite to eat.'

'Yep, I sure will,' he lied. 'A burger.' He could see from the young man's expression that he didn't believe him; not that it mattered. 'What's your name again, my friend?'

'My name's Steinn,' the boy laughed. 'As I tell you every time you come in here.'

'Names don't matter,' he mumbled on his way out. 'Just eyes. The eyes tell you everything you need to know about someone.'

This Steinn had friendly eyes, with a spark of mischief behind them; the eyes of a man rebellious enough to steal from the shop's cash register. But at the same time, friendly and charitable enough to give an old drunk small change. He strolled along Laugavegur, the snow settling on his head as he walked, forming a crown that melted until his thin hair was soaked and he began to shiver with the chill of it.

At the corner of Snorrabraut he crossed the street and went into one of the tourist shops; the thin, miserable man who worked there immediately threw him out. He tried to mutter that he only wanted to warm himself up a little, but that made no difference. The skinny guy was adamant that this wasn't the place for him, and glared at him with his blank eyes, threatening to call the police. That would be something, being pulled by the law in a shop in the middle of the day, as sober as a judge and without even losing his temper. That would be a waste of a ride in a car and an overnight stay, so he left and walked briskly down to Kjörgarður – the heating under the pavement along this part of the street was easily enough to melt the falling snow – and before he knew it he was indoors with a mug in his hands. He hadn't even needed to spend any of his stash of coins; the Asian lady who sold noodles there just handed him a mug and told him to sit down. She was loud and he didn't understand a word of what she said, but she had kind eyes. He could see in them that she missed her parents, in a distant land far away, so she was happy to do a favour for an old guy with no home to go to.

He sipped his coffee, which gave him a glow of warmth inside, and leafed through the newspaper on the table in front of him. On the first spread, there she was, Úrsúla Aradóttir, with the news that she had become a minister. Somehow it didn't seem quite right that she could be as grown up as she appeared in the picture, but there was no doubt that it was her. Once again he had the odd feeling he sometimes got – that the lives of other people moved ahead along straight lines while his own time went in circles. He took out his notebook and was about to write down these thoughts when his eyes strayed to the man at Úrsúla's side in the photograph. They both smiled as they looked at the camera. But while her eyes were lively and cheerful, as they always had been, his were as cold as ice. These were the coldest eyes in the whole world. He stared at the picture and failed to understand how Úrsúla, now a minister, and whatever else she might be, could stand there and shake the hand of this man, the devil incarnate.

2

They had just left the marriage guidance counsellor's office that Monday when Úrsúla's phone had rung and the prime minister gave her two hours to make up her mind about taking on the role of interior minister for a year, a post combining the Ministries of Justice and Transport. Her eyes were still red with tears after yelling at Nonni in front of the counsellor, and she was sure her voice betrayed her upset as she told the PM that she would call back before the deadline. But she didn't really need two hours, and she didn't need to discuss it with Nonni before reaching her decision. She knew that she would make the call in good time and that she would take the job.

Nonni became weirdly excited and dropped his voice almost to a whisper, as if he was now party to some kind of state secret. His hand cupped Úrsúla's elbow, steering her towards a coffee house on Skeifan, where he took her to a corner table by the window.

'So just what did the PM say?' he whispered, taking a seat opposite her.

'Well, that it's for one year, because the current minister has to step down for health reasons.'

'Wow.'

'It's a bit awkward,' Úrsúla said. 'Appointing a minister from outside parliament and from neither of the two parties means they haven't been able to agree on which of them should get the ministry.'

'It's a smart move to take a third option,' Nonni said, falling silent as the waitress appeared.

Úrsúla had ordered a coffee, but Nonni had asked for a beer, which was unusual for him in the middle of the day. He had to be more upset than he appeared.

'You'll do it,' he said. 'Maybe it's exactly what you need; what you need to be able to put down roots here again. Maybe this is something that's exciting enough for you.'

Úrsúla nodded and they sat in silence for a while. Nonni took a long swallow of beer, which emptied half his glass.

He was probably right. She hadn't been happy since they had

come home; she felt out of touch – in a daze while life passed her by. This wasn't the way she had foreseen things unfolding. She had expected to spend her whole life in charity work, somewhere sandy and hot, where the burning heat on her body would show her that she was making a difference.

'What about the children?' Úrsúla asked, although she didn't expect anything would change for them, whether she became a minister or not. Nonni had looked after them mostly and would continue to do so.

'I'm only teaching part-time and I can arrange my hours so I can do more preparation at home, so this isn't a bad time.'

'I should be able to help people out there,' Úrsúla said and looked absently out of the window. It was snowing again, and a fresh layer of white was covering the grey that already lay on the ground. That was what she desperately wanted: to make a difference. To turn chaos into order, to make a difference to someone's life, somewhere. Nonni reached across the table and laid a hand on hers.

'It'll be good for us as well,' he said quietly, looking into her eyes. The argument in the counsellor's office just now was already forgotten and the sparkle of humour had returned to his gaze. 'A happy Úrsúla means happy kids and a happy Nonni.'

'You're sure about that?' she asked. She wanted to hear his words of encouragement said out loud, to hear him speak his mind, to voice his decision to support her. She wanted to be re-assured that things wouldn't go back to the way they had been, with him criticising her decision to take on a demanding role, feeling sorry for himself for getting too little of her attention, turning his back on her.

'Quite sure,' he said. 'It's no coincidence that an opportunity like this should pop up right now. This is supposed to happen. I'm a hundred per cent behind you, my love.'

Úrsúla squeezed his hand in return. It was a relief to hear his unequivocal support, although it didn't affect her decision. She had already made up her mind. She had done that before the conversation with the PM had ended. This was what she had been waiting for, something that sparked a desire inside her. This would be something that would wrench her out of the daze she had been in since she had left Liberia, on her way to the refugee camps in Syria.

3

The meeting with Óðinn, the permanent secretary, was a relief after the stiff formality of that morning's State Council session. She had struggled to sit still while one minister after another had got to his feet to list his achievements in parliament to the president, who had been surprisingly successful in feigning a real interest in these long lists. Úrsúla had been badly nicotine starved and puffed the smoke of two cigarettes out of the car window as she hurtled back to the ministry to meet Óðinn.

He was impeccably turned out, a waistcoat buttoned under his jacket and his tie neatly knotted at his throat. As soon as the doors closed behind them, he shrugged off the jacket and hung it on the back of a chair; Úrsúla allowed herself to relax too, kicking off her heels beneath the table and drawing her feet under her chair. Óðinn started by passing her a little bottle of hand sanitiser.

'Make sure you use it all the time,' he said. 'Over the next month you'll have to shake more hands than you've shaken in your whole life so far, and the flu season's almost on us.'

She laughed, squirted it into one palm and handed it back to him. Then they sat each side of the conference table and kneaded the gel into their hands. The sweet menthol aroma from her palms reminded Úrsúla of how safe she was now. There was no infection here that an ordinary sanitiser couldn't cope with. In Liberia they had washed their hands in bleach.

He took care to work the gel in between his fingers. His hands were large, as was his whole frame. He had to be at least one metre ninety, and with a barrel of a chest, although he was slim with it, which indicated either manual labour in the past, or that he had been a sportsman. Once he had finished rubbing the sanitiser into his hands, he waved them a few times to dry them off. Úrsúla wanted to laugh – he resembled a giant, clumsy bird – but she held back.

'Being ill isn't an option, unless you are in hospital with a burst appendix,' he said.

She nodded. He was making such a point of this, she wondered if he had bad experiences with ministers who were susceptible to infections. Rúnar, her predecessor, had stood down from the post for health reasons, but she assumed that was a heart problem or something equally serious.

'Do you have high stomach-acid levels?' Óðinn asked, his expression so serious that she couldn't stop herself laughing.

'No. Why do you ask?'

'That's good. In that case I advise you to eat plenty of chilli with every meal to keep stomach infections at bay. A minister with bad guts is nothing but trouble.'

'Got you,' she agreed. 'I'll do everything I can to stay healthy. But isn't it time we took a look at the list?'

She pointed to a page of closely typed text on the table between them, listing all the matters they needed to attend to. Óðinn nodded, sat up straight in his chair and started at the top of the list: protocols for a non-governmental minister's relations with parliament.

She nodded her head and listened absently, examining his face. He had to be close to sixty, with grey in his hair and a network of fine lines around his eyes that suggested that he frequently smiled. His current formal manner had to be because bringing a new minister up to speed with the job was a serious matter.

'Then there are your assistants and their areas of work. Sometimes there's a political adviser and a personal assistant, but if they're the same person then it makes financial planning easier. Do you have any names in mind?'

'I haven't had time to think it over properly, but there are people from both parties who have made suggestions. I think one person will be enough,' she said.

It was quite true. There had hardly been time to draw breath since the prime minister's call on Monday giving her a two-hour deadline to decide whether or not to take the job.

'Then there's the car and the driver...'

'No, thanks,' she said, and Óðinn looked up in astonishment. 'What do you mean?'

'I can drive myself,' she said. She had strong opinions about ministerial cars. Of course there was a certain convenience about such an arrangement, and it saved time. But there was something a little too grand about being driven in a smart limousine among normal Icelanders who were paying for it. It was simply not her style.

Óðinn put the list aside and leaned back in his chair with a thoughtful look on his face.

'You realise that the only thing people miss once they're no longer a minister is the driver? You can deal with emails on the way to and from work, you can send him to run errands for you, and he's also responsible for your security. He'll shovel snow off the steps, change lightbulbs, all that stuff.'

'I'm married, you know,' she said, and at last Óðinn cracked a smile.

'We can discuss this later,' he said, and although she had not meant to leave it open to further discussion, she nodded her agreement so they could continue with the list. She was desperate for a cigarette and wanted to get the meeting over with.

All the same, a full hour had passed and Úrsúla was edgy from nicotine withdrawal by the time Óðinn crossed off the final item on the list and got to his feet. She felt him loom over her as he offered his hand.

'Welcome to the job,' he said. 'I'm here for you all the time, for anything, and I speak for the whole ministry when I say that we will do everything we can to ensure your tenure here is successful.'

She stood up and gripped his warm hand.

'Thank you very much,' she said. She had a feeling inside that they would work well together. He smiled and she saw the lines around his eyes deepen. For a second he reminded her of her father; not as he had been towards the end, but as she remembered him when she had been small and they had played together.

'One more thing,' she called after him as he was about to leave the conference room. 'There was a woman who called here this morning with a request for the ministry to look into a case. It's a rape accusation that seems to have been held up in the system. My secretary booked it as a formal request. Would you look into it and give me some advice on how to proceed?'

'Of course,' he said from the doorway. 'I'll check on it.'

Úrsúla accompanied him along the corridor towards her office, and as she was fumbling for her access card to open the minister's corridor, she noticed a very young dark-skinned woman pushing a cleaning trolley.

'*Hæ*,' Úrsúla said, putting out a hand. 'I'm the new minister. I don't suppose you can tell me where someone could sneak out for a quiet smoke?'

4

There had been a strange crackle of tension in the air the whole of the previous day, and Stella was still feeling its effects. Everyone went about their work more quietly than usual, and there had been more couriers and journalists about the place than usual.

The receptionist downstairs had asked Stella to mop the lobby especially thoroughly because of the snow that was brought in on coats and the soles of shoes, and melted into muddy pools on the floor. She did her best, making the occasional quick sortie down-stairs with a mop to wipe up the worst of the water. She didn't want to be caught out not doing as she had been asked, as that would un-doubtedly end up with the permanent secretary being called, as he seemed to be the top dog here. Stella found him frightening. She had encountered him once, when he had said hello, welcoming her to the ministry when she had started a few months ago. He had smiled amiably, but Stella had wanted to turn on her heel and run as fast as she could, as the touch of his hot hand gave her a feeling of pure, clear misery. This had taken her by surprise, as he seemed to be a man to whom life had been generous – tall, handsome with a senior job – so the dark sadness she sensed from him didn't fit. Or maybe this sensitivity of hers was playing tricks on her. Her mother had always said that the gift she had inherited from her grand-mother had come with a generous portion of imagination.

'It's always like this when there's a new minister,' the reception-ist said. 'Everyone's stressed and worried, and then it turns out that the new minister is always lovely. I saw her yesterday when she came to collect the key and she seemed relaxed and cheerful.'

Stella shrugged. She had hardly had anything to do with the former minister; she'd only ever seen him hurrying along the cor-ridors with a phone clamped to his ear. He had never spoken to her, and neither would the new minister. The receptionist was dif-ferent, as everyone said hello when they came in, but cleaners were as good as invisible.

'Well, she's here,' she heard people say as she passed by, empty-ing the bins. 'Have you seen her yet?'

The new minister was in the building and had started work, but nobody seemed to have caught sight of her. She would pro-bably not address the ministry staff until tomorrow, but people were sure they would recognise her, as last night's news covered the change of minister and there had been a short clip in which she was holding the key.

Some people seemed to know her from her background in

student politics, and someone mentioned that she had worked with refugees in foreign countries, organising aid in disaster areas, or something like that. But Stella neither watched the news nor read newspapers, so she knew nothing about this woman; she'd never even heard her name before.

It wasn't a bad place to work, but Stella realised that she wouldn't be here for long. Her job was part of a temporary initiative for young people who had 'come off the rails', and social security paid half of their wages. Mopping the corridors of the city's smartest buildings was supposed to be a way of getting people's lives back on track. The ministry's staff had accepted her; they were clearly accustomed to having people in the building doing things nobody quite understood. After the first week she seemed to blend into the daily routine and nobody paid her any attention anymore. She liked that. She also liked the fact that as long as she kept the lobby floor dry and emptied the bins on the third and fourth floors, nobody was aware that she was there, as long as she punched herself in and out morning and afternoon. At the end of the day a bunch of people appeared from some big cleaning contractor and cleaned the whole ministry, so what Stella did or didn't do made little difference. It was the easiest job she had ever had, and she had plenty to compare it against: in her nineteen years she had been through any number of jobs.

Her phone buzzed and she put the mop aside.

Party at our place tonight! read the message from Anna.

She didn't check to see which Anna it was from. It didn't matter. They were a couple, both called Anna. They were known as the Annas and threw regular lavish parties to which they invited only 'cute, exciting' girls. Stella knew that the colour of her skin alone put her in the right category; it was as if her golden-brown colouring worked like a magnet for lots of women. Normally she was quite happy to benefit from one of the few advantages of being one of the tiny minority of brown Icelanders. But after the last party the two Annas had thrown it had taken her a week to recover, and she had promised herself never to go back. But now it was Friday, and she was skint, with nothing to do but stay in her room and watch Netflix on the computer, so it didn't seem such a bad idea. What else were weekends for if not having a little fun?

I'm busy and will be late, if I can get there at all, she wrote back. It didn't do any harm to pretend that she actually had a social life; it added to her mystery. And anyway, she preferred to turn up late, when things were already in full swing and everyone had knocked back a few drinks. That way she wouldn't have to hold any conversations. She always felt that she was more in control that way, although she knew deep down that once she had put away some of what was on offer she was as good as out of control. That was even without the Annas passing around the smarties.

She ran her fingers over the new Helm of Awe tattooed on her forearm, hoping it would protect her from drinking herself into a stupor and going home with someone she really didn't want; such as the news reporter the Annas always invited and who was clearly in the 'exciting' class – courtesy of her TV fame, as she certainly wasn't cute. Stella harboured a suspicion that the Annas were trying to pair her up with this woman, but her enthusiasm for this was precisely zero. Pondering this, she pushed the cleaning trolley ahead of her along the corridor and practically ran into a woman. The woman took hold of the trolley and stopped it with a laugh.

She extended a hand.

'I'm the new minister,' the woman said, and dropped her voice to a whisper. 'I don't suppose you can tell me where someone could sneak out for a quiet smoke?'

The speech that Permanent Secretary Óðinn had made earlier that day, emphasising that staff, whatever their political persuasion, were here to assist the minister in shouldering a great responsibility, came to Stella's mind. So she took the minister to the fourth floor balcony, where she herself went to smoke. The minister could hardly be expected to shoulder all that responsibility without an occasional puff.

5

Gunnar put everything he had into that last lift. His shoulders screamed in pain and he was sure he could feel the tendons in his forearms tear under the strain. He was up to 150 kilos on the bench and while the fourth lift had been tough, the fifth was a bastard. He wasn't concerned about the weights dropping onto him, though, and he couldn't be bothered to ask a member of staff to watch over him, just in case things went badly. He was the competent, reliable type who fixed things alone when push came to shove. All his adult life had gone into preparing for this role, and he knew deep inside that a day of reckoning would come when the difference between life and death would be down to him alone.

'That's some proper punishment!' said a man who walked past, and Gunnar realised that a loud gasp must have accompanied the last lift. He had to take a couple of deep breaths before he dared sit up. The sweat had glued his back to the bench and there were black dots dancing before his eyes. He was satisfied with what he had achieved, and now he needed to eat well to feed his freshly trained muscles. He wished they were even bigger, but for his work, not through vanity. His job called for bulging muscles, although bulk alone wasn't the key; strength and courage had to go hand in hand.

He spent a long time under the shower, enjoying the feeling of his pores opening as the sweat washed away. Weightlifting was accompanied by a kind of spiritual wellbeing: the triumph of his will over his body never failed to make him proud of himself. It was more difficult with running though. He always had to force himself to run and generally didn't feel great afterwards. But it was also important for work that he could sprint, not that he would often have to do it. He pulled on his trousers and decided to do without a singlet under his shirt. He was so hot that he felt as if he was on fire.

He quickly pushed his stuff into his training bag, put on his shirt and buttoned it up, but dropped his tie into a pocket. He could put it on in the car. He picked up his shoes, and walked barefoot to the gym's lobby and out into the snow. To begin with the cold was pure pain, but this was followed by a chilled mist of satisfaction. The snow was soft, forcing itself up between his toes, and creaked with each step. By the time he reached the car his feet were numb, but the fire in his body had subsided and he felt good. Now his shirt wouldn't be soaked with sweat. He turned up the car's heater, directing it into the footwell to dry his feet while he knotted his tie. He'd put on his socks and shoes but hadn't tied the laces when his phone rang. As soon as he saw the number he checked his watch in a moment's panic, but there was nothing to worry about. He had a clear hour before he needed to be at the ministry.

Disappointment welled up in his chest as he put the phone aside, and the feeling that Iceland wasn't the right place for him returned yet again. All his bodyguard training – most recently a course in evasive driving – would probably never be of any real use to him in this little country. He had imagined that the government offices would be just the place for him, and indeed they had liked the look of him, especially after the national commissioner of police had said there should be a higher level of security around ministers. But there were very few jobs going and plenty of people after them. All he could look forward to now was the same as usual: security at the ministries. He swallowed his disappointment and swore to himself. What sort of minister didn't want a driver?

6

His feet carved a path through the snow as he ambled up and down Ingólfsstræti, keeping an eye on people going in and out of the ministry. He had tried to go in, but the security guard sitting in front of a computer at the reception desk told him to stay outside. He went round the corner of the building and climbed the steps under the balcony on the Sölvhólsgata side, but that door was locked, so he continued to wander around the building, peering through windows in the hope of seeing her inside.

Every now and again he stopped to look at the picture he had torn from the paper. There was no doubt whatever that this was the man: the devil incarnate. And he was holding on to little Úrsúla's hand. She was no longer a little girl with cropped hair but a grown woman in a smart jacket and her hair in a bun. What on earth had she been thinking, giving him her hand like that? Examining the scrap of newspaper, he tried to imagine what the look in her eye might mean, but the picture was too grainy for him to judge whether her expression was one of a little girl who had got lost somewhere along the line and joined hands with evil.

He stopped by the statue on the mound of Arnarhóll and gazed back along the street. It was late in the day and he had yet to see her emerge. Thinking it over, he had seen remarkably few people passing through the doors of the building. The same people who had gone inside earlier had now come out, on their way home he guessed, many of the lights had been turned off, and few staff were now to be seen. There had to be a rear entrance to the building. He hurried back along the street towards the ministry, past the entrance on Sölvhólsgata and into the car park at the back. That was it. Beyond the gate, between the hotel and the ministry building, he could see another entrance from the lower car park that couldn't be easily seen from the street. This lower car park was closed, with one of those electric gates that opened when a driver pointed a finger at it, but it was open to pedestrians, so he limped down the steps and into the car park. The spaces by the fence were unmarked, but right next to the building was a disabled space marked with a blue sign, and next to them the spaces he was looking for: those reserved for the minister and the permanent secretary.

There were cars in both spaces. One was big and black – a sleek 4x4 with darkened windows; it was in the permanent secretary's spot. The other was a pretty ordinary family car – a Toyota – and he knew immediately that this had to be Úrsúla's. He didn't even need to look at the sign in front of the car. The Toyota hadn't been properly cleaned for a long time and the roof was caked with hardened snow, as were the boot and bonnet. That was typical of little Úrsúla, whose mind was always on something other than where she was right now.

He pulled the sleeve of his coat over his hand and wiped snow from the windscreen. Soon Úrsúla would drive home and would be relieved not to have to wipe the snow off first. He cleared all of the windows with care, and then took out his notebook, tore out a page and wrote a message to Úrsúla. Unfortunately it had begun to snow again, so if he were to put the note under one of the wipers, it would quickly become soaked and illegible. He tried the door handle and found that luck was on his side. The door opened, so he could place the message to Úrsúla on the seat, where she would find it as soon as she went to get in the car. He smiled. It was typical of the little scatterbrain to forget to lock her car.

7

Úrsúla was surprised at her own surprise: she was taken aback by just how much of a shock the note was. She was already kicking herself for having forgotten to lock the car. It hadn't occurred to her that by parking in the spot marked *Minister*, she was telling everyone which vehicle was hers. Clearly every fruitcake in the country had an opinion on everything imaginable, and that seemed to include her appointment as minister of the interior.

The devil's friend loses his soul and brings down evil, the note read, the last few words an almost illegible scrawl. It looked like someone had decided she had made friends with the devil himself. There was nothing unusual about politicians being lambasted for entering into coalitions with people someone was unhappy with, but as she was not linked to any party, she had somehow imagined that this kind of criticism wouldn't come her way. All the same, people ought to be used to seeing political parties working together when the parliamentary term was so far advanced, and anyway she'd simply been called in to finish the work begun by Rúnar. She screwed the note into a ball and flicked it aside, and it was lost among the mess of paper, juice cartons and sweet wrappers that filled the footwell. She reminded herself that this weekend the car would need to be cleaned as the smell was becoming overpowering. She sighed and tried to relax, to let her racing heartbeat slow. She had been aware before taking the job that she wouldn't be popular with everyone and that she'd get to hear about it. But the note in the car had still been upsetting. Somehow it was too close to home, too personal. In future she'd leave the car in the other car park with all the others.

As she parked outside her house, she wound the window shut – the smell in the car had forced her to drive home with it halfway open. There had to be half a sandwich turning green somewhere down there, or something in the junk in the back. She'd have to ask Nonni to clean the car. Judging by the emails waiting for her and the long jobs list, there wouldn't be much opportunity to do it herself. This weekend would have to be spent getting herself up to speed on everything the ministry did.

'Congratulations, my love!' Nonni called out as she opened the front door. 'You made it through day one!'

Kátur bounced towards her, his furry body twitching with delight at seeing her again, and as usual she dropped to her knees to greet him. She held his little head in both hands, kissed the top of his head and breathed in the smell of newly bathed dog. Nonni regularly gave him a bath and used shampoo on him, even though Úrsúla had warned that it wasn't good for dogs.

'Lovely to see you, Kátur,' she whispered into his fur as his tail wagged furiously. There was no limit to how much she loved this little dog. He had kept her sane when she had moved back home, becoming the compass that showed her the way back to love. He had helped her put aside her weapons and lower the defences she had erected around herself somewhere between the Ebola epidemic in Liberia and the refugee camps in Syria.

The dog wriggled from her arms, ran halfway along the hall into the apartment, and then back to her. That was what he always did, scampering between her and the family, as if he were showing her the way home to them. This was guidance she certainly needed, as since moving back to Iceland she had felt at a distance from them, as if they were on the far side of some invisible barrier that she had been unable to break through.

She took a deep breath, taking in the warmth of the household, and for a moment she was gripped by a doubt that she had done the right thing by jumping into a ministerial role. There was no getting away from the fact that it would mean less time at home, less energy to devote to the children, less time for Nonni. There would be less time for her own emotional recovery. But it was only for a year, the twelve remaining months of the parliamentary term.

'Pizza!' the children chorused the moment she stepped into the kitchen. They were busy arranging toppings on pizza bases, and she could see Nonni was preparing a seafood pizza just for the two of them. There was an open bottle of white wine on the worktop, a glass had been poured for her, and the dining table was set with candles.

'You're a dream,' she sighed, kissing the children's heads and wrapping her arms around Nonni. He was warm to the touch, freshly shaved and sweet-smelling, and she felt her heart soften with gratitude, blended with doubt that she genuinely deserved such a perfect man. This was how it had been for more than a year. Every time she felt a surge of warmth and affection towards him, it was accompanied by an immediate surge of bad feeling. There was guilt, regret and self-loathing. Why couldn't she simply love him as she had loved him before?

'So how's it looking?' he whispered and handed her a glass of wine.

She sat on a barstool and sipped. She'd tell him tonight, when the children had taken themselves off to bed. She would tell him how the day had begun, how she had been prepared for the first interview of the day, expecting to be getting to grips with complex and demanding issues, only to be faced with such a painful and difficult personal case.

The face of the mother who had sat opposite her that morning, rigid with anger and sorrow, remained vividly in her mind. As she watched her own daughter arrange strips of pepper to form a pattern on a pizza, she felt a stab of pain in her heart: she was only two years younger than the girl who had been raped.

Saturday

8

The report was so powerful that Úrsúla couldn't be sure if it was the sheer loudness of it or the wave of air pressure generated by the explosion that pushed her eardrums in, leaving them numb, so that she lay face down on the ground in absolute silence. In her peripheral vision she could see some movement in the distance, but it was difficult to tell through the cloud of dust, so she lay still in the sand that now seemed to fill her whole consciousness, revelling in the joy at being alive that swept through her. She wanted to stay there and make the most of this feeling for as long as she could, because before long she would have to get to her feet and face the fact that the bomb must have gone off very close to the camp, perhaps right inside it, and there would be casualties. She would feel guilt at being alive and from there it would be a short stop to the deadness inside that had plagued her ever since Liberia.

The silence in her head dissipated gradually and she could hear faint shouts and moans. She flexed her arms, ready to stand up. It was high time to get the people who had sought shelter in the refugee camps over the border into Jordan.

Úrsúla was woken by the hammering of her own heartbeat. She was on the sofa at home in Reykjavík. There was a cartoon playing on the TV that had no doubt been put on for the children, who had woken ridiculously early. With a deep sigh, for a moment she wished she could be back in Syria, to the second after the explosion, when she had sensed the life force surge through her veins and felt that there was some reason for her existence. That was when she felt that she had a purpose, even a calling. She carried with her a responsibility to get living people – those who were frightened, hurt and in need – to shelter.

Now she wasn't sure whether she had been asleep or having a vivid daydream, as if her thoughts had sought out memories that might kick-start her dormant emotions, exercising and stretching them back into life. Kátur crawled on his belly off her feet, where he had been curled in a ball, and along the length of her body until his damp, cold nose lay at her throat and she could feel his breath on her cheek. It was as if the dog sensed her thoughts. The love he always had for her never failed to melt her heart. Her affection for him was bound up with certainty and comfort. If she could love this bundle of fur, then surely she still had the capacity to love her own offspring.

Úrsúla sat up and shook off her own self-indulgence. Kátur watched her, waiting for a signal. If she were to get up, he would greet her as if she had just come through the door, then run to the back door – his way of telling her that he wanted to be let outside to pee. She would stand in the doorway, taking lungfuls of cold Icelandic outdoor air before brewing coffee and getting herself ready for the day ahead. She needed to go through a whole stack of documents, bring herself up to speed with the rules and regulations that applied to foreigners, and work out a job list for the coming week. It was clear that not much of her time would be her own, so she needed to make good use of the hours she had.

9

His expectations had created his disappointment. If he hadn't so clearly envisaged himself doing his dream job, then he wouldn't be so frustrated now. Although Gunnar understood the principles of Buddhism and tried to devote himself to them through meditation and the solutions that this offered, he still struggled to come to terms with the train of thought that said it would be better for him to accept right away that the bowl was cracked – that his dream job had been lost and that his life was already over.

He sat with his legs crossed, hands limp in his lap, concentrating on inhaling and exhaling while thinking of nothing but the flow of air that he felt crossing his upper lip and entering his nostrils then slipping down into his lungs to feed his bloodstream with oxygen, before taking away the carbon dioxide and discarding it by the same route. Fragments of daydreams in which his strength and alertness protected someone important from evil found their way into his consciousness. He repeatedly had to decline these thoughts – banish them so that he could continue to concentrate on the flow of air entering and leaving his body.

Meditation always helped, even though he never managed to maintain it for more than five minutes, and he was much calmer now, as he stood up, than he had been when he sat down, in spite of the burning disappointment. In reality he was disgruntled. It was a relief that he felt no real anger though. Anger was what he feared most, as it would herald rage. But there was only disappointment. He had been looking forward to taking on this assignment, getting to know the car and the minister, relishing the prospect of taking this task seriously and doing it better than it had ever been done in Iceland.

The real pain lay in knowing that, regardless of all his dreams and wishes, he had everything needed to make him a first-class bodyguard. He understood the importance of the role, that it was crucial to create a feeling of security so that whoever he was looking after could do their work without fear. He also had insight. Insight, as his teacher on the personal protection course in America had said, was the most important part of the bodyguard's armoury. Insight meant feeling rather than knowing, and sensing rather than seeing. The key to all this was being able to trust these instincts.

He lifted both hands high above his head and bent forward to stretch his back after sitting. As he straightened up he felt a spark of hope deep inside him. Ministers come and go. In a year there would be another election, and then there would undoubtedly be a new government that would want drivers, and he could also start to look around for opportunities overseas.

'Where on earth is anyone supposed to sit in this apartment?' Íris asked as she came through the bedroom door into the living room, wearing one of his old singlets and with her hair awry. 'Not everyone can sit on the floor all the time like you do.'

He smiled and pointed at the sofa.

'Then the floor's better,' she said. 'That sofa's not something anyone would want to sit on.'

She was right that the sofa was neither smart nor particularly comfortable, but it was an excellent example of how to let a little suffice. This was something Íris didn't understand, and whenever she came over or stayed the night she always complained about how sparsely furnished the place was. He got to his feet and went over to the kitchen worktop, where she stood shaking a carton of some protein drink.

'Good morning, pretty lady,' he said, a hand in her dark hair as he kissed her.

'Good morning, handsome man,' she replied.

She was a delight when she was like this, and he felt the fluttering down in his belly that came when he hadn't seen her for a while, or when she was sweet and loving; when she had herself under control.

10

Time seemed to stand still, and when Stella looked at the clock in the living room it was always seven, every time. She wasn't sure if that was seven in the morning or the evening, though. She had been hanging on all night for everyone to make a move to somewhere they could dance, but nothing was happening; some of them had even started to dance in the living room. All of a sudden she was sick of it all and wanted to leave, but she was unsure if this was because there were no fun girls there, or because of the newsreader, who was always at her heels, trying to get her to talk, or just staring.

'Come on, sugar. Give this one a chance,' Anna A said in the tone of maternal concern the Annas always used when speaking to her, and she stroked Stella's cheek. Stella could feel from her touch that Anna was as high as a kite, and it didn't look like the party was going to shift to a nightspot anywhere. This was going to continue all the way through to Sunday morning.

'Want another smartie?' asked Anna.

Stella shook her head, sipped from the glass of water Anna handed her and sauntered back to the living room. Some of the girls were dancing and others were sitting on the sofa, including the newsreader, who seemed to have finally struck lucky. So at least she wouldn't be following her from one room to another. The double doors stood open and Stella went outside onto the deck, taking breaths of outdoor air. Three girls were singing in the hot tub, their efforts undoubtedly sounding better to them than they did in reality. She could jump into the pot and join in the singing, or go into the living room and dance, but she had done all this before. And somehow in this dead time between seven and seven she felt faint and so overheated her head seemed about to burst. She went back inside, took her coat from the hall, opened the front door and stepped out into the cool silence.

The newsreader was standing on the steps, her scarf covering half her face as if she wanted to disguise herself, probably already feeling the regret that was inevitable after stepping through these doors.

'Always the same crap,' she said through her scarf. 'I don't know why I keep coming back. I don't even like pills, or any other dope, for that matter.'

'Don't you come mainly to stare at me?' Stella said, buttoning her coat, aware of how soft the buttons were. She stood still and stroked them with the tip of her index finger. They were ordinary plastic buttons, and she wondered why she hadn't noticed before just how smooth they were.

'You can dream here,' the newsreader said. 'But that's pretty much all I get to do.'

'I saw you chatting to someone on the sofa just now; that looked promising,' Stella said, still stroking the buttons of her coat. They really were so smooth under her fingers.

'That only lasted until something better came along,' the newsreader said, placing her feet tentatively on the slippery steps, the bitterness plain in her voice. 'Bye,' she said, walking away without looking back.

Stella watched her go, wearing a thick coat and her scarf over her head, but in open-toed shoes so that she walked awkwardly and her feet had to be wet from the snow underfoot. There was something about the shoes that triggered a stab of sympathy in Stella. The newsreader had obviously come to the party in heels to look good, or at least to try and look her best, with her hair stiff and immaculate, as if she were in front of the cameras, apparently unaware that the style made her look twenty years older.

'Hey!' she called after her. 'Do you want to get something to eat?'

The newsreader stopped in her tracks and turned.

'Where?' she asked and Stella shrugged.

'Anywhere. I don't know if it's morning or evening, or what's open. Sushi or Hlölli, or whatever's around. I'm just starving all of a sudden.'

The newsreader checked her watch and coughed.

'It's seven in the evening. Saturday evening.'

'Wow. These parties always confuse me. I could have sworn it was Saturday morning.'

The newsreader smiled.

'How about we go to my place. The fridge is full of stuff and I can throw something together quickly. I live there.'

She pointed to the grey tower that overshadowed the whole district, and Stella stared at it. She hadn't noticed before what a handsome building it was. There was something about the stone of the walls with its shades of grey that reminded her of velvet or silk, or anything other than grey stone. She wanted to say something about the contrast of soft and hard, silk and stone, but the words evaded her.

'I'm not going to sleep with you,' she said instead, and the newsreader laughed in embarrassment.

'I know that,' she said. 'I'm only offering fried eggs and a chat.'

Sunday

11

'Hell … I was going to ask you to clean the car out for me, and I forgot all about it,' Úrsúla said as Nonni appeared, handing her a bowl of *skyr* as she sat at the computer.

'I can't be bothered to do it today,' he said, massaging her shoulders. 'Why don't you take my car tomorrow?'

'No, it's all right. I'll survive one more day. There's something in the back that's gone off, so it smells like a rubbish tip. Could you do it tomorrow evening?'

'I promise,' Nonni said as he kissed her temple.

She leaned against him, wishing the moment could stretch out so she could make the most of his lips against her skin. He stood up straight and the bad vibe grew inside her again, the feeling that he was too good for her, even if he wasn't able to see it for himself.

'You've been working all weekend,' he said. 'Won't you come for a Sunday-afternoon drive with us. I promised the kids that we'd go for a swim and an ice cream.'

She sighed. There were still emails to go through and work to be done to familiarise herself with the new South Coast Highway project, and then there was the new adviser.

'I'm waiting for a call from Eva Aðalbjörns. She's up for the job.'

'That's great,' Nonni said. 'You'll have someone whose fashion sense is as sharp as her political antenna.'

Úrsúla laughed.

'I could do with some fashion sense myself. I wish I could deal with the clothes thing like men do, just a new tie once in a while.'

'You always look great. But seriously, that's really good,' he said and kissed her temple again. 'She seems to be a hard worker. So next weekend you can send her home with the emails and you can come swimming with us.'

He turned in the doorway, smiled and winked at her, and for a second she felt a jolt of the electricity she had used to feel when he smiled at her. He became more handsome as the years passed and he would carry it well into old age. A hint of grey in his dark hair and stubble would just make him look even cooler. She couldn't fail to see how other women looked at him, and when they were out somewhere in company she was proud that he was her husband. But this flash of lightning was inevitably accompanied by the guilt that had coloured every aspect of their relationship since moving back home. He regularly asked what the problem was, but whether they were with the counsellor or alone at home, she was still unable to say out loud that she felt a kind of emotional shortfall when it came to him and the children, that she knew deep down that she loved them, but didn't truly feel it. She couldn't say that she felt an affection for them any more than for people in general; she liked people and wanted to help them, and that included these three people. But beyond that … nothing much.

She had been warned about this long ago, both in training and when being supervised during her first couple of years working in disaster relief, and by colleagues in the field, who told her that while some of them suffered from PTSD, with bouts of sweating, trembling and nightmares, others became hardened. She was clearly one of the second group. This wasn't something she had ever expected. She was resilient, with her head screwed on properly, or so she had thought: a sensible, down-to-earth, tough person. But when Médecins Sans Frontières had borrowed her from UNHCR to organise the emergency camps in Liberia during the Ebola epidemic, everything had changed.

It was in Liberia: after a few weeks of gulping back the fear, dressed in yellow coveralls in which the tears and the sweat mingled in the overpowering heat, and seeing through the goggles how a human body could shrivel into an anonymous pool of vomit and shit and slime and blood, it was as if this had become her only reality. This was the real human situation that nobody at home was aware of or capable of understanding. And she couldn't explain it to them. There was no way to tell the story. There were no words that could describe the Ebola epidemic. There was also no easy way to have this kind of thing stored away in your memory. She felt that she had been wearing those plastic coveralls ever since.

But she couldn't bring herself to tell Nonni all this. She couldn't tell him that she didn't feel she was really here at all, that part of her had been lost, dripping into the bloodstained earth in Liberia or blown up in Syria, and that she was no longer sure what feelings she still bore for him. She couldn't tell him, so she just shook her head.

'Nothing's wrong,' she said, unable to contemplate hurting him.

12

Daylight made its way in through the window, so it had to be around the middle of the day. Stella sat up on the sofa and was frozen with fright as fragments of the weekend appeared in her thoughts. She had the strange feeling that she hadn't been awake since Friday, but in fact, she had probably been awake more or less the whole weekend. It hadn't been a normal wakefulness though, more a semi-dreamworld that had taken command of her senses, while her mind took a holiday. Now she'd need to piece those thoughts back together.

'This is a fucking fantastic flat,' she said as Gréta the newsreader appeared in the living room, fully dressed, make-up on and smiling, as if she had been awake for hours.

'Thank you,' she said. 'I inherited fishing quotas. It takes more than a journalist's salary to pay for this.'

Stella admired the view from the floor-to-ceiling windows that overlooked the city in two directions. The old town looked grey with its covering of dirty snow, but the steep corrugated-iron roofs had thrown off their coverings and the bright colours stood out in the gloom. Gréta went to the kitchen and could be heard pottering about.

'I'll make some coffee,' she called out.

Stella tried to recall what had happened since she had come back here with the newsreader. She remembered bacon and eggs, a couple of cans of beer and some gales of laughter over something that in hindsight wasn't so funny. She went to the bathroom, peed, washed her face and gulped cold water from the tap until her belly was bursting, but somehow her thirst remained unslaked. When she went into the kitchen, Gréta was placing pastries on an oven tray to heat up.

'Hey, last night's not all that clear ... So I have to ask—' Stella began, before Gréta cut her off.

'I may be desperate, but I'm not a perv,' she said sharply. 'I've no interest in unconscious women.'

'Sorry,' Stella muttered, taking a seat on a barstool and wondering how the hell Gréta managed to look so immaculate – in her own, weird, old-lady kind of way.

'Did you take an upper to wake you up this morning?' she asked.

Gréta smiled. 'To tell you the truth, I don't always take the Es they offer. Somehow I don't trust myself to let go completely, so I just let the champagne do for the last part of the party yesterday.'

That explained how she could be on her feet as fresh as a daisy while Stella's mind was still a mess.

'Don't tell anyone,' she said. 'Not that it matters, because I'll not bother going again. That kind of atmosphere doesn't do me any good.'

Stella smiled to herself in sympathy. That was exactly what she always told herself as well – every time.

'Aren't you on any dating apps?' she asked.

Gréta shook her head. 'Ach. I was on Tinder, but it didn't work,' she said with an apologetic smile. 'The women I'm interested in don't fancy me.'

Stella felt the same pang she had the night before as they had left the party together, and a desire grew inside her to help this woman. Turning down the old-lady vibe just one per cent would go a long way to boosting her chances.

'I'll fix your profile for you,' she said, putting out a hand, and Gréta obediently passed across her phone.

Stella started by changing her profile picture to one that was newer and less formal. An ancient posed passport photo wasn't ideal bait. She added a couple more photos of her with more or less the same hairstyle.

'There's nothing that pisses you off more than going on a date and finding that the other person has been using some really old photo,' she said, with an accusing glance.

'I was trying to lose a few years and a couple of kilos.'

'That's crazy,' Stella said. 'Nobody wants to be deceived. If you're fooling women into thinking you're young and slim, then you're missing out on the ones who prefer them mature and broader.'

She said 'broader' even though a more straightforward adjective would have been appropriate; she didn't want to be too direct by saying that some girls prefer fat women.

'They really exist?' Gréta sniffed.

'Yep. The problem is you're presenting yourself as something you're not. Anyone meeting you would think you're the type that sits in an old armchair and knits socks in front of the telly, when you live in a white designer apartment with splash paintings on the walls.'

'Those are Jeff Elrods. Originals.'

'Whatever. But there you go. I wouldn't know which way up

these pictures go, but you do. But nobody looking at you would imagine that. See what I mean?'

'What? Is it the clothes, or what?'

Stella looked her up and down while she searched for the right words to tell the woman how to stop looking like a dork.

'Well, if you want to wear old-lady gear...'

'Trouser suits.'

'Yeah. But if you're going to wear a suit, then stick to black, dark blue, grey. Go for a power-lesbian vibe and get away from the granny look. Those pastel colours have to go.'

'Pastels work fine on television.'

'But do you always have to be dressed for work? Pastels just scream senior citizen.'

'I'm not even forty.'

'Exactly.'

Stella turned to the profile text on Gréta's Tinder profile and sighed. With a thumping hangover and with only half a mug of coffee inside her, she had thrown together a better bio than Gréta had managed to write – and no doubt had struggled with.

'It's about showing your strengths,' she said, 'instead of making light of the weaker points.'

She erased all the stuff about university degrees and political positions, and being interested in a 'steady relationship', and punched in a few words that would help Gréta start to reel them in. She handed the phone back and smiled with satisfaction as Gréta read the description of herself out loud, with wonder in her voice.

'"Strong-minded, culturally aware, financially independent, solidly built lady who dreams of a princess to pamper, share laughs with and have fun together."'

'Let me know how many swipes you get,' Stella said.

13

His nest was sheltered and dry. The temperature was just below zero but his padded boiler suit kept the cold out. He pulled the hood up before falling asleep and woke up with his whole body comfortably warm. As long as it stayed dry you could get through a heavy frost. This was something he knew from experience. He took a small torch from his breast pocket and shone its beam on the scrap torn from the newspaper. Úrsúla and the Devil. It was too painful a thought to imagine that this innocent creature had fallen into his grip. He was relieved that he had sent her a warning by leaving the note in her car. He hoped she would take notice of it. Once upon a time she had taken notice of everything he said, looking up at him with wide eyes, her face one big question as she waited uncertainly for a sign that he was joking or not. If he laughed, then so would she, out loud and with all her little heart. Now and again he had got things wrong, told her something confusing or even things that children shouldn't get to hear. The wretched booze didn't bring out the best in people, and in that respect he was no better than anyone else.

He opened a crack and peered out of his nest. He needed to pee, and to walk and stretch his legs, but he didn't want anyone to see him making his way out of his hiding place. This was his personal foxhole and the best place to keep a watchful eye on her, and he didn't want to be kicked out of it. Nobody seemed to be about, so he slipped out and set off through the snow, which crunched under his feet. The old churchyard was at the end of the street and he could pee there.

The guy in the little corner shop was amiable and heated up his sandwich under the grill, adding that coffee came free with it. So he made the most of the offer and gulped down three mugs with milk, crumbling a few lumps of sugar in there as well while he waited for his sandwich. He paid with the small change the lad at Hlemmur had given him. As soon as he was outside the shop, he bit into the sandwich. It was piping hot, so the melted cheese burned his lip, but he liked seeing the steam rising from it into the cold air.

He ate as he walked, and when he was outside Úrsúla's house he swept snow from one of the low concrete bollards across the street and gazed at her through the window as he finished his sandwich. She was sitting at her desk, a cheek turned towards him, and for a moment he felt she hadn't changed at all, was still the lively little girl with endless questions on her lips. Then that feeling fizzled out as he recalled that she was halfway to being in the devil's claws.

He felt the terror grip his heart as suddenly the golden light from her table lamp no longer seemed to be a warm and comforting glow that fell on her face, but was instead the glare from the burning fires of hell.

Monday

14.

'I have to confess that it completely slipped my mind,' Permanent Secretary Óðinn said. 'I'll ask for information from your secretary and look into it today.'

Úrsúla smiled to hide her impatience. It wasn't as if this was something major that he needed to be involved in. All that was needed was for him to look at the memo from the secretary, who had noted down the main points and supporting information from the mother on Friday, and then decide in whose hands to put the matter. This would take him two or three minutes at most. But to be fair, this was something she had mentioned to him in haste as he stood in the doorway after their first meeting, so he hadn't noted anything down.

She told herself that she would need to take a few deep breaths and adjust to the ministry's pace before she could demand that its staff shift up a gear to keep up with her. At any rate, that was her aim: a more efficient ministry that could deal with things fast. It was appalling how so many cases were caught up in the system, and that these mainly involved foreign citizens – which was her field of expertise. Asylum seekers could wait months for responses to appeals, and the endless uncertainty could drive people mad, with all the consequences that entailed.

She knew perfectly well how insecurity could affect people. If you didn't feel safe, mindfulness was just some kind of fad for westerners who had no need to fear what tomorrow might bring. It was the opposite of human dignity to be able to aim for nothing more than surviving from one day to the next. So this was at the top of her list: finding ways for the ministry to shorten the time it took to process cases. Of course, she only had a year, but twelve months ought to be enough to get things moving in the right direction.

She sat down with the heavy South Coast Highway folder in front of her. This was an issue that had been mentioned when she had been asked to take the job; tough decisions would need to be taken, she'd been told. Personally, she had little liking for this kind of private enterprise, but the state's lack of initiative regarding the road network had already cost too many lives, so it was clear that something had to be done to redevelop the most heavily used roads in the south-west.

By the time midday came around, she was dazed and felt sure she had already done a day's work. She had requested that the entire staff come to the open area on the third floor so she could speak to them all, but as she faced them she didn't feel inspired to make a stirring speech, so she simply thanked them for their warm welcome and hoped that they would work well together. She could see from the smile on Óðinn's face that she had said enough. He led the applause that morphed into general mutter as some people drifted back to work and others pulled on their coats to walk over the road to the ministry's staff canteen. She was starving so followed their example. When she arrived in the hall, though, her cheeks rosy from the brisk walk, one of the canteen staff hurried over with a look of distress on her face, and Úrsúla realised that it probably wasn't standard practice for ministers to use the canteen.

'Just sit there, dear,' she said. 'I'll bring you something to eat.'

'There's no need for that,' Úrsúla said, but then Óðinn was at her side, agreeing with the woman.

'Normally it's only the minister of finance who eats here, because it's convenient. But when other ministers come here for lunch, as they do sometimes, we don't want them to waste their time standing in a queue,' he said. 'So I arrange for the minister to sit down and their food is brought to them. You don't have any dietary foibles, do you?'

'I eat everything,' Úrsúla said, and noted the look of relief on the server's face as she hurried away while Óðinn lightly but firmly took her by the arm and steered her to a seat.

'This table is kept free for you and other ministers, and their closest colleagues,' he said. 'And they'll serve you here.'

Úrsúla sighed. She had no choice but to let this cloying attitude remain in place, at least to begin with, while people learned to trust her. Right now protesting could be taken as discourtesy, and she had no intention of offending anyone by trampling roughshod over their habits and customs.

She had hardly sat down when the server was back and placing a tray in front of her.

'Thank you so much,' she said. 'You're really looking after me.'

The server glowed, took a small bottle from the pocket of her apron and added it to the tray.

'Ministerial sauce,' she said.

Úrsúla looked blank.

'Chilli sauce,' Óðinn explained. 'It kills off stomach bugs.'

Úrsúla thanked them, and stifled a laugh, realising that the permanent secretary was entirely serious. She was not overly fond of spicy food, but for the first few days she would go along with it, although considering all the fuss, it didn't seem likely that she would use the canteen frequently. On the other hand, she was determined to stick to her guns on the ministerial car, whatever the police commissioner had to say about it. She hadn't even had a driver in Syria, so she certainly wasn't going to allow herself to be driven around the city like some princess.

Once she had finished eating, she needed a cigarette, so before she went back along the ministerial corridor to her office, she sneaked out to the fourth-floor balcony the cleaner had shown her, and found that she was already there. Maybe the girl didn't do much else, other than standing there, smoking on the balcony. It was good to know she didn't need to stand there alone in the wind getting her nicotine fix, though.

'How are you?' she asked, as the girl lit her cigarette for her.

'Fine,' the girl said. 'And you?'

'Oh, you know,' she replied and laughed. 'This morning I've become familiar with the permanent secretary's forgetfulness, the ministerial table in the canteen and the special ministerial sauce, so I'm looking forward to finding out what else I need to know to become a proper minister.'

'The ministerial rubbish,' the girl said.

'What?'

'You're only allowed to put documents, notes and suchlike in one bin. That's the black one in your office. I make sure everything gets shredded before it goes in the container for paper waste.'

15

She'd expected the start of the week was going to be tough, but it turned out to be worse. She could hardly keep her eyes open and was terrified that she would actually fall asleep pushing the cleaning trolley. That was the downside of party weekends, particularly if smarties had been consumed. She seemed to be able to sleep endlessly for a few days afterwards. She told herself she was never, ever going to drop those things again. From now on, she'd let a couple of beers do the job, she thought, also reminding herself that she was never going to one of the Annas' parties again.

She glanced around, and when she was sure there was nobody about, she went to the cleaners' store and shut the door behind her. She just had to close her eyes for a few minutes. She took two packs of paper towels, put them under her head for a pillow, lay down and was asleep before she had even closed her eyes.

She was startled awake on the cold floor by her phone buzzing at her. She sat up, with no idea of how much time had passed, and put it to her ear.

'Hello?'

'*Hæ*. It's Gréta.'

'Who?'

'Gréta. Thanks for your help the other day.'

Stella searched her dazed mind for fragments of the weekend. Had she met someone called Gréta at the party? Or was this someone at the ministry whose face she couldn't place?

'Yeah. *Hæ*. Thanks...' It was best to pretend nothing was wrong, and wait for whoever was on the line to let fall a hint of who they were. She stood up, feeling dizzy, and held on to the steel wash basin as a support. 'How are things?'

'Just fine,' the woman on the phone said. 'I was just going to let you know that I got two matches.'

'What?'

'On Tinder. Like you suggested.'

Stella sighed with relief. It had to be the newsreader. Her head was still so messed up after the weekend, the name hadn't rung any bells, but she did now have a vague recollection of giving the woman her phone number.

'Cool! Told you so,' she said. 'Good-looking?'

She was a tiny bit curious now: what kind of women were showing an interest in the newsreader, with the new information Stella had put on her profile?

'Yes,' Gréta said. 'One of them in particular looks really lovely.'

'That's cool,' Stella said. 'I hope it all goes well for you.'

She was ready to end the call; she wanted to check her phone for the time, so she could decide whether to go round with the mop again – enough to show she was working – or to lie back down on the floor.

'But ... how do I go about this?' Gréta asked, a note of desperation in her voice.

'Just chat to her,' Stella said. 'Give it a week and then invite her out on a date at the weekend.'

'But I have to go for a work dinner, it's a sort of annual thing.'

'Then invite her to go with you,' Stella said. 'Aren't you famous? Anyone who bites on the princess idea I put in your profile will have to be up for dinner with stars from the telly.'

She ended the call abruptly, as her stomach was suddenly turning somersaults. She turned and vomited into the steel basin. Fuck this. She was never, ever, ever going to one of those fucking Anna parties again. She never failed to overindulge in everything on offer: too much to drink, too much grass and too many pills.

When she had stopped retching, she drank some water from the tap and almost threw up again as the water was sickeningly warm. The hot and cold pipes had to be touching each other.

Her phone told her that it was twelve-thirty, so now she could go for lunch. Something to eat would calm her stomach, but first she needed a smoke. A dose of nicotine would banish the trembling and the dizziness, and the almost overwhelming urge to smoke more grass. That was a yearning she would have to tough out, as she was broke until the end of the month.

The cold air on the balcony was refreshing, even though she was dressed in a polo shirt and the chill left her shivering; at least she wasn't so drowsy.

'*Hæ*,' the new minister whispered as she stepped out onto the balcony at Stella's side. 'How are things?'

'*Hæ*,' Stella said, holding her lighter up to the minister's cigarette.

'What's that?' the minister asked as she drew down a lungful of smoke, one finger lightly touching the tattoo on Stella's arm. Stella started at the touch, as if a jolt of electricity had passed through her body. There was clearly some of the weekend's cocktail of drugs still in her system.

'It's a Helm of Awe,' she said. 'It's an old Icelandic rune that protects against black magic and enemies.'

The minister smiled and took another drag on her cigarette.

'Maybe I ought to get one,' she said. 'I wonder if it would work in politics as well?'

16

'What do you mean, you don't remember?'

Úrsúla had to make an effort to keep her irritation under control and suppress the urge to yell.

'Friday morning, the day after I received the keys, a woman came here and you showed her into my office. She'd booked an appointment with Rúnar. I gave you a list of points afterwards and asked you to make a note of the meeting.'

'I'm so sorry, but that was a very difficult day,' Freyja the secretary said. 'A new minister taking over...'

Úrsúla raised a hand to stop her. She wasn't going to listen to a lecture, the subtext of which would be that Freyja was the one with experience and Úrsúla was the rookie. Úrsúla opened her mouth, about to remind Freyja that on Friday she had asked her to look after the woman, who was in floods of tears, and had watched them go along the corridor together, when she was stopped by Eva bustling in with an armful of clothes.

'I've brought you everything in two sizes,' the adviser said. 'So you can try on both and return whatever you don't like or doesn't fit.'

Úrsúla followed her into the office and shut the door behind her. Eva dropped the bundle of clothes on the sofa.

'My secretary is on the stiff side,' Úrsúla said. 'What should I do about her?'

She picked up a blouse from the top of the pile.

'Give her a chance. The staff are always stressed out when a new minister is appointed, and you came in at pretty short notice. Let's see if she softens up in a couple of days. Otherwise you just get Óðinn to transfer her.'

Eva held up another blouse to show Úrsúla. It was a light brown, patterned with a motif of small flowers and made from some material that shone like satin.

'Pretty, isn't it?' Eva said.

'It's pretty,' Úrsúla agreed. She would wear whatever Eva told her to. Eva had a far more developed taste in clothes and had strong opinions on what women in politics should wear. 'Óðinn and my secretary both seem to have gaps in their memory, and I'm wondering if it's because it's this particular case – something I asked them to look into. I get the feeling that their selective memory is a way of telling me what kind of issues they want me to be dealing with.'

'What was it they decided to forget?' Eva asked, placing a jacket and trousers on the sofa and holding a top next to them for comparison.

'A woman who came here on Friday and asked me to check where in the system her daughter's rape case is.'

'Understood. Bad PR for you to start with. They're just trying to shield you,' Eva said, handing her trousers to try on.

Úrsúla took off the trousers she had come to work in, which were probably on the hippie side for a minister, and took the new trousers, tailored in a solid block of colour, from Eva.

'I didn't write down her name, phone number or address, or anything. I gave the whole thing to Freyja. All I remember is the woman's name is Rósa; I don't recall her other name.'

'If she came here to the ministry, then her name and ID number will have been registered at reception. Just ask the reception secretary downstairs.'

Úrsúla was relieved. She had completely forgotten about the main reception desk, as she always came in through the building's back door. She would find out the woman's name and prepare a new memo, which this time she would place directly in Óðinn's hands.

17

He woke up and bumped his head. His first thought was that he was in the shelter and someone was having a go at him, then he remembered that he was safe in his hiding place, his own personal foxhole. He felt dizzy, and was sure that he was being rocked back and forth, but in the darkness it was difficult to figure things out. He patted his pockets and found the torch, turned it on and lit up his refuge. All of a sudden he had the feeling that it was Christmas. This wasn't a Christmas like his recent ones, when he had been fed by the Salvation Army and psalms were sung, but a childhood Christmas. Back then his mother had lit candles and baked as the Christmas greetings were read out on the radio, and they had sat at the table and read out loud to each other from the books they had received as presents. It would be good to have a book here in his hiding place. All he had were newspapers, and of course the cutting of Úrsúla and the Devil. He shone the torch on it once again and tried to fathom what the look in her eyes meant, but it was as if she wouldn't give anything away. That was the problem with the picture. She was smiling, which indicated that she was happy, but how could she be happy in his company? It would be different if it was someone other than Úrsúla. Then he'd understand that she wouldn't know any better. But she, Úrsúla Aradóttir, ought to know that caution was needed around this man.

He felt his feet tingle, and knew that this was a precursor to cramp. He tried to shift himself around and stretch out his legs, but the space was too small. The cramp came on so he tried to shake his leg, kicking hard. That worked for a little while, but the cramp was obstinate and was back before long and he kicked out a few more times. This was the damned leg that had been broken all those years ago and had been nothing but trouble ever since. His breathing came fast and shallow as he tried to stop himself groaning with the pain, and he reached out to take hold of the luminous green handle that he used to get in and out of his hiding place. But everything rocked beneath him, and he knew he wouldn't be able to stand up right now. He would have to wait until the movement had stopped and the dizziness had abated. He took a piece of Danish pastry from his pocket and stuffed it in his mouth. Sometimes a bite of something sweet kept the pain in his feet at bay. But he had to spit it out. The anger welling up in his throat stopped him from swallowing. He was raging with fury that Úrsúla should be in cahoots with that man, the Devil incarnate, who would kick a man when he was down, the Devil who took people's lives.

He kicked hard a few times and the cramp passed, he could breathe easily again, and as he did so the whole place stopped moving and fell silent. Then he heard the sound of approaching footsteps.

18

Stella had put the rubbish into the garbage container and was emptying the shredding bin into the paper container when her phone rang. She saw the number from earlier in the day appear on the screen.

'It's me again. Gréta.'

'Yeah, *hæ*. Sorry I had to put the phone down earlier.'

'No problem. I was just wondering if you could give me a little advice...'

The grey tower in which Greta lived was nearby. Stella gazed at it now and saw that it was colourless and ugly in the gloom of falling snow. There were no velvets or silks in its rows of tones, just greyness, and she felt a sadness take hold of her heart, as it always did when the smarties wore off. Everything just turned so much lousier. This grey tower, which overshadowed the ministry's car park, had turned ugly, and the flakes of wet snow that fell from the sky and inevitably found their way down your neck had turned disgusting, and Gréta the newsreader was just plain irritating.

'Look, I'm a bit busy right now—' she said, but Gréta interrupted her.

'Haven't you finished work? Why don't you drop by on your way home? I'm cooking.'

Stella sighed. She was starving. This was all part of the aftermath of a heavy weekend. Maybe she had lost a load of vitamins or something, but it seemed that her body constantly demanded food. On top of that, she was skint, and there was nothing to eat at home but cup-a-soups and crispbread. She could eat with Gréta the newsreader and in return she could give her some pointers on how to pull this woman on Tinder.

Before she'd really had time to think about it she was there in the grey block, her coat on a chair in the hall, sitting in the kitchen, wolfing the appetisers along with the beer that Gréta had just given her.

'She could have used an old picture as well,' she said, trying to cool Gréta's expectations; she seemed to be buzzing with excitement over her first matches.

'I don't care if she's older and fatter than she looks,' Gréta said.

'A date is a date,' Stella said, nodding her agreement.

Although Gréta was something of a TV celebrity, she clearly wasn't the type who could afford to be too picky. But the woman who had indicated an interest was quite good-looking. In fact she was remarkably pretty – unexpectedly so, for someone showing an interest in Gréta's profile. She had to have just come out, had only just begun looking around and maybe had seen Gréta on television and had been intrigued by the well-known face.

'What should I say to start off?' Gréta said as she chopped mushrooms and dropped them into a saucepan. 'I need some kind of icebreaker.'

'Just say hello,' Stella said. That was what she always did, and so far it had worked well enough.

'Just hello?'

'Yep,' Stella said. 'You say hello, and she replies somehow or other, and then you just start to chat.'

Gréta put the knife down and picked up her phone. She stared at the screen for a moment as if she needed to screw up her courage, and Stella felt a pang of sympathy for her. This was a woman who wasn't usually on the back foot.

'Phew. I hope she replies soon, otherwise I'm going to be a bag of nerves,' Gréta said, tossing her phone onto the table as if it had burned her hand. She poured a whole carton of cream in with the mushrooms. 'Best to think about something else,' she muttered. 'What's she like, the new minister?'

'She's fine,' Stella said. 'We go for a smoke together on the balcony.'

'Really? I didn't think she looked like a smoker,' Gréta said. 'What do you talk about when you're having a smoke?'

'Y'know,' Stella said. 'This and that.'

'She comes across as a tough character.'

'How so?'

'Well, you know, cool jobs and all that. Refugee camps, Médecins Sans Frontières, crisis management. She comes across as an adrenaline junkie, not the type you'd expect would become a minister. It looks like there's a lot more paperwork than in the work she's used to.'

Gréta reached for the phone she had only just tossed aside.

'She's not answering,' she said with a frown.

'Don't worry about it,' Stella said, feeling her belly call out for food. 'If this one doesn't work out then there are plenty more fish in the sea. And you can always use old-fashioned Icelandic magic to pull a chick,' she added, pointing at the rune on her arm.

Gréta laughed.

'If you can work some magic that brings her to me, then that would be wonderful.'

'I'm not joking,' Stella said. 'There's an old spell you can use to attract girls. In fact, it's pretty simple.'

Gréta gazed at her curiously, as if she was trying to weigh up whether or not she was being serious.

'I'm not sure I believe in that kind of stuff,' she said, stirring the sauce.

Stella shrugged.

'It's like the placebo effect,' she said. 'If you believe it'll work, then it will.'

19

There was something otherworldly about the way the secretary at reception downstairs shook her head, as if Úrsúla lived on a separate plane from the rest of the ministry, so contact with them was impossible. But this couldn't be true. Every person who set foot inside the ministry was booked in and out of the building.

Úrsúla asked the woman to check again, both on the computer system and the paper record. She obediently did so, but there was no visit recorded on Friday morning.

'Could someone have forgotten to book her in?' she asked, knowing it was futile. All the same, it was worth asking; people were fallible and mistakes happened.

'It's unlikely,' the secretary said. 'Nobody is allowed in without a booked appointment or for a prearranged reason. And I always call upstairs and let the person concerned know that their visitor is here, and they say yes or no to them coming in. If they say no, or don't recognise the visitor's name, then they're simply not allowed in. But, of course, all kinds of things could happen.'

'This woman had booked an appointment. She was supposed to meet Rúnar, my predecessor. There has to be a record of that.'

The reception secretary went through the pages for Friday and shrugged her shoulders.

'This was a middle-aged woman who came to see me on Friday,' Úrsúla said in the hope that this would trigger a recollection. 'As far as I recall it was just before midday and she spent a quarter of an hour with me. Freyja took her back downstairs. Don't you remember?'

The reception secretary had begun to shake her head before Úrsúla had finished her sentence.

'That day was a very difficult one,' she said. 'It's always particularly fraught when a new minister takes over, with a lot of people coming and going. I'm terribly sorry.'

She looked down at the desk in front of her instead of meeting Úrsúla's eyes. Úrsúla felt the irritation building up inside her. It was practically the same speech she had heard from Freyja: tough day, new minister, blah, blah, terribly sorry. There was no way to argue with people who were so sorry.

Úrsúla sighed. Eva had certainly been right when she said that the staff were nervous about the new minister. Óðinn had undoubtedly laid down the law, telling them not to bother her with anything trivial, so most probably it was him who'd had the woman's name erased from the registration, to prevent Úrsúla from getting involved. He'd certainly have done it with the best of motives, but she would have to make it clear to him that she didn't appreciate this kind of manipulation.

She left the reception lobby and walked through the building to the staff entrance at the back. The snow had continued to pile up, but it melted as fast as it collected in the empty car park, so her car looked like a monument standing in the middle. She pulled the sleeve of the brand-new coat Eva had chosen over her hand and shoved snow off the edge of the car's roof so she could open the door without it falling inside. This time she had locked the car and left it in a free spot so there was no chance of finding an unpleasant message, but she still looked around the car to be sure. The stink inside was becoming unbearable; she'd ask Eva to take it to be valeted tomorrow. She couldn't expect Nonni to be outside cleaning the car in this weather. She dug through the junk in the footwell for a scraper and cleared the worst of the snow from the bonnet and windows, then sat in the car and started the engine.

The snow had reduced the traffic to a crawl, and it was obvious that the snow ploughs were only able to keep the main roads clear. Úrsúla opened a window to let some air in, but this brought with it flakes of snow, although it was hard to tell if these were coming from above or drifting in from the roof of the car. It was almost time for the news, so she switched on the radio, but almost immediately turned it off again, because she could hear a clanking sound coming from the back of the car. She listened for a while and then switched the radio back on. It was just as well to take in the news on the way home, as she wouldn't have to shush the children over dinner later. She could catch up properly online when things were quiet.

The newsreader was in the middle of an item about the criticism around the prime minister's decision to appoint her to a ministerial post – over the heads of experienced men from both government parties – when she heard the clank again. She turned down the radio, but turned it up again as she wanted to hear the rest of the news item. It had to be ice dropping from the wheel arches or something. On the radio the prime minister nimbly defended his position, saying that it was always possible to criticise the choice of ministers when there was such a pool of talent available, but his party was implacable in its support for equal rights, in addition to which, Úrsúla's specialist knowledge of issues concerning refugees was especially useful.

Úrsúla was startled by another clank. This time the sound was much louder, followed immediately by another. In fact, it sounded like distant gunfire, which was out of the question here. The sound was accompanied by a faint vibration; perhaps the noise was coming from the boot.

She'd have to check. It sounded as if something heavy had come adrift. Maybe she had forgotten about a gas bottle from the barbecue after the summer, or something else that had been there for a long time and which had now come adrift. She turned off the road and into the wide area by the harbour. She intended to stop right away, in the entrance, but the snow was piled so high on each side, she had to continue all the way to the open space that had been cleared. Here she would be able to turn the car around and get out without her shoes filling with snow.

She switched off the engine and got out, but another clank stopped her in her tracks. This time the car stood motionless, so there was no question of anything rolling from side to side. It was as if there was something alive in the boot. She glanced around, regretting that she had turned onto the quayside. Even though it was in the middle of the city, the place was poorly lit and the nearest people were some distance away. These days her gentler instincts seemed to be buried so deep that she sometimes felt that they had been lost, whereas fear was just below the surface and something like this was all it took to upset her equilibrium.

She considered simply getting back in the car, driving home and asking Nonni to check, but another clank stopped her in her tracks. She didn't dare drive off with something alive in the boot. She thought about calling the police, but then imagined standing in front of a bunch of uniformed men, all laughing at her for being hysterical, and dismissed the idea.

She summoned up her courage, stepped closer to the car and stretched out a hand to open the boot.

20

Gunnar had dressed in three minutes. He looked at his reflection in the minister's hallway mirror and saw that in spite of his haste, he looked fine. His tie was knotted at his throat and he had managed to smooth down his hair on the way here.

The call from the cabinet office had taken him by surprise, especially as he was just coming to terms with his disappointment.

He had abandoned his half-eaten dinner – a steamed chicken breast – and rushed out.

'Hello,' said the guy from the national commissioner of police who was in charge of ministers' security. Gunnar had met him a few times before but couldn't remember his name; it sounded Russian as he recalled. He followed him into the living room, where the new minister sat with one arm around a girl who had buried her head in her shoulder. Two uniformed officers sat opposite her. In the kitchen a tall, dark-haired man was fussing over making coffee. He had to be the husband.

'What's going on?' Gunnar murmured to the national commissioner's guy.

'There was a rough sleeper in the back of her car. He attacked her when she opened the boot.'

'Christ.'

'Yeah. Not pleasant. He had clearly made himself at home there for a few days. She had refused the national commissioner's recommendation that she have a driver. But now she's changed her mind. Welcome to the job.'

The minister was still busy giving a statement to the uniformed officers, so the national commissioner's guy beckoned Gunnar to go with him.

'From now on you collect her from the front door every morning and go with her to the door when you bring her home. If there's nobody home, then you come inside with her and carry out these security checks.'

The guy handed him a list, reading out from a copy of it as Gunnar followed him through the house.

'Back door: locked and glass undamaged. Ground floor windows: undamaged. Ground floor lights: working. First floor: windows undamaged, lights working, balcony door locked and windows undamaged.'

'Got it,' Gunnar said, and that was enough to stop the guy from reading out the whole list.

'These are the new working guidelines. We feel there's a greater risk of ministers being harassed, so it's as well as to keep to these,' he said. 'Being a minister's driver isn't what it was a few years ago.'

'I'm a trained bodyguard,' Gunnar said. 'I know this stuff.'

As they returned to the living room, the uniformed officers were leaving and the husband had just brought in a tray.

'Would you like this coffee?' he asked, and Gunnar shook his head. He didn't drink coffee. Coffee put him on edge.

'Here's your driver, at your service,' the national commissioner's guy said, jerking a thumb towards Gunnar, who leaned forward and extended a hand.

'Gunnar,' he said.

'Úrsúla,' she replied. Her handshake was strong and warm. 'This is my husband, Nonni, and our daughter Herdís. We have a ten-year-old son who is staying with a friend overnight, fortunately.'

'I understand you've had an unpleasant experience.'

'Yes. I imagine Boris has told you what happened. I'm unhurt, but had something of a roll in the snow,' she said. 'And the self-confidence has had a battering. You know that I was going to drive myself?'

Gunnar nodded, relieved that the minister had reminded him of the national commissioner's guy's name.

'My last job was in Syria, and there was gunfire all day long, and before that I was in Liberia during the Ebola outbreak. So I'm no shrinking violet, but somehow you don't expect this kind of thing here in Iceland. I have to confess I'm shaken.'

Gunnar nodded. It was clear that the woman felt a need to excuse herself, make it plain that she was no pushover, but that didn't matter to Gunnar. He was delighted to be in his dream job.

'Gunnar will handle all your security,' Boris said. 'And it's best if you don't open the door in the morning until Gunnar has rung the bell.'

'Why's that?' the girl asked with a curious expression on her face.

'It's because recently ministers have experienced unpleasant things at home. Offal or paint on their doors, that kind of thing.'

The girl's eyes widened in surprise and fear, and she looked beseechingly at Gunnar.

'Are you going to look after my mummy?' she asked.

'Yes,' Gunnar said, sending the child a smile. 'I'm going to take very good care of her.'

Tuesday

21

Úrsúla took the neat plastic sleeve that Eva handed her and lifted a corner to look at the printouts. *Fréttablaðið, DV, Morgunblaðið* and many online news outlets had covered the case at the time, six months ago, but there had been nothing recently. The latest clipping was five months old.

'These state that a formal accusation has been lodged, but there are no names – neither the mother's nor the girl's,' Eva said.

'This should be enough for Óðinn to find out more. There can't be that many police officers in Selfoss with rape accusations made against them. This must be documented somewhere.'

'Yes, according to the reports, the girl went to the local health centre, which ordered a rape kit from the National Hospital in Reykjavík, and after that there was a request for assistance from the Reykjavík city police in making a formal accusation, because it was against a police officer who came under the authority of the Southern Region.'

'OK, that's perfect, Eva,' Úrsúla said and handed the plastic sleeve back to her. 'Will you take this to Óðinn and make it clear that I want this followed up, with a formal request for an update on the progress of this case?'

Eva nodded, turned and was gone, and Úrsúla sat at the computer to check her emails. Eva had already filtered them efficiently, marking the ones that she ought to deal with personally. She would be able to get through a few of them before the cabinet meeting.

She was just finishing the coffee the secretary had brought her and had made progress on the unanswered emails when Eva appeared in the doorway.

'I've called the driver,' she said. 'Cabinet meeting, and a quick chat with the PM afterwards.'

'He'll want to talk about the South Coast Highway,' Úrsúla said. 'And I'm hardly halfway through it. There's a whole stack of material to go through.'

'You could ask Rúnar for information, if you need it,' Eva said, opening the door for her. 'And I can read through material and give you a digest.'

Úrsúla nodded. There was every likelihood she would do just that. There didn't seem to be many spare hours for work that required concentration in this job.

'It's plain idiotic to be driven from one building to the next when it would be quicker to walk,' she said. In the light of day, yesterday's fear now seemed pointless and she was already regretting having agreed to this ridiculous ministerial-car-and-driver idea.

'The last thing you need is to meet the media outside when you're out of breath and have wet feet from trudging across Arnarhóll in the snow,' Eva said, holding Úrsúla's coat so she could slip into it.

'I can dress myself,' she said, but Eva laughed.

'Get used to being waited on,' she said. 'It'll do you good.'

Úrsúla scowled. Nonni told her the same thing. He enjoyed looking after her, even though she knew that he did this partly to show her how pleasant their home life was and that she'd be better off with him and the children than in some disaster area, trying to put things to rights. She knew it was also a declaration of love: his way of showing her how dear she was to him.

She took the cabinet meeting agenda from Eva's hand and scanned it while they walked to the lift.

'And what did our excellent permanent secretary have to say

about this morning's message?' she asked as the lift doors closed behind them.

'He just mansplained to me that this kind of case couldn't be prioritised while there's other important ministry work waiting to be dealt with, but he would naturally acquiesce to the minister's wishes and examine the case.'

'Ach. Poor man,' Úrsúla sighed. 'I'll give him a gentle reminder later today, and again tomorrow, and again after that until he gives up and does what I ask him.'

'Welcome to politics,' Eva said and Úrsúla laughed.

'Somehow I don't think I'm going to be here long. This is just a temporary role, but hopefully I can achieve something useful and then move on to something else.'

She had always imagined that she would spend most of her working life dirty and sweaty as she tried to impose order on chaos and relieve suffering. Having children hadn't exactly fitted in with such a career, so when she had been pregnant with Herdís she had agreed to a desk job with UNHCR. But that hadn't lasted. Before long she was back in the field, going to refugee camps to gather information for the commission. After that, she had taken occasional unpaid leave as other organisations and bodies offered her assignments, and that was how it had been until a year ago, when Nonni had finally had enough and made it plain that it was time for her to move back to Iceland and find a job that didn't take her away from the family for extended periods. It had to be a job that didn't involve lethal epidemics and falling bombs. But all the same, her idea of the future still included dust, baking heat and an all-encompassing hopelessness that she could help alleviate.

'Just you wait and see,' Eva said. 'Politics is a bug. Once you're bitten, you can't get rid of it.'

Úrsúla laughed.

'I managed to not get Ebola when I was in Liberia, so I'm sure I can steer clear of the political bug at the Interior Ministry,' she said.

22

Last night they had made him take a shower with soap, and gave him clean trousers and a T-shirt to put on before locking him in a cell. Then there was breakfast, and he was read the riot act about keeping away from the minister. Lovely lads, these policeman today. In the old days he'd have been more likely to get roughed up for no reason at all.

The copper who took his statement had a serious look on his face, asking if he knew whose car it was that he'd made himself at home in, but he had shaken his head and acted as if it had been a complete coincidence that it had been Úrsúla's car and not some other one.

He wanted to trust this sincere young policeman and tell him that Úrsúla was in danger if the Devil himself had hooked his claws into her, but he didn't dare. There was every chance that he had his spies here as well. His lies and intrigue stretched out in every direction.

He walked past the bus station at Hlemmur, which was now too smart a place for him to be allowed inside. The smell of him made people lose their appetites, as one of the doormen had informed him, so he went straight to the kiosk.

'Good morning, and may it be a fine day,' he said as he went inside and heard the man behind the counter sigh. The old guy was working there today. He went straight to the coffee urn and filled a paper cup.

'Had a night in the cells?' the old guy asked as he handed him the coffee.

'Five-star accommodation,' he said, sipping coffee as he stood at the counter and watched two men feeding coins into the fruit machines. 'Do they ever win anything on those machines?'

'Pah. A handful of change now and again. I reckon it's more about the game than the money, whatever they think.'

He thanked the man for the coffee, dropped the paper cup in

the bin and set off into the falling snow that was coming from the west and seemed to be building itself up for a blizzard. He set off along Laugavegur, heading for the shelter. Although it would be locked until later in the day, sometimes the guys would gather outside, taking slugs from their bottles; surely someone would give him a dram now that he had started to shiver.

23

As soon as the photographers had left the conference room, Úrsúla realised that this was the moment she had been dreading: sitting at this table that had so often been in the news, as one of the participants, among the chosen ones who posed and smiled in their seats, hands in their laps, but who then shut the doors on the rest of the world while they took decisions. It was a relief to find that when the doors closed behind the photographers the atmosphere became informal.

'So where are the doughnuts?' the prime minister called out and the government laughed. This was clearly part of the routine. The tray was quickly brought in, most of those present reached for one of the twisted doughnuts and followed the prime minister's example by dunking them in their coffee. Two of the women present didn't join in, leaving the doughnuts untouched and making do with sparkling water. Úrsúla guessed they were watching their waistlines, as one of them, Guðrún, the minister for social affairs, looked to be on the tubby side. Women in politics had to look good, while the men didn't seem to need to worry about it, unbuttoning jackets and happily letting their bellies strain their shirt buttons.

She was relieved and delighted to find out how much this first cabinet meeting was like a management meeting at any other organisation – something she had plenty of experience of. The only difference between this and the meetings she had taken part in before was that the mode of address was formal. All of the ministers addressed each other by title and not by name. That would need some practice.

'Can I offer you more coffee?' the prime minister asked when the meeting was over and they were the only two left.

Úrsúla shook her head. She had moved to a seat next to him at a corner of the table. Through the window she could see the buildings at Lækjartorg, and if she were to crane her neck, she could see the square itself, where a small snowplough was scraping the ground and salting it for the benefit of pedestrians.

'The more I think about it,' he said, stretching to take one more of the twisted doughnuts and dipping it carefully into his coffee, 'the more I'm convinced we absolutely did the right thing by bringing transport, local government and justice under one roof in a single interior ministry.' Chewing the doughnut, he continued to speak from the corner of his mouth. 'Rúnar probably wasn't the right man for the job. But I have a strong suspicion that you're the person who can take this on.'

'Thank you,' Úrsúla said. 'I hope I can meet your expectations, and those of both parties.'

'No question,' the prime minister said, his mouth full of doughnut.

Úrsúla cleared her throat and drew a deep breath.

'Let's get down to business,' she said and the PM nodded.

'Although the South Coast Highway was one of our main election pledges, we need to find a good reason to dump it,' he said. 'We have to come up with something along the lines of the financing having fallen through, or that the whole matter has been put on hold until after the next election, or whatever, so that we can quietly put the whole thing to bed. You can rely on Óðinn to come up with some bullshit that sounds convincing but which can't be looked into too closely.' Úrsúla opened her mouth to speak, but the prime minister continued. 'Or, if you dare, you can take this decision on your own initiative, but you'll be in the firing line from every direction.'

'That's exactly the problem. There's cross-party agreement on this, all the polls show that the public is in favour, the environmental assessment has been done and the finance is there. So why pull out?'

'Do you think it's acceptable that a social-democratic party should be behind an initiative that means people have to pay a road toll for travelling around the country?' he asked and reached for another of the doughnuts. Úrsúla wondered if he had had any breakfast that morning.

'Of course private enterprise isn't the ideal option,' she said. 'But can you see this being done any other way in the foreseeable future?'

The PM put his half-eaten doughnut aside, sighed and stared into his coffee cup as if he was looking for fragments.

'I watched you on the TV when you presented this initiative,' Úrsúla added. 'You sold it to me, just like you sold it to everyone else. So why has your position changed now?'

The prime minister turned the cup around in his hands a few times then slurped down the remaining coffee. He put the cup down in its saucer, cleared his throat and looked at Úrsúla, who was taken aback by the intense blue of his eyes. She had often noticed them in pictures, but never face to face. There had to be something in the cold winter light coming through the window that intensified their striking sky-blue colour.

'There's a problem,' he said in a low voice. 'We have to get out of this, and the sooner the better.' He shifted in his seat, placed his elbows on the table and leaned closer to Úrsúla. 'There's a hitch in the financing,' he said. 'The bulk of it comes from pension funds and the state makes a small contribution, but there's a substantial chunk that comes from overseas investment funds.'

'I've looked through it,' Úrsúla said. 'As far as I could see, it all looks fine.'

'That's just it,' the PM said. 'It's extremely problematic; it's come to light that one of these funds – the largest one, in fact – is an overseas investor in name only. In reality, it's held by an Icelandic individual.' The prime minister coughed again. 'Ingimar Magnússon.'

Úrsúla stared at him and felt her jaw drop in astonishment.

'The one and only Ingimar Magnússon?' she asked.

'Hmm. Yep.'

'Shit.'

It was the only comment Úrsúla could think of.

'Yes.' The prime minister leaned back in his chair and looked down at the table like a small child with a guilty conscience. 'That pretty much sums it up.'

24

Úrsúla's frame of mind was grim as she stepped out of the portico of the prime minister's offices, but she had to stop herself laughing when the driver jumped out of the car and hurried around it to open the door for her. He didn't seem to be in a humorous mood though. He was dressed like a bodyguard in some foreign country, in a dark suit, white shirt with a black tie, and a white wire that snaked from his collar up to one ear.

'It's a bit silly not to walk the few metres from one building to the next,' she said, as if she felt a need to excuse herself, although this was his job and he was the last person she needed to apologise to.

'Pretty much everyone who has had a driver misses it afterwards,' he said.

Óðinn had said the same thing. Maybe this was a standard civil-service answer: a way to persuade ministers to have a driver at their disposal, with the same mixture of bossiness and concern that she had encountered more than a few times over the last few days.

'I imagine I'll get used to it,' she said, and realised as soon as she had said them that the words sounded odd. 'That doesn't mean I don't appreciate your work,' she added quickly. 'It's just a very strange feeling – I seem to have become the kind of figure everyone buzzes around.'

The driver nodded. 'I understand,' he said. 'But it'll become part of the routine.'

They were outside the ministry, and as he had instructed, she waited while he got out of the car, went around it and opened the door for her. Then he accompanied her to the door, not turning away until Eva came to meet them, a phone in her hand, which she handed to Úrsúla.

'I feel like a child being babysat,' she whispered to Eva as she took the phone.

'It's Rósa,' Eva whispered. 'The woman who came to see you that first morning. The one whose daughter...'

Úrsúla needed no further information and sighed as she took the phone.

'I'm so relieved to hear from you,' she said, as the woman began to apologise down the line.

'I hope I'm not being too pushy by going through your assistant. Your own number goes straight to the government offices and I didn't want to call your home number...'

'That's all right,' Úrsúla assured her. 'I wanted to get in touch with you. I didn't take your number the other day and it seems the assistant got things wrong. I'm sorry about that.'

'Please don't apologise,' the woman said. 'I'm so grateful that someone's prepared to help us. Everyone seems to have lined themselves up against us. There are kids online who have been calling my daughter a whore. And she's never even done it ... apart from ... except when...'

The woman's voice cracked and for a moment Úrsúla had no idea what to say. There were no words of comfort that would suffice.

'I'm deeply sorry to hear it,' she said in a low voice. 'It's a hard world, and it's painful to see our children experiencing the bad side of it.' She heard the woman sigh and sniff. 'Give me your full name and ID number, and your daughter's as well,' she said, trying to sound cheerful. 'This isn't going through an assistant. I put everything in the hands of the permanent secretary this morning, so it should go through the system quickly.'

Úrsúla started at the woman's snort of derision.

'If it's still the same permanent secretary, then not much will happen,' the woman said. 'I've spoken to him time and again, and every time he's just about to put things in motion, and nothing ever happens.'

25

'Why don't you make something of this fascination with ancient Icelandic stuff and study it properly?' Stefán asked with the questioning look in his eyes that always made Stella take what he said seriously. She always took careful notice of his advice and had done so ever since he had become her social worker when she was ten years old. This was why she continued to meet him at a coffee house once a month, even though he was long retired. The mystery was, why on earth he was still happy to give her his time. He was so generous with it, there had to be real concern there.

'I thought studying it would kill the enjoyment,' Stella said, and looked out of the coffee house's window. The driven snow seemed to be piling up against the pane so that soon there would be no way to see outside. 'School makes everything such a drag.'

He smiled through his grey beard, and Stella smiled back.

He still seemed to enjoy her company. She was grateful for that, even though his unasked-for advice and interference could irritate her.

'Academics don't even believe in magic. They just want to find out where it came from and how it was used,' she said. 'I've read loads of articles; there's nobody left who uses magic.'

'Why do you think that is?' he asked, a hint of a smile reaching those questioning eyes of his.

'Because people don't believe it works, that it's just some old junk.'

'Old wives' tales.'

'Yes. I understand why people think that, but what if this is an unexploited resource? What if the magic does work and can be used?'

Stefán sighed and grinned, but his smile vanished when the waitress appeared and asked Stella in English if there was anything more they wanted.

'She may be brown, but she's Icelandic,' Stefán snapped in irritation.

Stella gave the girl a smile and shook her head.

'Oh, I'm sorry,' the girl apologised. 'I didn't know you spoke Icelandic.'

'That's all right,' Stella said. She was used to this and was no longer surprised when someone addressed her in English. This had become more frequent after all the tourists had begun to arrive and there were more foreigners than locals around the town. 'Were you about to say something?' she asked Stefán, who had a sour look on his face.

'When people were cold and hungry – and beset by sickness, superstition and the fear of trolls and ghosts – they needed something they could believe in that would give them a little control over their lives,' Stefán said. 'I have to say I don't quite see how trousers made of a dead man's skin or farting runes have any relevance to people today.'

Stella laughed. It was just like him to come up with the farting runes. She had to admit some of the ancient Icelandic spells were hilariously funny, in their own sick way. But others were useful, no less so today.

'All right,' she said. 'But just imagine how useful it would be to be invisible. Or if you needed to find a girlfriend,' she added. 'I could help you out there.'

'I'm happy as it is with my Ása,' Stefán smiled, but reached forward and placed a hand on Stella's arm. 'But I can well imagine how you would have wanted to be invisible when you were a little girl.'

The questioning look was back, as was the concern in his voice.

'Could it be that, just like those people in the seventeenth century, this fascination with magic is just you trying to make sense of your life?'

26

As Úrsúla cleared her desk at the end of the day, she thought over a few other strategies she could have used to ensure the rape accusation received proper treatment. But it was too late now. What was done was done, and she had to admit that she felt her blood pumping faster through her veins. She needed to direct her thoughts elsewhere; after the meeting with the prime minister, the whole South Coast Highway headache had created a knot of tension inside her. Or maybe the tension was because she simply wanted to see Thorbjörn again; apart from the dog, he was the only one who had moved her on any emotional level since she'd been home. It was as if his proximity set off a turmoil within her that she hadn't felt for far too long, and she was unable to explain to herself why he had this effect on her. He'd been in her office less than a quarter of an hour before he'd pulled her close and kissed her.

As soon as he had come in she had begun to explain the complexities of the rape case. He had replied that it wasn't a problem, was easy to deal with. Then he'd taken the newspaper articles and the online coverage that Eva had printed out, along with the mother's phone number, folded it all together and stuffed it into his jacket pocket. His careless demeanour both fascinated and irritated Úrsúla.

'I can do an interview with the mother,' he said. 'That would attract attention.'

'Sounds good,' Úrsúla said. 'And you can send a request to the ministry to ask what progress has been made on the case, and then I'll have no choice but to make my own formal request, and push it hard. That way it can't keep getting pushed to the back of the queue.'

When she had spoken to the mother on the phone, she had come to the conclusion the usual methods weren't going to work. She would have to do something to crack the ministry's deep inertia when it came to uncomfortable cases. She would make it plain that she had no intention of tolerating such working practices. If her year in the job resulted in people who brought accusations to the ministry getting better treatment, her time would have been well spent. Some cleaning up was needed, and she wasn't going to shy away from it. But it was questionable whether Thorbjörn was the best tool for the job.

'How are you feeling?' he had asked. His voice was warm, and she had to swallow the lump in her throat as she recalled how understanding he had been when she had frozen, shrivelling up inside herself, in the middle of an interview about Liberia. That had been just after her return, after her time in the refugee camps in Syria, which would be any normal person's vision of hell. It was supposed to have been a prominent interview, but she had put a stop to it, feeling that it was the wrong approach, in view of all the suffering she had witnessed. She was also sure she could not describe in words what her work was all about, and wasn't convinced that anyone would be better off for reading about it. Some things were simply so terrible that it was better for people not to know about them; the results of an Ebola infection were exactly those things. Thorbjörn had said he understood her position and hadn't applied any pressure, despite having spent two days gathering material and preparing himself, and even though *Vefpressan* had already flagged up the interview.

Ever since then, thinking of Thorbjörn had given her a warm feeling inside, and as he stood in her office, looked at her with concern in his eyes and asked how she was feeling, she felt the turmoil inside and her feelings coming alive.

'I'm just fine,' she had said, coughing awkwardly; but he shook his head, took her hand and pulled her to him, and for a moment Úrsúla let his lips rest on hers, until she pushed him away. She longed to rest her head on his chest, nestle in his strong embrace, mould herself to him and forget.

She finished sorting the stuff on her desk, and sat down again, shaking the mouse to wake her computer from sleep. She would have to recover her equilibrium before going home. The guilt that had been a sharp pain in her belly for more than a year had built up. It was no surprise: not only had she become bereft of feelings for her own family, she had allowed Thorbjörn to kiss her, and in all truthfulness, she had returned his kiss. That was completely wrong, whichever way you looked at it. But at the same time, her heart pumped faster than it had for a long time. Alongside her regular heartbeat was another beat, with a rhythm that sent waves of delight through her. She closed her eyes and relived the moment.

Thorbjörn was just as he had been the last time they had met: stocky, hair cropped close to his skull and two days' worth of stubble on his face. He might well have been in the same checked shirt as when he was supposed to interview her.

'You're not all right,' he had whispered, pulling her into his arms, and her heart filled with gratitude. It was so good to feel the understanding, to feel the sympathy. 'You're not all right,' he whispered. 'But I can heal you.'

27

The drill's battery was flat, so Gunnar finished the job with a manual screwdriver borrowed from Jón, or Nonni, as the minister referred to her husband. That closed up their letterbox, so the minister's husband would have to do without the morning free-sheets. The note that had waited on the mat for the minister when she arrived home had clearly been written by some oddball; it was in an angular script with ugly letters in all different sizes, surrounded by marks and blotches. Gunnar could understand why she had been shaken by the message:

Remember, Death is the Devil's Handmaiden.

Gunnar had taken the note from Úrsúla's hand and put it in an envelope. It would be passed to the commissioner's department, as they collected all the threats received by ministers for analysis, to decide how each minister's security should be managed. Sometimes it was the same idiots who made a habit of pestering government figures, while there were others who had a particular axe to grind and were relentless in their efforts.

'I'll go to the post office tomorrow and arrange for your mail to be kept there. I'll collect it two or three times a week and bring it to you,' Gunnar said.

The minister's husband stared at him in astonishment.

'Can you do the grocery shopping for us as well?' he asked, and Gunnar laughed.

'No problem,' he replied, and shook his head at the open beer bottle the minister's husband made to hand him. 'I don't drink.'

It was one of the things he had weaned himself off. He didn't like to be a prisoner to desire, even if it was just the innocent fancy for a cold one at the end of the working day. His personal development aim was to be rid of all worldly ties; to be a slave to nothing, neither the buzz of a drug nor his own pride. The phone ringing excused him from explaining all this to the minister's husband. Normally a questioning look appeared on people's faces if you turned down a drink, almost as if it was admission that there was something wrong with you. Most people asked if he had dried out in rehab, and shook their heads, unable to grasp that he had given up alcohol without having to.

'Hello?'

Boris, his police contact, was on the line. Gunnar had been waiting for the call and went out onto the steps, keeping close to the wall where the porch around the door sheltered him from the worst of the snow; it had now eased off, merely falling from above instead of being driven sideways by the storm.

'You were right,' he said. 'The old guy's been let out. They let him go around lunchtime, so it could well be him who dropped the note in her letterbox.'

'I guessed as much,' Gunnar replied. 'I've sealed up the letterbox now, so we'll see what happens.'

'The police reckon the old guy was just looking for somewhere to shelter from the weather when he got in her car. He seems to be a couple of sandwiches short of a picnic, so they don't see much point in charging him or taking out an injunction. If he keeps on pestering her, we'll just have to talk him out of it.'

28

Úrsúla felt a stab of guilt in her belly as she silently reproached herself for the kiss, and no less for the feelings that welled up inside her when she was close to Thorbjörn. What on earth was wrong with her, being so emotionally numb towards Nonni, who she had loved and trusted more than anyone alive, while burning with passion for a man she hardly knew? Lying in bed with Nonni, close to him and in the warmth of his body, was so comforting, so safe, that she failed to understand herself.

If she were to apply a little pop psychology to herself, she was sure she'd find that this was some form of PTSD, manifesting itself as a bizarre lack of feelings for the people who she knew deep inside she loved the most. It was as if a disconnect had appeared between her mind and her body, between emotion and good sense, so that what she knew seemed to have no effect on what she felt in her heart. Now, deep in her heart, she felt a pulsing joy, the extra beat that Thorbjörn had set ticking and which she resented. There would be no more meetings. She had given in to temptation and she was determined not to go near the man again. There was too much at stake and the thought that she might hurt Nonni was heartbreaking.

She gazed at him as he sat in bed with his tablet in front of him, going through his emails. So that they could move home, he had resigned from a good position at the university in Geneva, taking on part-time teaching at the economics faculty at the University of Iceland. This was so that she could regain her balance in a safe, quiet, familiar environment.

These days he used reading glasses, and as they were cheap ones he had bought at a petrol station, they didn't fit and slipped down his nose, making him look cute as he tilted his head back so he could see the screen through them. He sensed that she was looking at him and glanced down at her.

'How are you feeling?' he asked, and she swallowed the lump in her throat; he wasn't asking a big life question about their marriage or her emotions. He was asking how she felt after seeing the note – the death-and-the-devil message that had been waiting for her when she came home.

'Oh, fine,' she replied. 'I'm with the police on this: it's not worth making a drama out of it with charges and whatnot. The poor old boy just isn't right in the head.'

'Hmm.' Nonni took off his glasses. 'You reckon the note came from him – the bum who was in the boot of the car?'

'Yes.'

Úrsúla didn't think twice. She simply took it for granted that the note had come from him. 'I don't want him charged or anything like that, but I'm not sure I agree with the police – that he was just looking for somewhere to get out of the weather. And I think the note today proves that.'

'What do you mean?'

'I mean that he seems to have some unfinished business with me. Not with just any woman, but me in particular. I had the feeling when he jumped out of the car that there was something he was looking for.'

Nonni put the tablet aside, clearly disturbed by what she said.

'Don't even start thinking like that,' he said, his voice grave.

'Ach, well. I know,' Úrsúla said. 'But with the note today—'

Nonni interrupted her.

'It's understandable that men like that trigger an emotional response in you, what with your father and all that, but you really have to make sure that you don't become an enabler. Don't start to feel sorry for some nutcase who could be dangerous.'

'I know,' Úrsúla said. 'I know.'

She shifted closer to him and pushed him back in the bed so she could rest her head on his shoulder and breathe in the scent of him. Contentment suffused her as she was surrounded by the warm security of his presence, and in response she instantly felt a new burst of guilt. But this was mixed with another and even more disquieting feeling, which grew the more she paid attention to it. This was her intuition that the street bum in the boot of the car knew her.

She tried to think back to the moment she had opened the boot and he had burst from it like an uncoiled spring. Had he called out her name as he leaped at her and sent her flying into the damp snow?

Had he called her Úrsúla?

Wednesday

29

It seemed there would be no respite. Now the whole thing had re-surfaced, just as they seemed to be getting things back on track. Kiddi had raged into the kitchen, his voice still breaking, going from bass to falsetto, as he yelled that he was never going back to school, and this fucking house could go to hell. Right now, Marita was almost ready to agree with him.

She scrolled through the news on the internet and saw that to-morrow there would be interviews with Rósa, Katrín Eva's mother, and with the newly appointed interior minister, Úrsúla Aradóttir. So this tension would continue for the rest of the week. She emptied her coffee into the sink. Since Kiddi had burst out of his bedroom and banged the laptop down on the table in front of her, it had gone cold.

She refilled her cup with hot coffee, added a dash of cream and sighed. She'd drink her coffee while she mustered the courage to call the school and let them know that Kiddi was ill. Then she'd have to call the bank and let them know she wouldn't be coming to work. Sitting in the cashier's booth and watching people divide into two groups was unbearable. There were those who knew nothing, or behaved as if nothing was amiss as they waited for their numbers to be called. Then there were those who ignored the numbering system and either chose a different cashier or made their way straight for her, to tell her that they were on her side; that it was all the fantasy of an attention-seeking teenage girl, and that Jónatan was a good man who would never do such a thing.

Then she'd have to call her mother back home in the Faroes, tell her the whole story and ask her to let Klemens stay with her a few more weeks. It wasn't because she was concerned he'd find something out, or because the nursery-school staff weren't wonderful; it was more because she doubted her own ability to cope with what the four-year-old might get up to. The day the police from Reykjavík had arrived to take Jónatan's statement, Klemmi had thrown a tantrum. Normally she could calm him down fairly easily, but this time she had barely managed to stop herself slapping the boy's face. His demanding presence had become unbearable, now that she hardly had the energy to keep herself going. And now Kiddi really needed her full attention as he was old enough to understand perfectly well what was going on.

Marita scrolled back through the news coverage. The circumstances were described in the same words across every media outlet, as if they were simply copying each other. The story was that the victim had been babysitting the police officer's four-year-old son one evening when he came home late from a shift. He had offered her beer, and as she was unused to alcohol she was soon drunk. The policeman was then supposed to have forced her to have sex with him. The girl had gone home, half dressed and in tears, and from there to the health centre with her mother, after which police officers were called in from Reykjavík to handle the accusation of rape. To a stranger who didn't know Jónatan and Katrín Eva, it might all sound very plausible.

But she remembered that evening clearly, and it hadn't been anything like Katrín Eva had described to the police. Coming home from the annual work get-together, Marita had met Katrín Eva in the doorway, and while the girl was clearly in a hurry, she had been neither in tears nor half dressed. She had been wearing that huge parka of hers and had said hello to Marita as they met at the door. Marita had asked if Klemmi had been good and Katrín Eva had said that he had, and that he had fallen asleep some time ago. Then they had said goodbye, Marita had taken off her shoes and her coat, fetched herself a glass of water and gone into the living room where Jónatan was asleep on the sofa, still in his uniform. She had lifted his feet, waking him up, and had sat on the sofa to drink her water while she told him about the skits that had been performed at the staff party. She didn't recall that he had been under the influence, although she couldn't swear that he hadn't had any beer. He listened to her account of the party, sniggered at one or two of the jokes that she repeated for him, and yawned. His feet were bare and lay in her lap. She had slipped a hand inside one trouser leg and ran it over the hairs on his shin, feeling his warmth.

Marita closed the laptop and picked up her phone. It was almost eight-thirty and she had finished her coffee. She would have to brazen it out with the school secretary and the receptionist at the bank, both of whom would act as if nothing untoward had happened, but of course both would know something had. She took a deep breath and tried to calm down as the hand that held the phone began to tremble.

30

Úrsúla should have remembered that Thorbjörn worked through the night and worked fast. But she hadn't expected his article to appear online until the next day. Now all the other media had picked it up, and an interview with Rósa, the mother of the rape victim, was set to appear the following day. Thorbjörn had also booked an interview with Úrsúla so he could give her side of the story and explain where in the system the case was. Eva had pushed the interview to as late in the day as she could to give Úrsúla time to prepare.

Freyja, the secretary, put her head around the door to tell her that Óðinn had arrived.

'Show him in, please,' Úrsúla said, and gestured to Eva to stay where she was. It would be better to have her present for this conversation.

Óðinn held his smartphone in front of him as he came in and held it up for her as he sat down.

Thorbjörn's headline could be seen on the screen: 'Police Rape. Fifteen-Year-Old's Case Lost in the System'.

'What's this supposed to mean?' he asked.

She didn't even try to pretend to be surprised. Óðinn was an experienced official and knew all the system's horse-trading tricks.

'I need to respond to the media to explain just where in the system this case is, so I'm asking you to make a formal status request.'

Óðinn nodded and opened his mouth as if he was about to say something, but Úrsúla forestalled him.

'Immediately. This happens right away.'

'I see,' he said and stood up with a sour smile on his face. He hesitated, as if he had something more to say, but said nothing, turned on his heel and left.

This wasn't the way Úrsúla wanted things done, but she needed him to learn the lesson – to take on board that he wasn't to sweep cases under the carpet because they could turn out to be an embarrassment for the minister.

'Óðinn,' Úrsúla said before he disappeared through the door. 'Just so you know: you don't need to shield me. I can take no end of flak. That doesn't matter. What matters is that people get their grievances handled by the authorities. I promised the girl's mother that I would examine the case and I want it examined.'

He turned in the doorway, looked at her for a moment and nodded. She could see that he was hurt, that by using this stratagem she had humiliated him, but she had needed to do something to kick-start this case, which seemed to have been repeatedly stifled.

'Was that all right?' she asked Eva as the door closed behind Óðinn.

She nodded her agreement.

'A reasonable mixture of firmness and explanation,' she said. 'But this is going to be all over the media, so that promise about taking flak is going to be tested.'

'I can take it. Transparency is a good thing,' Úrsúla said. 'I made the promise on the first day in the job to look into this case, and I don't break my promises.'

She had hardly finished her sentence before Freyja showed Thorbjörn in and Úrsúla felt the guilt overwhelm her, along with a rush of desire. She was about to break a promise; the most important promise she had ever made.

31

Gunnar was startled to see the minister looking so miserable. She sat in the passenger seat next to him with her phone in her hand, reading something on the screen that clearly wasn't pleasant.

'Something wrong?' he asked.

They were on their way to the opening of some exhibition of ancient legal texts in the National Library, where she was to give a speech. But now she wasn't looking at all cheerful, and every drop of blood seemed to have drained from her face.

'It's something you should probably take a look at,' she said and handed him the phone.

He slowed down and looked for a space that had been cleared of snow. The piles of it were that deep each side of the street, if he were to pull over he would have trouble freeing the car again, spinning its wheels in the drifts.

He finally pulled into a bus stop, took the phone and read the fine detail of what 'bitches who stick their noses where they're not wanted' can expect. The description was both foul and showed a level of imagination regarding how a female body could be abused; in particular, Úrsúla's body. The sender was fossi@gmail.com. That could be just about anyone.

'Keep hold of that,' he said, handing the phone back. 'We'll let the analysts at the commissioner's office see it. That's a direct threat.'

Úrsúla nodded, shut her phone and dropped it into her pocket.

'Are you OK?' he asked before pulling away again.

'Yes. Sure,' she said and took a deep breath. 'It's just unsettling.'

He set off into the traffic again, inching along the icy roads as he tried to work out how to tell her to protect herself from such messages, without appearing to be telling her what to do.

'Wouldn't it be better to let your assistant filter your messages?' he said cautiously. 'Most ministers do that. There's no need for you to read that kind of filth.'

'Hmm.' She appeared to be thinking it over. 'Eva does filter my mail, but I check it as well. Maybe I shouldn't.' She stared out of the passenger window and seemed to be talking to herself. 'But isn't it better if I'm aware that someone has such a deep hatred for me? Isn't it better to be prepared?' she asked, and turned to him with a look that showed her question was sincere. It was obvious that this aspect of the job was something she hadn't been prepared for.

'Eva and I will collect all the hate mail and threats, and we can pass them over to the commissioner's department. They'll produce a monthly digest for you and they'll be in touch with me if there's anything in particular that I need to watch out for. That makes the risk analysis more realistic, and you don't have to read the filth.'

She hummed to herself and looked out over the city's lake. It's surface had frozen and thawed several times in the last few days, so it had taken on a sheen that made it almost luminous in the midday brightness.

'I suppose it's part of the job and I ought to just get used to it,' she said. 'I should have known digging into a rape case would turn up something like this. It's as if some people can't hear the word rape without their hatred for women boiling over.'

'True,' Gunnar agreed. 'In the profiling course I was on we were taught that there are two social issues that can send people completely insane with anger: sex crimes and immigration.'

'Shit,' Úrsúla said. 'So I'm going to have all the racists coming after me as well when I start getting involved in immigration? That's where my expertise lies – it's the main reason I agreed to take on the job, to try and get those issues into some sort of order.'

At the Skothús bridge he decided to take a right turn, go over it and along Suðurgata to avoid the worst of the traffic, which was all keeping to the main roads, as the side roads hadn't been sufficiently cleared of snow. The ministerial 4x4 was on nail tyres, so it would cope where less well-equipped family cars wouldn't.

'This kind of hate mail simply goes with the job,' Úrsúla said, again sounding as if she were talking to herself.

Gunnar took the turning off the roundabout and the car sped up the slope to where the National Library sat, immovable.

'It's not just the job,' he said, recalling what he'd learned about high-risk groups. 'Women in this kind of role get double the hatred. That's something else I picked up on the course. Powerful women arouse some extremely odd emotions in people.'

32

Stella had shredded everything, tied the bag closed and was on the way out with the rubbish when her phone rang. She stopped by the door and fished her phone from the waistband of her knickers, where she had stowed it because there were no pockets in her grey tracksuit trousers.

'Gréta, again.'

'Hæ Gréta,' Stella said and barely managed to stifle a yawn. The woman had cooked a three-course meal the day before yesterday, and given her leftovers to take home, so she couldn't make it obvious how dull she found her.

'We've chatted every now and again since the other evening,

like you suggested, and I was wondering if it's time to meet up, or wait a while?'

Stella let out a low groan. The woman seemed to need to be guided every single step of the way to getting a date.

'No, meet her right away,' she said. 'You don't want to waste time on someone who's no good. You need to find out if there's a spark there or not. There's no point spending time on some woman if there's no spark.'

'OK, I see what you mean,' Gréta said. 'Should I invite her to the annual get-together at work, or out to dinner somewhere?'

'No!' Stella yelped. 'Absolutely not dinner for a first date. You don't want to be too eager. And it would be a pain if you ended up having to sit through a whole dinner with some misery guts.'

'She doesn't come across as miserable,' Gréta said, and Stella bit her lip. She was also thinking that it might not be easy for this apparently normal and rather pretty girl to be lumbered with Gréta for a whole evening.

'Coffee,' she said. 'Ask her to meet for coffee, and be casual, y'know? Say, "Shall we get a coffee sometime this week?" Don't come across as desperate; be confident, like you're out on dates all the time. Girls like that.'

'So just coffee, or coffee and cake? Or some kind of healthy cake so she can get the impression right away that I'm making an effort to not be too ... solid?'

'Jesus, Gréta! Just have what you want! Have cake, so at least she'll get to see that you're someone who enjoys life.'

Gréta laughed awkwardly. 'OK, yes. I'm just stressed and then I overthink everything.'

Stella's feeling was that once the girl had met Gréta in person, there would be no further dates, so it would be as well for Gréta to get some satisfaction out of the date; and that would be the cake.

'Just try to relax,' Stella said. 'And just be yourself.'

'OK,' Gréta said, and Stella could hear her take a deep breath. 'How are things at the ministry?'

'How do you mean?'

'Well, there's that scandal over the rape case that seems to have got bogged down in the justice system. Have you heard anything about it?'

'You know I'm just a cleaner here,' Stella said. 'I'm not a permanent secretary.'

'Just wondering if you've heard anything in passing, when you're having a smoke with the minister.'

'Fuck off,' Stella said, and ended the call, stowed her phone back in the waistband of her pants, unlocked the door using her card and backed through it, pushing it open as she went. Her arms were full of bags of waste and shredded paper, so she couldn't see over them as she took the usual couple of steps to the container.

'What would it cost for you to forget to shred stuff from a couple of bins and let me have it instead?'

The man asking the question was leaning against the waste-paper container, chewing gum with his mouth open. Stella started as if she was unconsciously about to defend herself and dropped the bags on the ground.

'It's OK, you're safe with me,' the guy said, and as if to demonstrate this, he raised his hands and took a few steps back into the car park.

'What the hell do you want rubbish for?' she asked. This had to be either a journalist or a creep of some kind. Or both: a creepy journalist.

'You don't need to worry about that,' he said. 'Just think about how much you want. Seven hundred krónur a bag? A thousand?'

She didn't have to think too hard to know that this would break all sorts of rules and she'd be sacked on the spot if anyone found out. But at the same time, the sums ticked over in Stella's mind. She was always so miserably skint at the end of each month, so a few extra notes wouldn't come amiss. How much would depend on how many bags he would want.

'Which bins are we talking about?'

'The permanent secretary's. And the minister's, of course.'

33

Úrsúla had already let herself out of the car by the time Gunnar had made his way around it to open the door for her. She would have to talk this over with him; she was perfectly capable of getting out of a car by herself, at least here, outside her own house. There was something deeply ridiculous about sitting still, waiting for him to open the door for her.

There was a light in the window; it warmed her heart to see the cheerful yellow glow behind the glass. Nonni had to be home, and probably the children as well, and all of them crowded into the kitchen most likely, the children playing a game or doing homework, and Nonni conjuring up something wonderful in a saucepan. She was thinking about discussing the South Coast Highway dilemma with Nonni this evening. She could always rely on him to have a sensible, grounded opinion and to keep things to himself. That at least was a feeling that hadn't faded: that she could trust Nonni.

The evening gloom made the street greyer than ever. The row of concrete-walled houses, of which theirs was the fourth from the corner, had been coarsely rendered in shell sand, as had the whole street. On the other side, directly opposite their place, was one of the large, white-painted detached houses that broke up the greyness of the street. In bright weather, myriad grey shades could be seen in the shell sand, and it sometimes glittered if the sunshine was strong, but now, in the darkness, the houses had a heavy, dark feel to them.

She and Gunnar walked side-by-side over the slippery pavement to the steps then stopped as a police car came to a halt next to the ministerial car.

'We roll past every couple of hours,' said the police officer who stepped out of the patrol car. 'So the chief told me to bring this, as I was coming this way anyway.'

He handed her a large envelope.

'It's the statement about the incident with the car for you to sign,' he said, walking with them to the front door. 'I can take it back with me.'

Úrsúla went into the hall, kicked off her shoes and opened the drawer of junk in the phone table. She rooted through and found a purple felt-tip; it would do to sign the document. She scanned the statement as she stood there, reading the detailed description of how the homeless man had hidden in the boot of her car, and had jumped out and pushed her to the ground when she had found him there. She pulled off the cap of the felt-tip with her teeth and leaned over the old telephone table to scrawl her signature on the document. Then she straightened up sharply at the sight of the homeless man's name.

Her heart raced and a feeling of helpless fear swept through her. This was a name she knew; a name she knew very well.

34

Stella inspected her mother's plump face and smiled. Her mother smiled back at her with the enigmatic look that meant she knew something Stella didn't, but the drug-induced fog prevented her from saying what it might be. Stella sometimes wished her sedation could be reduced so that they could talk together properly and she could find out what was behind that mysterious smirk. But the doctors said that it was out of the question. Her mother would just become hysterical again, and possibly injure herself or someone else. That was the nature of the damage to her brain, they said.

Sometimes when she sat with her mother, which she had to confess to herself was becoming increasingly seldom, questions about their whole existence came to her mind. Her mother was the only one at the care home who wasn't as pale as snow, and sometimes Stella felt that she was in completely the wrong place. The round Aztec features seemed to be so impossibly far from their proper environment Stella couldn't help but retreat to her childhood memories of her mother wrapped in a colourful poncho, with flowers in her hair and a long necklace made of bean pods around her neck. She wondered if everything they had fled – Stella's father and his criminal gang – could in fact have been worse than this.

'*Tienes trabajo?*' her mother asked – *You're working?*

She asked the same question every time. There was nothing strange about this, of course; Stella had never been great at holding down a job.

'Yes, Mama,' she said and stroked her mother's hand. 'I have a good job now.'

Her mother smiled mysteriously and her almond eyes narrowed even further. It was no surprise that new staff at the care home assumed she was Asian and wanted to talk to her about Thailand and Vietnam. Stella's own looks were more mixed as her father had been practically white. Her curly hair had come from him, although when her mother was in a bad mood, she would sometimes say that Stella was the child of a black delivery man who had appeared in the kitchen one day, and that was where the curls had come from. Of course that wasn't the truth, and her golden skin was evidence of that. She was fair enough for people to assume, after they had moved to Iceland, that she was Guðmundur's daughter. She had been proud of that, back when she had been a little girl and they had only just arrived in Iceland, but her attitude changed fast after she saw what Guðmundur did to her mother. Since then the misunderstanding was one she was always at pains to correct. She much preferred the thought that her father was a hit man in Mexico, rather than Guðmundur.

'It's your birthday soon,' her mother said, and Stella felt her heart leap with delight. Her mother would sometimes forget Christmas and Easter, and normally she didn't know what day of the week it was, but she always remembered Stella's birthday – always, without fail.

'Yes,' Stella said. 'Soon. I'll be twenty.'

'And then your grandmother will come flying to us,' her mother said, and it was as if the drugged mist parted for a moment; she sat upright in her chair and leaned towards Stella. 'She'll come flying all that way on a broomstick to visit you on your birthday.'

Joy made Stella's heart beat faster as she looked into her mother's eyes; they were now alive and the mysterious smirk had spread across her face into a real, clear and shining smile. It was the way her mother had smiled at her when she was little.

'Yes,' she said, gently stroking the back of her mother's hand. 'Grandmother will come soon.'

'Flying on her broomstick,' her mother said.

'Yes,' Stella said, and sniffed. This was a rare genuine conversation, which for a while banished her loneliness.

'Your grandmother the flying witch.'

'Yes.'

'Please give her my regards.'

'I'll do that, Mama,' Stella promised and laughed as her mother giggled quietly.

'You'll have to tell me about everything she does and says when she visits you on your birthday.'

'Of course.'

It went without saying that Stella would tell her mother the news after her birthday. But she knew, as always, that there was no guarantee her mother would be in any condition to listen to her then.

'Remember to tell her that I sent her my regards,' her mother repeated, and smiled as the joy glittered in her eyes. 'Remember to tell her that her daughter sends her regards. Tell her that, when she comes flying to you on her broomstick, your grandmother the witch. *La bruja.*'

35

The phone call had left Marita exhausted. Jónatan had been drunk and in tears, which she found even harder to cope with than the rage over all this that burst out of him when he was sober.

'Maybe I deserve this,' he said, and she shushed him.

There was no point starting to think like that. He just mustn't think or talk along those lines. If he were to say anything like this to anyone else, it could be misunderstood and seen as an admission of guilt. So she repeatedly shushed him and told him to go to bed and sleep it off. Tomorrow everything would look better. But that was just something she said, as tomorrow things would be no better. If anything, it would all be half as bad again.

Tomorrow the interview with Rósa, Katrín Eva's mother, would be published, undoubtedly a gut-wrenching, tearful interview full of the crap that the girl had fed her. And tomorrow Jónatan would call again and either yell or whine, and again she would have to calm him down and comfort him. She did feel sympathy for him, but it was painful.

He had been temporarily transferred to another station after the accusation, and he was lonely, missing her and the boys. Although she felt sorry for him, she was also relieved in many ways not to have him there all the time, as regardless of how hard she tried to convince herself, there was always the same irritation with him deep inside her. He had got them into this mess. He had given the girl a beer, and that was what seemed to have set this whole crazy thing off.

It wasn't yet midnight when she sat at the computer to see if the pdfs of any of tomorrow's papers were online yet. Over the last few months she had found that sometimes you didn't have to wait until past midnight for the next day's paper to be ready. She checked the main media outlets, but so far there was nothing. Midnight was half an hour away, so she wouldn't have to wait long. She opened Facebook and scrolled through the news feed.

She couldn't see anything about the case, as she had blocked anyone who had commented negatively on it. That left only a few people, mainly from back home in the Faroes, who didn't follow Icelandic news. Of those who were local, there were just some colleagues from the bank and a few youngsters, friends of Kiddi's.

Her heart skipped a beat when Katrín Eva appeared in a picture. It was one of her own photos that by some evil coincidence had shown up in Marita's 'memories'. Klemmi was in Katrín Eva's arms; she guessed that he was around three years old, so she had just started babysitting him. It had been beneath Kiddi's dignity to look after his little brother, even though they had offered to pay him. He had wanted to get a proper summer job, outside the house, so he had spent the summer on one of the tills at Bónus. Katrín Eva had looked after Klemmi all that summer, and sat for them every now and then over the winter, and had continued to do so right up until ... Right up to when she had decided to go home howling to her mother, saying that Jónatan had raped her.

Marita deleted the memory, then searched for the picture and deleted that as well. If only it was as easy to delete people in real life as it was on Facebook.

She checked the papers again and saw that the first one had appeared online. She downloaded it and scanned it quickly. There was nothing on the front or back covers, or on the first couple of pages. And then it was there; almost half of the fourth page. It was yet another digest of the reported circumstances and the interior minister's short response to the paper's questions, with a pledge to find out what progress had been made on the case – as if there was anything to check on.

Why didn't the police write this off like any other stupidity? Surely they received dozens of complaints every day about this or that. One from a pissed-off mother, clearly angry that her daughter had been given a beer, could hardly be any more serious than anything else. This interior minister ought to have better ways to spend her time.

Marita went back to Facebook and looked up the minister's profile. She seemed to have trained as an engineer and had been involved in aid work. She had clearly changed her profile picture the day she had taken over as minister. The previous picture had shown her with a glass of red wine in her hand, obviously at some party, while the new picture was something more dignified, almost a passport photo with a blank background. Marita clicked on the picture and examined the minister's face. If this woman had any sense, she would see soon enough that the accusations against Jónatan were based on lies, and that the wretched girl and her mother were both crazy. Marita saw that the minister's email address was displayed on her Facebook page, and wondered whether she should write to her.

36

Gunnar stared at the empty text box and wondered how to begin the message he had already addressed to fossi@gmail.com. He needed to be courteous, but firm. His intention was to make this person aware that Úrsúla was not an unaccompanied, defenceless woman, that a team of men was in place to protect her. Guys like this, who loved to terrify women, only had respect for other men.

Good evening, he began. *My name is Gunnar and I am Interior Minister Úrsúla Aradóttir's bodyguard. The permanent secretary and the minister's assistant drew your message to my attention and requested that I reply to you.*

Of course, this was completely untrue. To begin with, his role wasn't that of a bodyguard but primarily her driver, and he hadn't discussed replying to the message with anyone, but he wasn't going to let this thug know that his email had reached Úrsúla, or give him the pleasure of knowing that it had done its job by causing her discomfort and fear.

It is clear from your words that you are struggling with a great

deal of anger that appears to have little to do with the interior min-
ister. I would urge you to find other outlets for your feelings and
request that you do not contact the minister again.
With kind regards,
Gunnar

He hit send and heard the whoosh as the message set off on its electronic journey to its anonymous recipient. Gunnar lay on the floor and worked on his abdominal stretches. He did thirty crunches, rested for a while, and did another thirty. He was able to empty his mind while he exercised and focused his thoughts on counting the crunches. As he felt the muscles in his belly begin to tire, he slowed down, making the same movements, but as slowly as he could, to make them even harder. His muscles howled with the effort. No pain, no gain, he thought, as he dug deeper.

'What are you doing up so late?' Íris asked sleepily as she came out of the bedroom. They had fallen asleep after they'd made love, but he had woken after a few minutes and had not been able to get back to sleep.

'Crunches,' he said.

'Why's your laptop switched on?'

'Just because. Some work I had to do.'

'What work do you need to do in the middle of the night?' she asked and stepped closer to the sofa where the laptop lay, bending to see the screen.

Gunnar rolled over, reaching out to shut it.

'What was that for?' Íris said and he could hear the tone in her voice that he knew so well. This was the sharp, tense tone that preceded the storm. 'What are you hiding?' she asked.

'It's confidential,' he said. 'It's work stuff.'

'Liar,' she hissed.

'Not at all,' he said calmly. 'I work for the Cabinet Office. So I'm not at liberty to let anyone see my emails.'

'You're a fucking chauffeur!' she snapped. Gunnar imagined that the tourists who had rented the flat next door would be awake by now. 'What can a fucking chauffeur be doing that's so secret? Well?'

'It's confidential,' he said in the same calm voice, feeling the need to correct her growing inside him. He wanted to tell her that he was also a bodyguard, that he oversaw the minister's security, and that he was working directly with the commissioner of police. But she knew all that; she was simply trying to provoke a response. But a response was what she wasn't going to get.

'If you're messaging someone else then I'm going to go fucking crazy,' she yelled, storming into the bedroom and throwing things around.

He wanted to call after her that she was already crazy, but instead said, 'I'm not messaging anyone else. I'm telling the truth.'

It was indeed the truth, but now that her anger had been triggered, there was nothing he could do. And he had no inclination to try to do anything. He took up his position on the floor to go back to his abdominal exercises, but hadn't even begun when he heard the front door slam shut behind her. Now the tourists next door would definitely be awake.

He filled his lungs and pumped out his breaths. Tearing each muscle made it stronger, so he had to push them beyond their limits if he wanted to increase his strength. He was close to two hundred repetitions, and the sweat was cascading down his forehead and into his eyes when he heard the whoosh from his computer that told him he had a message.

Breathless, he got to his feet and shook the mouse to wake the computer; as expected, he saw a reply from fossi@gmail.com.

He opened it and saw immediately that his courteous approach had not had a positive effect. If anything, the wording told him that his efforts had rather served to infuriate this lunatic still further.

You can request all you like, you idiot. You don't tell me what to do. I'll bite her fucking tits off if I feel like it, and fuck her posh arsehole after I've beaten her head to a pulp. Go to hell and take the fucking whore with you.

37

Time passed in a crazy, recurring whirl, repeating itself, but at the same time constantly bringing new things for him to deal with. He had gone to a funeral in the cathedral with Eddi, who was so tanked and such a sensitive soul that he began to weep after the eulogy for a man he didn't know from Adam.

'After that, I feel like I know the fellow,' Eddi said, and sniffed.

They had probably sung the hymns a little too enthusiastically because it wasn't long before the undertaker came and told them to keep it down. The undertaker was a good guy, though; he let them stay where they were, on the pew at the back, as long as they didn't cause any bother. Some undertakers wouldn't let them in, but this one was always good to them.

After, they had gone to the wake held in the cathedral's hall, but they had struggled with the stairs; Eddi because of how drunk he was, and him because of his wretched bad foot. They stuffed themselves at the cold buffet and announced that 'he was always a friend to me' in sob-choked voices to anyone who would listen. Nobody had the heart to throw them out, and nobody wanted to dishonour the departed by being less than charitable. It always worked.

Eddi had puked the whole lot up on the steps outside, after they tumbled down them on their arses. It was strange how it was always harder coming down steps than climbing up them. He had helped Eddi, miserable, nauseous and wailing with artificial sorrow, up to the shelter, where they washed their faces at the sink and got ready to get some sleep.

He woke with the sermon echoing in his head, and crossed himself, thankful for this power against the evil that had pursued him ever since the Devil had brought little Úrsúla under his sway.

The warden suddenly appeared before him, anger in his eyes, and ordered him to get to his feet.

'You know we don't tolerate any trouble here!' he said, and

added that Eddi was in a state because of him and had been taken to A&E. 'You've given him a black eye and fat lips, not to mention knocking out one of the few teeth he had left! And the bathroom's awash with blood. What the hell's that about – beating the shit out of your pal?'

The anger in the warden's eyes was shot through with disappointment. He was all right, this guy, but like everyone who worked there, he was strict.

'I won't deny what I don't remember,' he muttered as he pulled on his coat.

It was clear that the Devil's works were gathering around him. And now that the Devil had his hooks in the interior minister herself, nothing and nobody was safe.

'You need to have a word with yourself, Pétur. You're not coming in here again unless you abide by the house rules,' the warden yelled at him as he set off into the snow.

Dawn wasn't far off and there was nobody about in the city so there was a silent stillness to the place. It wasn't long before his feet were wet, as the snow was thawing and the footsteps of those who had walked this way before him had become a million little foot-shaped puddles. He tried to avoid them, but slid and stepped in them now and again.

All the lights were off at Úrsúla's house and the letterbox had been screwed shut. It was just as well her car was parked outside so he could leave his message for her on the windscreen; his warning for her to turn aside from the path of the Devil.

Thursday

38

Úrsúla looked up from her laptop and was about to say something to Nonni as he returned from dropping the children off at school, but was startled by the expression on his face.

'There's another note!' he hissed, angrily waving the piece of paper in Úrsúla's face. 'It was on the windscreen this morning. Under one of the wipers. It's obviously meant for you.'

Devil's-mini-ster reaps death, the note read.

'Looks to me like a direct murder threat,' Nonni said, fidgeting as he stood by the desk, too agitated to sit down.

Úrsúla nodded her agreement.

'I'll have Gunnar look into it,' she said, but that was as good as adding fuel to the fire.

'Have Gunnar look into it? What on earth does the driver have to do with this? We need an injunction on this weirdo to stop them from coming near us. We can't live with daily threats. You need to have the police deal with this right away!'

Úrsúla stood up, pulled Nonni close and wrapped her arms around him. His body was stiff with tension, and it took a little while before he began to relax. She laid her face against his chest and felt his rapid heartbeat through his shirt.

'I do take this seriously, my love, I promise,' she said. 'Gunnar has a direct line to the national commissioner's office, which makes sure that government people like us aren't troubled by weirdos. They collect all the evidence and do some kind of assessment of what level of security is needed.'

Nonni squeezed her tight, once, and let her go.

'I have to admit that it scares me a bit,' he whispered.

'I know,' she said. 'Me too.'

She stroked his face. He was so agitated that she didn't dare mention the email she had received the day before. That would wreck all his ideas about protecting her. He had been certain that they would be safe in Iceland, that here nothing bad ever happened and evil was restricted to comments online. And anyway, she had a hunch that the email was less significant than the scrawled notes, a feeling that was especially true, now that she knew the note-writer's identity. She would have to tough it out and tell Nonni she knew who it was.

'I'll take this very seriously,' she said. 'In fact, the feeling I had was right: the down-and-out in the boot of the car did know me. I saw in the police report last night that he's Pétur Pétursson. Now that he's lost all his teeth and has a beard, I didn't recognise him.'

'Úrsúla! And it's only now that you're telling me this?' Nonni snapped.

'I only realised last night,' she said. 'I didn't want you to have a sleepless night.'

This was a half-truth. The reality was that she had first wanted to think it over for herself. She had preferred to examine the fear and the sorrow in her mind before tackling Nonni's reactions. They were what she expected: he strode back and forth across the kitchen, his face flushed and a look in his eyes that could have been panic, anger or fear.

'Pétur Pétursson?' he asked.

'Yes.'

'Pétur Pétursson has been holed up in the boot of your car and has been sending you death threats?'

The tension made his voice so high, it was ready to crack.

Úrsúla nodded.

'The Pétur Pétursson who murdered your father?'

39

Stella swore with disgust as the bus she couldn't afford to take shot past, splashing her with slush as it went on its way. She sketched the Óttastafur fear symbol in the air and angrily sent it to the driver, although she knew it wouldn't change anything. She would have to walk further from the kerb wherever she could, but the snow was piled in such a way that the only clear part of the pavement was right by the road, which was just where anyone making their way on foot would get splashed as inconsiderate drivers hurtled past without slowing down. Right now she had seen enough snow to last her a lifetime.

She had been captivated by it when she had seen it for the first time, not long after they had come to Iceland. Guðmundur had woken them up to see the falling snow, and she hadn't been able to contain her excitement, rushing out into the little garden in her nightdress, where she danced and tried to catch flakes of snow on her tongue as they fluttered to earth. Then she had rolled in the white, soft snow until her teeth had begun to chatter with cold. Her mother and Guðmundur had laughed and kissed, and for breakfast Guðmundur had made pancakes using the leftover rice pudding from the day before.

She recalled sitting, looking out through the window at the snow, with the sugary, oily residue of the pancakes running down her chin, and thinking that she and her mother were just too lucky for words. It seemed too good to be true that they were in a safe place where they would never again need to be frightened. And that was the way it had turned out: too good to be true. Just as the snow that fell to earth – pure, white and beautiful, with promises of bright winter days to come – soon turned into a slippery, grey-brown mess on the streets, getting in everyone's way, so her mother's marriage to Guðmundur soon turned sour, and then it became dangerous.

Stella turned down onto Sæbraut and crossed over at the lights. She clambered over a high mound of piled-up snow to reach the cycle lane that ran along the shore; it had been cleared and scattered with sand, so she could make reasonably fast progress here. The snow falling from the storm-pink sky was wet and would undoubtedly turn to rain by daylight. At any rate, she hoped so. It would be great to have a few days of rain to clear away the dirty snow and the ice beneath it.

Not far from the ministry, just as she was going to cross over Sæbraut again, she slipped on the ice. She put out a hand to save herself, and felt the pain shoot up her arm as her palm landed on the sand-strewn ice and she found herself sitting in the snow. She screamed to stop herself from crying, and when she stood up she realised that her behind was soaked and the legs of her trousers were still wet through from the bus splashing her earlier. But she had taken a decision. She was going to sell this creepy guy all the rubbish he wanted, as long as he'd pay a thousand krónur a bag on the spot. At least she'd be able to afford to take the bus and have something left for a hot dog and a Coke for dinner.

40

Gunnar finished scraping the wet slush off the steps with a shovel and took a big bag of salt from the boot of the car to scatter on the path. Úrsúla's husband, Jón, had told him there was no need to clear the snow, but it was in his job description and he had no intention of having the minister slip on the ice and injure herself. As well as that, he was pretty sure that the husband had enough on his plate, as the minister was hardly going to be doing any household duties considering she left for work early in the morning and came home late in the evening. He thought of Fossi's message as he salted the steps and reproached himself for having got in touch. He should have known that there was little point appealing to the good sense of a man who could write that kind of thing.

He was just about to ring the doorbell when Úrsúla opened the door.

'Come in and have a cup of coffee,' she said. 'Nonni has just made some.'

'I can wait in the car if you're busy,' he said. He wanted Úrsúla to understand that she had no need to be concerned about his wellbeing, or to worry about whether he was properly fed and rested. But sometimes people who weren't used to having others looking after them found this difficult, and according to the bodyguard's handbook, this could lead to increased tension.

'I need a word with you,' she said, gesturing for him to follow her inside.

His heart lurched and he felt a knot of anxiety form in his belly. He had no doubt she was going to get rid of him and go back to driving herself. He had noticed how uncomfortable she was being driven around, her every footstep followed. He took off his shoes and tiptoed into the kitchen, where she was sitting at the table.

'Good morning. Fresh coffee,' Nonni said, placing the coffee pot on the table in front of him.

He nodded, smiled but left the coffee untouched.

'Good morning,' he replied quietly and took in their expressions. It was obvious that something was wrong. The veins in Nonni's neck were bulging as he moved nervously behind his wife, who pushed a shabby scrap of paper across the table towards Gunnar.

He read *Devil's-mini-ster reaps death* and felt a strange surge of relief. She wasn't going to get rid of him. In fact, she needed him. It was clear that they were both upset by the note.

'It seems to be from our friend who was in the boot of the car,' he said.

Úrsúla nodded, and Nonni cleared his throat, as if encouraging her to say something.

'Our so-called friend is probably no friend of mine,' she said and slid a sheet of paper across the table. He quickly recognised it as the police report about Úrsúla finding the down-and-out in the back of her car. 'Look at the man's name.'

Gunnar did so. He had heard the police mention that the man's name was Pétur, but other than that there was nothing familiar about it.

'Begin at the beginning,' Nonni said, standing behind her, and Úrsúla coughed.

'There's some back story here,' she said, and took a deep breath. 'My late father struggled with alcoholism and ended up more or less on the street. So most of my memories of him from when I was small are of seeing him downtown with his mates, who were all in much the same boat – dirty and drunk, sometimes causing trouble; other times battered and bruised by fights or accidents. A lot of the time he hung around with Pétur. They were friends.'

She picked up her mug and sipped, several times in a row, as if she was trying to swallow a lump in her throat.

'And Pétur was in a cell with my father, up at Hverfisgata, the night he died.'

'Pétur Pétursson, the man who has been sending Úrsúla clear death threats, is the man who murdered her father in a police cell,' Nonni said.

He was obviously deeply upset, and it manifested itself in this burst of anger, as if he had been keeping his rage under control until an opportunity arose to let it go. His wife sat silent, though, and stared into her coffee mug. Gunnar could see no anger in her expression. There was only sadness.

'He was judged unfit to stand trial,' she said. 'It must be years since he was released from the psychiatric detention unit at Sogn. It's deeply disconcerting that he's showing this interest in me now.'

'Showing interest!' Nonni snapped. 'Saying it's disconcerting that your father's murderer is sending you death threats is putting it mildly!'

41

In that moment between sleep and waking, the same string of thoughts ran repeatedly through Marita's mind. Opening her eyes and waking up fully, she sighed. She had been back in that nightmare situation when all this had first happened. Her mind was going through the events of that evening again and again in the hope of finding some overlooked detail that could shine a light on Jónatan's innocence.

Marita had met Katrín Eva in the doorway when she came in, wrapped up in her down jacket, and had greeted her:

'Hello, love. How was the evening?'

Katrín Eva had mumbled a reply, which Marita had taken as confirming that the evening had been fine.

'Was Klemmi all right?'

'Yes. He went to sleep ages ago.'

Katrín Eva had not looked up, and she guessed that the girl was sleepy and clearly wanted to be on her way home rather than hanging about in the cold.

'I'll pay the money into your account, love,' Marita had called after her.

Katrín Eva had turned and waved the notes she had in her hand, indicating that Jónatan had already paid her for the evening's babysitting. There was nothing unusual about that. It looked to be three five-thousand krónur notes, much more than she was owed, but Jónatan had always liked to be generous. Katrín Eva was normally cheery and would spend some time chatting to Marita before leaving, but that evening she had seemed taciturn, but it had been late and she must have been tired. On top of having drunk a beer.

Maybe that was why she hadn't stopped to tell Marita what Klemmi had got up to as she sometimes did, and hadn't asked how the staff dinner had been. Perhaps she was trying to disguise the fact that she was feeling the effects of the beer, and that was why she had avoided Marita's eye and kept her face deep in the fur collar of that ridiculously expensive coat she was so proud of.

Even though she had not seen Katrín Eva's face properly, she had still been able to tell the police officers from Reykjavík, when they asked her repeatedly, that she was certain the girl hadn't been in tears. If that had been the case, she would have heard it in her voice. Instead, she had just said, in a normal voice, that Klemmi had gone to sleep ages ago, then she waved a couple of notes in the air and left. If anything untoward had been going on, then Marita would have felt it as soon as she came in. But that couldn't have been the case as the living room was quiet, everything was in its place and Jónatan was asleep on the sofa.

If Jónatan had just raped the babysitter, he would hardly have been so relaxed as he sniggered at her account of the staff dinner and sighed with satisfaction as she massaged his feet. The whole thing was completely ridiculous.

Marita sighed again and stretched. The day ahead of her was going to demand all her courage and determination. She would have to call the school to let them know that Kiddi wouldn't be coming in again, then call in sick at the bank, and then she would check the news media and go through the comments on the online news articles.

It was just as well that most people seemed to believe their side of the story and doubted that the rape accusation could be true, although she was secretly ashamed of her delight when some referred to Katrín Eva as a lying slut. At least it provided her with an outlet, albeit meagre, for the anger that she had been bottling up inside as she did her best to keep a lid on everything.

Most of all today, she was not looking forward to reading the interview with Rósa, Katrín Eva's mother. She dreaded what she would have to say. They had been such good friends before. That was why Katrín Eva had come to babysit for them: her mother had offered the girl's services were they ever to need a babysitter.

Marita got to her feet and reached for the clothes she had taken off and thrown on a chair the night before. This would be another day of tracksuit trousers. She couldn't be bothered to get properly dressed, and she wasn't going to draw the curtains. Whether people really were gawping at them as they drove along the street, or she was just imagining it, it was as well to shut the world out, behind thick curtains. At any rate, it was the dark dead of winter both outside and inside the house.

42

Úrsúla almost began to regret having put Gunnar in the picture when they arrived at the ministry to find Boris, the national commissioner's representative, and Óðinn waiting for them with serious looks on their faces.

'We'll start the day with a meeting focusing on the minister's security,' Óðinn said, leading the way into the meeting room. She and Gunnar sat side by side, with Óðinn and Boris facing them.

'Coffee? Tea?' Óðinn asked, and when they had all shaken their heads he sent the secretary out of the room with a vague gesture that she clearly understood.

Gunnar handed Boris the scrap of paper that was now dry and wrinkled, and he read it.

'Yes, that could certainly be interpreted as a death threat,' he said. 'Particularly considering what we know about his background.'

'Agreed,' Óðinn said, leaning towards Boris to read the wording on the note. 'Somehow or other the man needs to be taken out of circulation. This isn't something that can be tolerated.'

Úrsúla's feeling of discomfort, which had begun as she entered the ministry building, had disappeared now that she saw them taking this seriously. Somehow she had feared they would think she was making a mountain out of a molehill. In comparison to Ebola, bombs and bullets, a note from a mentally ill down-and-out seemed trivial. But this fear seemed in some way unreal. What had happened to the woman who had pulled on a plastic overall and ski goggles every morning to bustle into the quarantine zone in Monrovia to organise the camp's expansion? Where was the woman who had been able to stand up and explain co-operation between NGOs on transferring whole refugee camps across the border into Jordan, maintaining her concentration as bombs could be heard going off in the background?

'Taking someone out of circulation isn't that easy,' Boris said. 'But I'll see what can be done about having him sectioned and kept on a closed ward.'

'And we need to get an injunction to keep him away from the minister, so the legal side of this is clear and there's a reason to call in the police if he tries to come close,' Gunnar said.

'I'll put the legal department on to it,' Óðinn said, scribbling a note.

'Gunnar, we'll be treating this as the highest level of security risk as long as this man is free,' Boris said. 'You make the necessary arrangements, ensuring the children don't answer the door alone, that sort of thing. Then there's the question of getting the security camera fitted outside so they can see who rings the doorbell. It's a disgrace how long that's taking.' Boris tapped notes on his tablet as he spoke.

Gunnar nodded.

'I'll go over all this stuff with the whole family this evening,' he said to Úrsúla. 'I'll inform the school and your husband that I'll collect the children for the next few days and bring them home.' He turned to Óðinn. 'We can co-ordinate that with the minister's schedule, can't we?'

'Of course,' Óðinn said. 'Our primary priorities are the minister's security, and alleviating any concerns she has about her family's safety.'

Úrsúla felt a wave of gratitude, because Óðinn was taking this development so seriously, which told her that this really was something grave, and not least because he appeared to have forgiven her for the day before.

'There's something I'm wondering about,' Úrsúla began, and the men all looked up. This was the first time since they had sat down that she had spoken. 'Could I get information on Pétur's detention, or rather, his treatment? It occurred to me that I have no idea how long he was in detention at Sogn, or what his medical notes say about his condition when he was released; whether or not he was considered dangerous.'

Óðinn nodded and made another note, while Boris again tapped at his tablet. Then they all stood up. Óðinn nodded to her before he opened the door and went out into the corridor, but Boris stopped in the doorway and turned to Úrsúla.

'There's one more thing,' he said thoughtfully. 'Do you know who this devil is that Pétur seems to be warning you about?'

43

Boris's question had echoed at the back of her mind all morning, but without properly becoming the subject of her attention: *Who is he, this devil?*

She had lunch sent up to her office and ate it while going through the South Coast Highway documents, but there was nothing in the paperwork that linked Ingimar Magnússon to the project. The usual due-diligence research into the financial backers merely showed overseas ownership. If Ingimar really was financing part of the road construction, then they would have to cancel it. She would have to find a way out of this – some way out of the trap.

Then there had been a visit by a group from the Coast Guard to discuss the possibility of increasing government funding. They had been accompanied by a corpulent, red-haired official called Adolf who lobbied so hard on their behalf that the Coast Guard people had been embarrassed.

'This is something that has to happen,' he had said with finality at the end of the meeting, standing up and taking a position at the door so that Úrsúla, who had intended to politely usher the guests out into the corridor herself, and to use the opportunity to go for a smoke, wasn't able to get past him.

'I repeat my promise that this will be examined in detail,' she said, trying to inject a firmness into her voice and stepping closer in the hope that he would get the hint from her body language and move aside. But he seemed immune to such unspoken messages.

'A promise is just a promise—' he began, and was clearly about to add something when Úrsúla interrupted, her voice sharper.

'When I promise something, I mean it,' she said, catching Adolf's eye and holding it until he looked away. Then she turned to the Coast Guard officials, who stood watching with embarrassment on their faces. 'I keep my promises, and what I'm promising now is that this will be considered in every detail.'

The Coast Guard men nodded their heads; as far as Úrsúla could see, they didn't welcome Adolf's overbearing manner. She turned back and came one step closer to him, so that they were almost touching, and he finally moved aside so she could open the door out into the corridor.

Her hope of snatching a cigarette break between meetings vanished when she saw that the next set of visitors were already waiting. A delegation of philologists wanted to speak to her about the Icelandic naming committee, which accepted or rejected the new first names that could be used when registering births. She reiterated her well-known opinion that it wasn't the state's job to be interfering in people's personal lives.

'We had hoped that the new minister would be more receptive to traditional arguments, and might even support maintaining the committee,' said one of the academics, frowning, and deepening still further the chasm that had formed between his eyes the moment they had stepped into her office.

'As I said, my opinion is that the Icelandic naming committee should be disbanded and we should be able to trust the good sense of the general public and allow them to choose names for their own children.'

'That could mean that there might have to be changes to child-protection legislation,' said one of the women, in alarm, and as far as Úrsúla could see, all three of them sat thunderstruck.

'Isn't that a good thing?' she asked, making an effort to speak lightly to counterbalance her guests' deep concern. 'If someone really wants to give their child a name that's so bad, it's damaging to that child, surely there's something going on already in that household that the child-welfare authorities should be taking an interest in. Wouldn't it be best for the wellbeing of a child saddled with a terrible name to be examined by the authorities responsible for child welfare?'

They went through the usual arguments – the language-preservation policy, the endless delight young parents took in concocting new names and the situation in neighbouring countries – but this discussion seemed to do nothing to lessen the concerns of her guests. They would undoubtedly have stayed longer if Freyja had not come in and announced that the allotted time was up. The academics got to their feet, and Úrsúla shook their hands, promising that she would examine their arguments in detail.

Eva came in as the trio departed, and handed Úrsúla a mug of coffee and a doughnut.

'Nothing but chaos?' she asked through a mouthful of her own doughnut.

Úrsúla laughed. 'No, not at all. I want to be able to help everyone, but I'm struggling to balance state regulation with the interests of parents who can't get a passport for their child because they've come up with an unacceptable name. I can't stand this nanny-state shit.'

'So you're going along with the Rúnar's decision to shut down the naming committee?'

'Oh, yes.'

Úrsúla dipped the doughnut into her coffee and bit into it. Its sweetness barely balanced the sour taste of the coffee, which had clearly spent far too long on the hot plate.

'Could you fix me a coffee machine for this office?' she asked, and Eva immediately tapped a note into her phone. 'One of those that just makes one cup at a time and won't give me endless environmental guilt.'

Eva grinned.

'You're getting the knack of all this luxury. First a car and a driver, and now a personal coffee machine!'

'That's right,' Úrsúla said. 'I've got used to the ministerial sauce, the ministerial car and the ministerial rubbish. All I need to complete the set is the ministerial coffee machine.'

They were still laughing as the door opened and Óðinn came in, knocking as he did so.

'What's so funny?' he asked.

Úrsúla shook her head, and Eva's expression instantly became deadly serious as she muttered an excuse. He looked at them inquiringly, one after the other, as if ready to stave off some blast of aggressive laughter, then moved closer to Úrsúla's desk and placed a sheet of paper on it.

'It's a press statement about this rape accusation,' he said. 'It's the usual stuff: the ministry regrets and the minister will ensure ... blah, blah. I'll send it out if you're happy with it.'

Úrsúla took the sheet of paper and scanned it.

'I'd have liked to have met the journalist to discuss this with him. Statements like this are a way of buying time, avoiding giving an answer,' Úrsúla said, and could see from Óðinn's expression that he didn't agree with her.

'I would strongly advise that we stick to the statement,' he said. 'We do need to buy ourselves some time so we can find out how far this case has gone. I don't think it's advisable to discuss things with journalists at this juncture.'

'What do you think, Eva?' Úrsúla asked, in the faint hope of some support from that direction.

But it didn't matter what either of them had to say. She was determined to meet the journalist. Because that journalist was Thorbjörn.

44

Stella's pulse pumped as she jogged down the stairs towards the ministry's back door, even though there was no chance that anyone could have seen her putting the waste paper in the bag unshredded. This late in the day the building was half empty, and it wasn't as if anyone kept tabs on her work. The creepy guy was waiting by the container, as they had agreed. She hurled the bag of shredded paper into it and handed him the other two bags, glancing up at the building to check that nobody was watching from any of the windows.

'That's the minister's and the permanent secretary's?' the guy asked as he took the bags.

'Yeah,' Stella replied. 'The minister's rubbish is in the bag that's tied. The one that's taped up is the permanent secretary's.'

He nodded and handed her some notes. She took them and stuffed them in a pocket, relieved to have the security of having some cash, but at the same time with a faint remorse deep in her belly. There was no question that she would be sacked if anyone were to find out. This was, without doubt, the easiest job she had attempted, and she shuddered at the thought of going down to the social security office to sign herself on as unemployed, knowing that she'd have to accept whatever lousy job they offered her once her benefits had run out.

The guy got in his car without a word, and Stella walked out of the car park and down towards Sæbraut, undecided whether to spend some of the cash on a bus home or to use it all to get something decent to eat. Most of all she longed to go up to Laugavegur and use every penny to drink beer in Dillon until DJ Andrea started to play. Then Andrea would buy her more beer; if she could drink beer all evening she wouldn't need to eat. But her plans hadn't gone further than that when her phone rang; it was Gréta's number on the screen. She seemed to be the only person who called these days, now that Stella's closest friends were spoken for and had lost all interest in the world outside their relationships.

'She wants to meet for a drink! This evening, right after my broadcast!' a flustered Gréta said. 'And I don't know what to suggest. Where do young, fashionable types who know what's *in* right now want to go?'

Stella grimaced at the image Gréta seemed to have of her. She didn't feel remotely fashionable or *in* as she trudged through the slush with two thousand krónur in her pocket that she had got for selling rubbish. But Gréta had never seen her at home in her little bedsit with mould on the walls and a bathroom she shared with four other people.

'I'm walking past your block right now,' Stella said. 'How about I come up and we can talk this over?'

In her mind she could see the glow of the little glass-fronted fridge in Gréta's kitchen, full of beer and champagne.

'Yes, please!' Gréta said. 'I'm getting myself ready for tonight's news and just popped home to change. But come on up. I'm so nervous about this date or whatever it is. Or maybe she swiped by mistake. She might be one of those people who can't tell left from right...'

Stella ended the call without saying anything. It wasn't good for Gréta to dig herself deep into desperation. In the lobby Stella nudged the up button. Hopefully Gréta would have a snack of some kind to offer her, like last time. Maybe some of those Greek olives that she ordered for herself specially.

45

He could sense that something had changed when he returned with the cans of sparkling water in a bag, but he wasn't able to put his finger on it right away. She had sent him out to buy lime-flavoured water that came in aluminium cans, and while he thought it was ridiculous to be buying canned water in Iceland, where the water from the tap was as clear and fresh as it could be, he gave in. He enjoyed spoiling her. But now there was something strange brewing. She stood by the kitchen worktop sipping from a glass of water.

'Didn't you just send me out to buy the super-special water because you didn't want to drink from the tap?'

'Gotcha,' she said, emptying her glass into the sink. 'Just winding you up.' She did it hurriedly, and there was an awkward look on her face, as if she had been taken by surprise. This wasn't just teasing, as she referred to the ways she provoked him. She had something to hide. His eyes scanned the living room and stopped at the laptop on the coffee table. He was sure he had left it on the sofa.

'Have you been snooping in my computer?' he asked.

'No, I just...' she shrugged. 'I just wanted to look something up on the net, see what's on at the pictures. Shall we go and see a movie tonight?'

'That's my work laptop,' he said. 'I told you to leave it alone.'

'Come on. I was just checking the movie listings,' she said. 'What's the problem?'

'I told you to use the iPad for the internet when you're here. And I told you that I'm the only one who uses the laptop. In my line of work I can't share a computer.'

'Right! A chauffeur,' she snapped and stalked to the door. 'That's a really special job!'

She slammed the door and Gunnar wondered how long the door frame was going to last. If they were going to be together much longer he'd better start looking for a steel one.

He popped open one of the aluminium cans and tasted the sparkling water. It was surprisingly good and certainly made a change from tap water, although he wouldn't have bothered with anything so trivial. He picked up the laptop and sat on the floor with it.

The email from fossi@gmail.com to Úrsúla that Eva had forwarded to him was remarkably similar to the one that Gunnar had received from him the previous evening. Now he bitterly regretted having written to him, to say the least. His email had fallen on stony ground and he wondered if it could even have been counterproductive. Maybe it had stirred up this lunatic's hatred of the minister even more. No doubt it was best to leave that kind of thing unanswered, but there was something about this kind of spinelessness, people who threatened violence but didn't dare do it under their own names, that Gunnar found deeply infuriating. He knew it was his weak point, his Achilles' heel, and that was precisely why he should not have allowed himself to write to Fossi.

Just to let you fucking Feminazi know that your hole isn't any more special than any other whore's hole. Sometime you're not expecting it I'm going to grab hold of you in the dark and batter you with a knuckleduster and fuck you until you beg for mercy you cunt.

Gunnar tried to force a smile, trying to find some kind of levity inside himself that would allow him to laugh it off, dismiss it, but it didn't work. The smile turned to a scowl and before he managed to stop himself, he had tapped in a reply and sent it:

So you know, you meatheaded idiot, your messages never reach the minister, so you can write whatever you like – everything goes from me straight to the police, so the only results you'll see are the police knocking on your door when they've traced this. PS. Wash your mouth out. Soap helps.

Gunnar leaned back and felt the buzz that his reply had given him. He closed his eyes and conjured up an image of Fossi that he felt fitted the philosophy that came through in his messages: a sweaty badly shaved man with an inferiority complex, sitting in a tattered armchair with a laptop on his knees, wanking over torture porn.

He had hardly any time to enjoy his feeling of victory, as a reply appeared after only a few minutes.

What makes you think I'm frightened of the police? I'm not scared of the cops. Your whore who thinks she can be a minister is the one who should fear me, and you should fear me too, you fuckwit.

46

For the first time since returning to Iceland, Úrsúla had a clear feeling of being alive. Her daze had given way to a hot rush that swept through her body like lava spreading under a glacier, thawing her out and bringing her to boiling point as she thought of Thorbjörn and their meeting that day. The relief that she could still feel emotion was so powerful, it almost brought her to tears. It was as if the guilt was somewhere far away, somewhere downtown at the work meeting Nonni was having – it wasn't something that troubled her right now, although she was pretty sure it would accompany him home.

But until then she was determined to enjoy feeling good for the first time in many months. As she sat in front of a cop show on the television, a stack of South Coast Highway paperwork on her knees, she knew it was a betrayal to be cultivating this relationship – it was completely wrong – but all the same, she couldn't stop herself sending Thorbjörn a message:

It was good to see you...

Her heart fluttered as the message went on its way, and she wondered where he would be when it arrived. Maybe he was out at some bar with a beer in his hand – she knew he was a dedicated barfly – or maybe he was at work on an article. Or maybe he was sitting alone, as she was, on the sofa, trying to erase from his memory those kisses and their heaving sweaty delight in each other.

Likewise, his reply read.

She felt a stab of disappointment. One flat word wasn't enough to satisfy her hungry mind. 'Likewise' was something so impersonal; a word that people would use after meeting at a birthday gathering or a party conference. Her phone buzzed again and her heart leaped as she read a second message:

I don't want to take a shower. Want to keep the smell of you on me tonight.

She replied with a heart emoji and closed her eyes as she thought back to their meeting, which seemed to have been so long ago, even though only a few hours had passed. She had asked Gunnar to drive her to Thorbjörn's home for what she described as a 'short meeting' without any further explanation. Forty minutes later she had come rushing back out to the car and sat in the back. Gunnar's expression had remained completely impassive, with no indication that he had noticed anything as she repaired her makeup and brushed her hair on the way home.

Úrsúla was startled by a knock. She couldn't be sure if she had been deep in a daydream, or somewhere between sleep and wakefulness, but now she was wide awake and her heart hammered in her chest. She got to her feet and went into the hall, then stopped and stood still, listening. Maybe it had been her imagination, a warning from her conscience, which had been sleeping deep inside her and was now stirring. Nonni wouldn't knock – he had a key – and the children were in their beds. She tiptoed to the door of Ari's room and looked inside. He was fast asleep, face down as usual, the duvet kicked off and the floor scattered with toys.

Maybe he had kicked one of his toys out of the bed and it had landed on the floor, waking her up. It wouldn't be the first time he had fallen asleep over his Lego. Úrsúla slipped into his room, picked up the duvet, laid it over him and gently stroked his hair. He was a beautiful boy and would grow into a handsome man like his father.

The knock was repeated. Úrsúla stiffened. It came from the front door. Unmistakeable. Someone was at the door.

47

Stella was pleased with how her evening had gone. She had resisted the temptation of a pub crawl, mainly because she had chugged a couple of beers in the half-hour she had spent with Gréta, and taken a couple more with her for later. She had also made herself a sandwich and heated it up under the grill while a stressed-out Gréta had made her check out one top after another, until Stella finally nodded her approval at a pleated blouse, which she told Gréta to wear under her jacket. Gréta rolled up the top and the jacket and stuffed them in her bag. She would change into them before meeting the woman for a drink. Stella told her to arrange to meet at the Slipway Bar, and to take care to leave after two drinks, saying that she had another appointment. It was always best to be the one to call time.

'If you fancy her,' Stella went on, 'go somewhere by yourself, to the bar or the toilet, and draw this symbol in spit on your palm, then shake her hand with it as you say goodbye; hold on for as long as you can.'

Stella drew the magic symbol on a piece of paper and handed it to Gréta.

'What's that?'

'It's an old Icelandic spell to hook a girl.'

Gréta sniffed, but took the scrap of paper all the same.

'You really know your stuff, considering you're pretty much a foreigner,' she said, rushing to the bathroom to brush her teeth.

Stella finished her sandwich, took a chunk of chocolate from the kitchen cupboard, and dropped a can of beer into each coat pocket, then accompanied Gréta, dressed in a mint-green jacket and with her hair tousled and in a short ponytail at the back of her neck, to the lift. As the lift reached the ground floor, she offered Stella her hand then leaned in and kissed her cheek.

'Thank you for all your help,' she said tenderly, and looked into her eyes, smiling with an expression that reminded Stella more than anything of Stefán, her social worker. He would sometimes gaze into her eyes with a mixture of sincerity and inquiry that she could never completely work out.

Stella was startled. She retrieved her hand and wrinkled her nose.

'Can't you get the hairdresser who sorts you out before the broadcast to do something a bit more sexy with your hair?'

'Such as what?' Gréta asked sharply, and Stella immediately regretted having said anything. She'd only added to the woman's nervousness. But the words had tumbled out of her somehow; she'd needed some way to break the uncomfortable eye contact that seemed to demand of her something she couldn't understand.

'I don't know. Something a bit more rock 'n' roll. Something younger.'

'Fuck. This is going to be a proper mess. She's not going to fancy me,' Gréta grumbled as she marched towards her car.

Stella went the other way, downhill towards Sæbraut to catch a bus, perfectly satisfied with a free meal and some free beer.

When she got home she took a shower and lay on her mattress, intending to take a quick nap. Instead she fell into a deep sleep, not waking until late in the evening when her phone pinged as a message was delivered.

She wants another date! Gréta's message read, triumphant, judging by the string of smiling faces and love hearts. Stella sent her a thumbs-up in reply, got to her feet and went to the shared kitchen, which also served as a living room for the Polish construction workers who lived there. She switched on the television to see if Gréta had taken her advice and done something new with her hair. She found the replay, punched the *play* button and it went to the middle of the news bulletin that ended with Gréta saying good night and reading out the headlines.

This was a different person from the one she had seen in the car park earlier in the evening; the woman who read the news and conducted the programme was confident and relaxed, with a smile on her face. Her hair was different, a little wilder – a spikier look instead of the helmet-like hair she usually had, and it made her appear livelier somehow. She asked the weather guy what they could expect and she asked the sports reporter what that evening's sport roundup would be covering, before looking straight into the camera and thanking people for watching.

Stella paused the replay and rewound to watch that part again. She had never taken a good look at Gréta before, never watched her carefully. She paused the replay right at the end of the broadcast, with Gréta looking directly into the camera, just as she had looked into her eyes in the lift, and Stella had to admit to herself that, although on the screen Gréta appeared even tubbier and you couldn't say that she was exactly pretty, she exuded a sexy energy. Maybe there was nothing so surprising about the pretty woman on Tinder wanting to see her again.

48

Úrsúla tiptoed to the front door and put her ear to it, listening for any sound outside. She held her breath and took care not to make the slightest sound with her every movement. She had no desire to have visitors, and whoever it was could hardly be paying a friendly call; these days people had the manners to call ahead, as everyone knew how busy her family was now. It could hardly be anyone selling stuff from door-to-door as it was getting on for eleven o'clock, and knocking after ten was seen as the height of bad manners.

She was startled by another knock; she felt its force pass through the wood and into her cheek. All that was between her and whoever stood outside were these hardwood planks. She wondered who was so determined they continued knocking when there had been no response after the first two attempts.

Of course, it might be something completely innocent: a neighbour needing to borrow some milk or some such everyday errand. But Úrsúla was feeling the effects of the comments below the articles in the online newspapers, which she had been unable to resist reading, so she was terrified that whoever was standing outside meant her harm. At the same time she was furious with herself for being so frightened. This was the woman who hadn't turned a hair when faced with an Ebola outbreak or a burst of machine-gun fire. She was the woman who could drive into a famine zone, step out of the car and start organising emergency relief without letting the sight of the children's swollen bellies or the wailing of the mothers with dying children in the arms get to her. She could see how ridiculous this situation was and couldn't help an ironic smile at the thought of their direction the online debate would take if people could see the new minister of the interior, the heroine of overseas aid, shaking with fear, too scared to open her own front door.

She heard a deep cough beyond the door, followed by a throat being cleared. Now Úrsúla's fear crystallised into the image of the bearded man she had once trusted and then deeply hated with a child's single-mindedness, and who had now made a new appearance in her life, dogging her steps at every opportunity. Only an old man would cough like that, so it was obviously Pétur. She wanted to fetch her phone and call the police, but her feet seemed to have no energy in them and refused to obey her. She sank to the floor with her back against the door. Right now the emergency button she had been promised would have been worth having. She could have pressed it and had Pétur arrested. She longed to have him locked away so there would be no more horrible notes on her car, or anyone hiding in the boot, or anyone knocking at the door when she was alone at home with the children asleep.

As if from a far distance, she heard a key being inserted into the lock and the door began to open. She instinctively leaned back against it. She pressed her feet into the floor and pushed her back against the door with every ounce of her strength, but she wasn't strong enough. The door forced her back and before she realised it, Nonni was crouching at her side, her face in his hands as she wept through gritted teeth.

'Hey, Úrsúla! It's all right, calm down,' Nonni said in his soothing voice, but somehow she couldn't pull her mind out of the panic mode it had switched into to prevent Pétur from reaching her sleeping children.

'Someone was knocking,' she gasped. 'There was someone at the door before you who knocked and I could hear him cough. It was Pétur, trying to get to us.'

'No, Úrsúla. It was the old dried-fish guy, the one from Grindavík who comes once a month. He said he'd knocked but hadn't wanted to ring the bell because it's late and the children might be asleep. I ran into him just down the street.'

Úrsúla stared in confusion into Nonni's eyes. She felt her heart sink, and the tears flowed down her cheeks. It had to have been the tryst with Thorbjörn earlier in the day that had broken down her defences, the gateway to her heart that she had these last few months kept locked and bolted.

'Hey. There, there, sweetheart,' Nonni said, his voice soothing, holding up a sizeable bag of dried fish.

49

Marita was relieved that Kiddi seemed to have spent most of the day asleep, only appearing to wolf down a couple of slices of bread smeared with peanut butter and jam, then disappearing back into his room without saying a word to her. She had tried to stroke his shoulder while he sat hunched over the kitchen table, but he shrank from her touch so she immediately held back. She didn't know how she could approach him, unsure if she had enough energy to give him even a little of herself. She was simply glad of every hour that she didn't have to deal with his reactions to the interview with Katrín Eva's mother. It had left her shaking with fear and anger when she had read it that morning, and the comments that appeared below the online version hadn't helped. Most of them seemed to support the standpoint of the woman and her daughter. The public's sympathy lay with those who whined the loudest, it seemed. She felt as if anyone could say whatever they liked about her family. Many of them pointed out that Jónatan had a son the same age as the girl in question, as if that had any bearing on the matter. Others wondered why they had needed a child minder when the family had a teenage son, as if there was something suspicious about that. Reading between the lines, Marita thought she saw a suggestion that she had asked Katrín Eva to babysit for some underhanded reason, when the truth of it was that she had given in to Kiddi's laziness, as every time he was asked to look after Klemmi, he moaned as if his life were on the line.

The comment that irritated her most of all was the one from a woman who asked what the man's wife thought about all this, as if she was supposed to be somehow standing against her own husband on behalf of all women.

Rósa, Katrín Eva's mother, had said in the interview that that evening ruined her daughter's life as well as her own, that nothing would be the same again. Marita agreed – this applied to her own family as well. Neither she, Jónatan or Kiddi would ever get over this, and she wondered what had prompted Katrín Eva to level this false accusation at Jónatan. What on earth had changed, after the two families had got on so well for more than a year, that had put something like that in her head?

The television was on and Marita realised that the cop show she had been sure had just started was over. Her knitting lay untouched in her lap, so she must have been sitting staring into space for ages. She was startled by her needles clicking against each other as they tumbled out of her hands to the floor, and at the same moment Kiddi stormed out of his room.

'It's a fucking lie that she's a virgin!' he yelled. 'She's definitely been fucked, and I know at least two guys whose dicks she's sucked!'

He spat his words out over her where she sat, unable to move, and he punched the air like a boxer, then spun on his heel to march back to his room and slam the door behind him.

Marita wanted to get to her feet, to follow him and ask him more, to find some words to comfort him, anything that could soothe the boiling fury that seemed to rage increasingly fiercely inside him. But she couldn't find the strength. His anger was one thing, but the crudeness of his words, describing sexual acts in such a casual way, left her paralysed.

In spite of his deepening voice and his frame, which seemed to be growing in every direction by the week, her little boy speaking of fucking and sucking, as if these were something everyday in his youthful existence, had taken her completely off guard.

Friday

50

Adolf moved one step closer to her as she entered the lift, and she immediately had the feeling he had been waiting for her. She said 'good morning' as a sneering smile appeared on his face. He folded his arms across his chest and she felt that he was deliberately flexing to place an emphasis on his physique. She felt uncomfortable, but she knew that she was still tense after the previous evening. It had been a very long time since she had broken down like that. She hadn't freaked out even when Pétur had leaped at her from the car's boot. But at that time she hadn't known that it was Pétur coming at her. When it came, that realisation had filled her with a searing mixture of fear and sorrow that had opened a weakness she seemed to have spent her life trying to conceal. It was the sensitive and immature weakness of a child. She moved to the far end of the lift and repeated her 'good morning' in a firmer tone.

'Has the matter got to committee stage?' Adolf asked in a derisive voice, without returning her greeting. The lift came to a halt and Úrsúla stepped out with relief.

'Not to committee,' she replied and smiled amiably. 'But an informal working group has been put together to work with the Coast Guard on finding a solution.'

Adolf put out a hand to stop the lift door from closing.

'Really? I haven't heard about a working group,' he said, and Úrsúla's smile broadened.

'No, I don't think you're part of it,' she said, turning and walking quickly into the minister's corridor, hearing the door lock behind her. She went directly to her office and told Freyja that she wanted no interruptions for the next hour.

Her breath was coming fast and as soon as she was in her office she leaned against the door. Eva was sitting with her nose almost against the screen of her laptop.

'I'm pretty much in shock,' Eva whispered.

Úrsúla nodded her agreement.

'Yes,' she said. 'I read the interview with that poor girl's mother when I got home yesterday. It's such a tragic description of the whole thing.'

Eva shook her head, and there was something about the look on her face that sent a chill down Úrsúla's back.

'I don't mean that,' Eva said. 'I'm looking at the item that popped up online a few minutes ago. It's about you.'

51

'According to our sources, the minister requested at a meeting with ministry staff and police that Pétur Pétursson's medical records should be handed over, as well as records of any psychiatric treatment he may have undergone. Such records are confidential and are not considered to be publicly available.'

Óðinn read from the screen in front of him in a voice that was so powerful and resounding that Gunnar found it almost painful. Then he slammed the laptop shut with a bang.

'There were three of us at this meeting,' he hissed, staring at Gunnar. 'How the hell was this leaked?'

'I have no idea,' Gunnar said and shrugged. 'I know as much about this as you do.'

Óðinn glared at him for a while, then sighed and slumped back in his chair. Gunnar had always felt that Óðinn was a friendly, reliable type, but now his manner was sharp and irritated.

'I don't understand it,' he said. 'I've spoken to Boris and he was as surprised as I was – said he hadn't even started looking for these documents so there's nobody else inside the police who knows about the minister's request, and I haven't mentioned it to anyone.'

'So it has to be me?'

Gunnar squeezed out a smile in a weak attempt to highlight how ridiculous this half-accusation sounded, but it made no difference. Óðinn's expression didn't change, but he twisted slightly in his chair to stare out of the window at the dark sky that would hardly have time to turn a real blue before dusk again set in.

'Maybe you mentioned this in passing to someone who could have then leaked it?' he said, still gazing out of the window.

'No,' Gunnar said.

'We're talking about a meeting that took place yesterday,' Óðinn said, turning back to face Gunnar. 'It can't be a long trail in such a short time.'

Gunnar shrugged again. There was no satisfactory explanation that he could give the permanent secretary; he couldn't think of any way Úrsúla's innocent and, in fact, understandable request could have triggered such a media storm.

'You have a girlfriend?' Óðinn asked. 'Could you have inadvertently mentioned this to anyone you trust?'

'No,' Gunnar said. 'I haven't mentioned this to anyone at all. It's as simple as that.'

Óðinn sighed and turned his gaze back to the window.

'It's a clusterfuck, the minister getting a kick in the teeth like this after only a week in the job.'

'What can we do?' Gunnar asked as he stood up.

Óðinn spun his chair in a semi-circle and got to his feet.

'What you do is precisely nothing,' he said with determination. 'The ministry will issue a statement explaining that this is all a misunderstanding.'

Gunnar nodded, turned and could feel Óðinn's eyes were on him as he left the office, along with his suspicion. It was obvious that Óðinn thought Gunnar was the source of the leak.

Gunnar walked along the minister's corridor to the lift. While he waited, he opened his phone and checked the news. It didn't look good, and the comments were vicious. He scrolled through one thread back to the beginning.

Guðmundur Jónsson: *Officials misusing their power, again and again.*

Abbi Stabbi Ólason: *Who the hell does this old bitch think she is? Medical records are confidential!!*

Óli Gunnars: *Hey, pal. This Pétur is the man who murdered her father, so maybe she just wants to make sure her kids are safe.*

Ingigerður Adamsdóttir: *Then she should be at home looking after her children instead of getting involved in politics that she obviously knows nothing about.*

Hulda Ýr: *Hey, 1950 called and it wants its opinions back. Seriously, you think women should just stay at home?*

Emma Björk Eyfells: *It doesn't matter who this man is. She has no right to see medical records, and especially not psychiatric records. This is sensitive information!!*

Grallaraspói: *All this one needs is rock-hard dick :)*

Hulda Ýr: *Really? There's something political you're unhappy with and this is the best you can come up with? Good luck being revolting.*

Einar Einarsson: *This overprivileged scum think they can do what they like! And they don't hesitate to walk all over the sick and break every rule of human rights! Úrsúla Aradóttir should resign immediately!*

Guðmundur Jónsson: *Hang on, Einar. Aren't you 'good guys' happy with your bitch now?*

Gunnar shook his head and got into the lift. He would get more satisfaction from vacuuming the car than from seeing any more comments.

52

'Pleeease. Please come home,' she had said in the most imploring voice she could manage. But her father merely leaned back against the plinth that supported the statue of Ingólfur Arnarson on the Arnarhóll hillock in the centre of the city, looked out over the harbour and lifted the bottle of spirit high in a toast.

'A bourgeois lifestyle isn't for me,' he said, and Pétur voiced his agreement.

'This man's a bohemian!' he said, slapping her father's shoulder. 'You can't lock up a free spirit inside a terraced house.'

Then they went back to singing 'Little Boxes', as they always did whenever she came to ask her father to come home. By the time they finished, Úrsúla was in tears. She was gripped by an overwhelming helplessness and wished she had some way to force her father to come back home, to take a shower, sleep it off and have a decent meal, and then everything would be fine. After a few days he would go back to work and bring home money for her mother. That was the way it had been up to now. But that autumn he hadn't come home with after his usual summer-long bender.

'Mum's so tired,' Úrsúla said. 'She works all day and knits sweaters all evening for extra money, but there's still hardly a thing in the fridge.'

'That's the old girl all over! Wasting time knitting when she could be reading the ancient sagas and nourishing her soul!' Pétur piped up, and her father patted his shoulder.

'How old are you now, little Úrsúla?' he asked gently, and she couldn't understand how he could have forgotten something like that.

'Ten,' she said, and tears began to roll down her father's grubby face. 'Please. Come home and help us.'

'I'm no good,' he said, took a swig from the bottle and wept some more.

That was the last time Úrsúla went to him for help. After that she had become the one who helped him, slipping him the change from her piggy bank or an extra sandwich she made for lunch without her mother noticing, and which she'd take to him at either Arnarhóll or down at Hlemmur.

'Are you all right?'

Eva placed a hand on her shoulder and stooped over her. Úrsúla was sat at her desk. She hadn't noticed the door open and Eva come into the room. She shook herself, still half dazed.

'Yes. Fine. I was just thinking about my dad. All this Pétur business has stirred it up again.'

'I can well believe it,' Eva said. 'You know I'm here for you whenever you need me. I have a shoulder to cry on.'

Úrsúla gave her a smile. It was a generous offer, but she wasn't inclined to accept it. She didn't make a habit of shedding tears, especially not over things from the distant past. It was a side of her that nobody other than Nonni had seen; the fear, sorrow and powerlessness, which were often so illogical but sometimes possessed her – just as they had the night before when the dried-fish guy had called.

'Thanks, Eva. You really are the best. But ... moving on. Would you be so good as to set up an informal working group to consult with the Coast Guard to figure out what additional funding we can find for them? And would you make sure that Adolf isn't part of it? He's been far too pushy with me.'

Eva tapped notes into her phone at lightning speed.

'Start the working group off with a visit to the Coast Guard, and count me in. I'd like to show them that I'm taking their request for funding seriously. And will you book me a visit to the Directorate of Immigration? Going there was supposed to be the first thing I was going to do, but then other stuff got in the way.'

As the door closed behind Eva, Úrsúla found the weight of her memories returning. She had no idea how long she spent staring into space. In her mind the doorbell buzzed, heralding the arrival of the priest, along with two police officers, who took seats in their living room, told them the news that her father was dead, and that Pétur was suspected of having murdered him.

Her mother had cried, asking why on earth they had placed the two men together in a cell. One of the policemen had explained that it had been Saturday night with a full moon, and every cell had been full. They had all said how sorry they were, and the priest had laid a hand on Úrsúla's head and muttered a short prayer. She recalled that she had found it uncomfortable, as if the priest was treating her like a little girl, as if he thought of her as an innocent child when in fact she was twelve years old and had lost any belief in God.

She had often thought back to how that moment had been so different from her mother's death more than a decade later. She had sat with her, holding her hand, as her mother's life ebbed away, and the peace and proximity blended with the sorrow and gratitude in her heart. There had been nothing painful about her mother's death. It had seemed to be completely natural, although it had come early, and there had been no questions or doubts.

Úrsúla was startled by the ringing of her phone. She had promised herself not to reply to any of Thorbjörn's calls, but she was unable to resist.

'That was a dirty trick,' she snarled into the phone.

Thorbjörn was immediately on the defensive.

'I knew nothing about it until a minute before it went live, I swear! Otherwise I'd have warned you,' he said.

'How can a story be kept secret on a paper with a staff of only four, all of them working in the same room?'

'That's exactly it,' Thorbjörn said. 'There aren't enough of us; we're loaded down with work and don't get an opportunity to compare notes. You have no idea how sorry I am about this, Úrsúla. I'm devastated.'

'Who the fuck leaked this to you?' Úrsúla hissed, her anger towards him already cooling and her longing for his body against her bare skin building, along with the desire to feel her emotions at work.

'I'll find out for you,' he said. 'I'm at home now. Come to me.'

'No,' Úrsúla said.

'Yes. Come.'

53

There was no doubt that it had been a tough day for Úrsúla. If he hadn't known better, he would have said that she had lost weight since the morning. She seemed somehow thinner and slighter in the seat next to him, and was oddly absent-minded, her thoughts apparently far from reality.

Gunnar drove slowly. It wasn't far but he dragged the journey out as far as he could, as if he was giving her a chance to change her mind. He knew exactly what she was up to. It was pretty obvious. This was the second time in two days she had asked him to drive her to this man's home for what she called a 'very quick meeting'.

He had looked up the address in the National Registry, and that was where he found Thorbjörn's name. It was gut-wrenching to know that the minister was privately visiting this man, who worked for an online media outfit that seemed to have as its primary objective besmirching the reputations of government ministers.

'Are you sure you can trust this ... journalist?' he asked cautiously as he brought the car to a halt outside a building that he had always thought was all student apartments.

'Yes.' Úrsúla didn't catch his eye as she got out of the car. 'I won't be long,' she added.

She clearly didn't want to be accompanied to the door on this occasion, so he watched until she had ascended the steps to the door, which opened as she approached, and vanished inside. He moved the car to a position at the far end of the gloomy car park, but made sure he could still watch the entrance for her to reappear. There was no need for the ministerial car to be obvious to everyone passing by.

At one time he had dreamed of living in this district, on the western side of the university, in a community of students and academics. That had been back when he had been aiming for academe. He had once imagined that he would find happiness in deep discussions with professors who were the diametric opposite of his father: men who would respect him, listening to him as they guided him. Instead he had seen during his teens that what would set him free would be his physique. Exceptional strength and agility would give him the self-confidence to meet any challenge. He had managed to find a way to make a living out of this obsession with muscles, as his father had called it, a sour expression on the old man's face as Gunnar had twisted his arm yet again in an attempt to prevent one of his drunken furies.

What are you doing tonight? The message on his phone was from Íris.

Nothing, he replied.

Shall I come to yours? Her reply came right back and Gunnar felt he could sense the optimism in the phone's ping.

No. I'm tired, he wrote back. *Let's make it tomorrow.*
Are you meeting someone else?

This time the phone seemed to have a harsher, louder tone to it, and the message came with an icon of a man with horns and a trident in his hand.

No, sweetie, he wrote back. *I'm just tired.*

It was a joke on his part to call her sweetie, honey, darling or doll, but she seemed to fail to realise that these weren't words that could be applied to her. She was as far as could be imagined from being a sweetie or a darling.

He glanced at the clock. Only ten minutes had passed since Úrsúla had gone inside. Reckoning that she was going to be as long as the last time, he thought he had another half-hour, so he checked his email. There was one message from Fossi, sent to Úrsúla's email address, but Eva had intercepted it and forwarded it to him:

> *Resign, you cunt, and I'll think twice about coming round to your house and raping you, feminazi wrecker bitch.*

Gunnar read the message again and again. What could have triggered such strong feelings in this lunatic? Maybe it couldn't exactly be called progress, but for the first time Fossi had stated what he wanted from Úrsúla. He had finally spelled out the point he wanted to make with these disgusting messages. He wanted her to resign from her post as minister.

54

Úrsúla's breathing had barely started to slow as she lay her head on Thorbjörn's shoulder on his living-room floor, when she caught herself comparing him to Nonni. Thorbjörn was no match for Nonni; he wasn't even close. She couldn't understand herself; she had a handsome, wonderful husband at home, who had stood by her through thick and thin over the years, and who she knew loved her, but she was throwing herself at this rough guy she hardly knew. Maybe that was what it was all about. Perhaps it was the primitive nature of their relationship that allowed her a freedom she couldn't find with Nonni. Or perhaps she was simply too terrified of letting herself connect with Nonni again; if she allowed him past her defences and into her feelings, then she would have to tell him about Liberia. She would have to tell him that the explosions and the bursts of gunfire in Syria had almost been light relief after dealing with Ebola; that an enemy in sight was child's play compared to the enemy who could hide inside you. But this was something she couldn't trust herself to do. She couldn't bring herself to see him lose his childish belief that the world would be a wonderful place if everyone just behaved decently.

Úrsúla sat up and rolled her singlet down as she glanced around Thorbjörn's flat. It was laid out in the same way as most student apartments, with an open-plan kitchen and living room, a bedroom to one side and a small bathroom opposite the front door. What was considered acceptable temporary accommodation for a student in Iceland would have been welcomed as a permanent home by a whole family in Syria.

Úrsúla wondered how a middle-aged man like Thorbjörn with a full-time job managed to hold on to a student flat, but she didn't like to ask. His personal arrangements were none of her business.

'You're leaving already?' he asked, stroking her thigh and sending a shiver of pleasure through her.

'My driver's waiting for me outside.'

'How are you feeling?' he asked.

She shrugged.

'I don't make a habit of this,' she said. 'I've never been unfaithful to my husband before.'

Thorbjörn was silent, but continued to run his fingers along her leg until she pushed his hand away.

'Are you all right?' he asked, and instead of replying in the same way she spoke to Nonni, with a shake of the head and a forced smile to tell him that everything was fine, she told Thorbjörn the truth. It was easy, so painless, and with no repercussions.

'No, I'm not all right,' she said. 'I haven't been all right for a long time.'

Saturday

55

'So,' was all the prime minister said as soon as Úrsúla answered the phone.

She knew exactly where this was going. He wanted to hear what ideas she had come up with for canning the South Coast Highway initiative. She mouthed an apologetic *sorry* to Eva, who sat opposite her at the desk. They had been going over next week's commitments and Úrsúla had been speaking as the phone rang.

'Nothing to tell you,' she said into the phone, leaning back in her chair and turning it away from the desk so she could look through the window at the pale-blue mountains in the distance. 'I'm working on it.'

A burst of golden-pink rays of sunshine broke through the clouds and bathed the mountain slopes of Akrafjall; the light was so bright it seemed almost to belong to another world.

'Talk to Óðinn,' the prime minister advised. 'He can cook up some kind of justification that's totally impenetrable, but looks completely plausible.'

'Yes, I don't doubt that eventually I'll be going to Óðinn for advice,' she said. 'But I'd like to hold off for the moment. The contracts are just waiting for me to sign them, and I can delay that for quite a while. I'd like to let the media storm over the street guy die down before I stir things up again.'

'It's fine to let one scandal drown out another,' the prime minister said. 'The more dust you kick up, the better.'

'I'm not sure I agree with you there, Mr Machiavelli,' she said, hoping that a lighter note would cut through the tension she could sense in his voice. But it had the opposite effect; the prime minister seemed in no mood for jokes.

'Rúnar couldn't handle the media and gave way under the strain before he scuttled away on sick leave. Now we'll see if his successor can stick up for herself or not!'

Before Úrsúla could begin to digest his words, he had hung up, leaving her in no doubt: the call hadn't been made to find out what the state of play was. He was cracking the whip.

'What was that?' Eva asked, staring at Úrsúla in astonishment. The call must have sounded as strange to Eva as it had been to her.

'That was our prime minister,' Úrsúla said with a sigh. 'He wants the South Coast Highway shelved.'

'What?' The astonishment shone from Eva's face as her jaw dropped. 'What the hell?'

'I know,' Úrsúla said, turning over in her mind whether she should spare Eva the explanation or not. But she desperately needed someone to talk to. She needed someone else's judgement and to think the matter through out loud. 'There's a problem with the finance,' she said. 'It seems that Ingimar Magnússon is one of the backers.'

'Fuck,' Eva said. 'Fucking hell, in fact.'

Úrsúla laughed and sighed at the same time.

'That's putting it mildly. If this gets out, the government is going to be under fire for allowing negotiations for a state project to get this far without knowing who they were dealing with. If we keep quiet and carry on, and it comes out that we knew we were negotiating with Ingimar the Terrorist, then we have even more of a scandal on our hands. Ingimar isn't the most popular person in Iceland.'

'Hell and damnation,' Eva said. Úrsúla wanted to ask her to swear some more, as it seemed to provide an outlet for the tension. She longed to sink the whole miserable business in a pit of fury and cursing.

'The worst of it is that I think I was appointed minister of the interior to do just this. I'm here to be the unpopular bitch who wrecks the vital transport initiative that the whole country has been looking forward to for far too long. That's why both parties buried their differences and accepted a minister from outside the government.'

'Shi—' Eva began, and paused. 'There must be a way around this. We can't stop this going ahead. The whole south coast is alive with tourists and can't cope with the traffic, and there's just one accident after another.'

Úrsúla looked at her thoughtfully. Eva's disappointment over the South Coast Highway being abandoned would be nothing compared to the rage that would erupt from people living along the south coast, as well as commercial drivers and the whole tourist industry.

'I really need to speak to this Ingimar directly,' Úrsúla said. 'I need to hear from him in person that he's behind the finance, and I need to be sure that the prime minister is telling me the truth. There's something about this that stinks, and I'm wondering if I'm a pawn in it all.'

Eva nodded.

'You can't just take responsibility for canning the highway without saying a word. You'll just be clearing up someone else's mess. But you can't let anyone find out that you're in personal contact with Ingimar. The man's a terrorist.'

56

Úrsúla could see the irritation on Nonni's face, so she quickly finished her conversation with Eva, switched off her phone and put it in her pocket. It was a cold, still day, and the snow crackled underfoot as they walked around the Árbær open-air museum.

'To start with you're back from work two hours later than you said you'd be. Then you're on the phone non-stop, and then there's this,' he muttered, so the children didn't hear.

'This' meant her long conversation with the chief executive of the Directorate of Immigration, who had happened to be buying his family tickets for the museum just as they turned up. Nonni and the man's wife, after a few pleasantries, had each herded their children into the yard, and Úrsúla had seen Nonni and the children playing on the swings in the corner while she convinced the chief executive of the need for co-operation.

'The phone's off,' she said, hooking a hand into the crook of Nonni's elbow.

She'd been surprised by how reserved the chief executive of the Directorate of Immigration was. He had mumbled and hesitated a few half-sentences that conveyed neither any particular interest in what Úrsúla had to say, nor even minimal respect for the ministry to which his department answered. More than likely a minister with a one-year term in office didn't carry a great deal of weight.

The children were happy and skipped down the steps. Today they had pancake-making and a guided tour around the old turf house to look forward to. This was a place they had visited regularly with the children every summer and Christmas holiday they'd spent in Iceland. Initially the toy collection had been the biggest attraction; later on it had been the animals; and now Herdís had developed a genuine interest in old houses and the lives of those who had lived in them. Ari's interest was mostly in anything edible, but otherwise he seemed happy just to join in, satisfied they were all together. Úrsúla would have been even happier if Kátur had been with them. He always helped lighten the atmosphere, his doggy delight in everything making them all laugh.

The trip to the ministry this morning had been worthwhile: a chance to clear up minor tasks, deal with emails, answer questions from the staff and start preparing responses to parliamentary questions on a variety of matters. Parliament made her nervous so she was determined to be well prepared for her first public appearance there and she had wanted time to concentrate. There were fewer people in the building on a Saturday and less pressure from the media, so this had given her space to think. At any rate, nothing had changed over the last twenty-four hours, and the newspapers were stuck in the same groove as before, lapping up each other's coverage and publishing interviews with legal experts who failed to agree on what documents the minister had a right to see. With any luck, it would all have blown over by Monday.

A tempting aroma met them as they stepped over the threshold of the turf house. The children were there ahead of them, and Ari was making pancakes over an open fire under the careful tutelage of a lady in national dress. They tasted the pancakes and heaped praise on Ari for his skill in turning them over, and for a moment everything was perfect, the four of them together, laughing and happy.

'This is a sight to see! The minister in person, here for a tour of the turf house,' a man exclaimed as he came in to the kitchen.

Úrsúla had a moment's discomfort as she recognised the man's face but was unable to recollect where she had met him before.

He solved the mystery himself by offering a hand to Nonni and introducing himself.

'Bergmundur. Professor of Icelandic language and folklore.'

'I'm Jón,' Nonni said. 'These are our children, Herdís and Ari.'

The man didn't pay any attention to the children, but instead he gazed intently at Úrsúla, who realised that he was one of the group of academics who had come to see her about the naming committee. The groove between his eyes looked deeper than ever, and judging by his tone of voice, Úrsúla hadn't been forgiven.

'I'd have thought that Disneyland would be more your thing,' he said, and Úrsúla couldn't be sure if his tone was sarcastic or simply curious. He took off his coat and Úrsúla was startled to see his woollen sweater, knitted in shades of grey, with buttons and black bands on the sleeves.

'Everything in moderation,' she muttered. 'We like the children to experience everything.'

'Is there Disneyland in Iceland?' Ari asked, giving his sister a hard nudge.

'Of course not, you idiot!'

'Shh! None of that, kids,' Nonni scolded.

'Then why did he say it?' Ari asked loudly, and there was a desperation in his voice, as if he feared that somewhere in Iceland lurked an American-style theme park that nobody had told him about.

'So is there Disneyland in Iceland or not?' Ari demanded again, and this time nobody replied, as Úrsúla shepherded him out through the kitchen door and into the yard.

'Let's go and get ourselves some waffles in the café,' Úrsúla said, and the children galloped across the frozen pasture.

'You could have spoken to that man a little more politely,' Nonni said as he followed her out into the yard. She could almost hear the anger boiling inside him.

His temper had been on edge since that morning, when he had seen the new house rules. He was the only one who should answer the door, and only after checking the screen connected to the camera that had been rigged above the door.

They walked side by side, following the children to the café. Úrsúla was surprised at herself for not giving the man a proper answer, for not even showing him minimal courtesy, but the pattern on his sweater had left her in shock. It was a complex and rarely seen pattern: an octagonal rosette in grey and black across the chest. It was exactly the same one her father had worn.

57

Marita rubbed oil into the frozen leg of lamb and salted it generously. Her mother had always roasted a joint of lamb from frozen, but Jónatan had showed Marita how to let it defrost over two or three days in the fridge and a whole day at room temperature on the kitchen worktop before it went into the oven.

'In this case, it doesn't need to be rock hard before we slip it in,' he had said, and they had laughed and giggled, and then he had kissed her and pinched her bottom, and she had been happy.

Now she felt slightly sick at the memory. This wretched case hanging over them wasn't just poisoning the present, but all their memories as well; all the fun, and everything they had done together, was now veiled in pain and disappointment that she couldn't be sure would ever be lifted. Everything had been ruined, you could say. The case had destroyed their life together – past, present and future.

Marita sprinkled paprika and curry powder over the joint and worked the red and yellow powder together with her hands until the spices had blended into an orange covering and her fingers were left numb by the frozen meat. Jónatan would just have to make do with a leg of lamb that had been roasted from frozen when he came home that night for a break between a round of shifts. She didn't trust herself to go to the shop to buy something else for dinner. She'd just make a meal from what there was in the house.

She poured herself coffee from the flask. These days she was making a full flask of coffee in the mornings just for herself, because she was always getting herself cups and leaving them here and there around the house, and generally didn't come across them again until the coffee was cold. She didn't seem able to finish anything she started. She was halfway through folding the washing, so that there was a stack of folded clothes next to a pile of clothes just from the dryer, and the vacuum cleaner was in the corridor between the bedrooms because she didn't have the energy to hoover more than one room at a time.

She sat at the computer and opened Facebook. There was a message from her mother and a couple of pictures of Klemmi. She missed him so much that her heart felt fit to burst when she saw the boy's apple cheeks and joyful smile. She replied with a couple of lines of thanks. She knew there was no need for them, as her mother was delighted to have the lad, but somehow it assuaged her guilt at sending him away. She opened her gallery to see more pictures of Klemmi. He was changing so fast that she could practically see him grow as she looked through the last year's worth of pictures. Her eyes locked on to a picture of Jónatan with the boys and she clicked to open it. He sat in the garden with Klemmi on his knee and Kiddi in shorts standing beside him. It was strange to see how alike the boys and their father were in this picture. There were a few comments, including one posted by Katrín Eva.

Good-looking guys, she had written, and had added a little red heart.

Underneath, Jónatan had added a comment:

The old guy is the best-looking, though, isn't he?

Yes, Katrín Eva had replied, adding a string of hearts.

'Look at this,' Marita said, pointing to the screen as Kiddi appeared in the kitchen, wearing nothing but underpants.

'I know. Fucking whore. She told everyone at school that she thought Dad was hot.'

Marita felt sick. How on earth could she be hearing this for the first time now, not least after all the long conversations she and Jónatan had had about the possible reasons behind Katrín Eva's accusations. This shone a new light on the whole thing; on everything.

'Hang on...' she stammered. 'Don't the police know about this?'

'Yeah,' Kiddi said. 'When they came from Reykjavík to talk to Dad, they talked to me as well, remember? And Dad sat in as the responsible adult. You could tell Katrín Eva had been flirting with Dad for months on end, and we told the cops that. Are you completely clueless about what's going on around you?'

He spat out the last few words angrily, turned to open the fridge, grabbed a carton of chocolate milk and disappeared into his room.

Marita's thoughts seemed to be coming out of the daze they had been in, and now she felt that she could understand Katrín Eva's manner when she'd left the house that evening, before she had lodged her accusations against Jónatan.

Maybe she had been in tears, as the police had said, when Marita had met her in the doorway. Could Katrín Eva have tried it on with Jónatan, and then gone home angry and hurt. Had she told her mother that he had raped her as revenge for his rejection?

58

'You've dropped a few!' Stella said, looking into Gréta's fluttering eyes.

She had already taken one tab herself, but that was clearly nothing to what Gréta must have swallowed. Gréta had already been at the dinner at the Annas' place when Stella arrived. As usual, she had taken care to be late, so that the women had softened up and she wouldn't have to take part in the conversation over the dinner table. But she needn't have worried, as Gréta and another woman took turns spouting monologues that the others listened to with rapt attention. It was amazing how a tab of Molly could make even the worst kind of bullshit sound inspired.

'I'm just so free now,' Gréta said. 'I just say exactly what I mean. For example, I'm going to ask you to let me know if the minister says anything about those medical records she requested. Or if she mentions her father and how he died – or anything else. You'll let me know? Because I'm your friend, aren't I?'

'I have a duty to keep confidences,' Stella said, and that was quite true. There was some piece of paper she had signed when she took the job. There was something uncomfortable about the way Gréta asked her again and again for gossip from inside the ministry. She always gave the same response: it sounded better than saying she never heard anything because she was just a cleaner.

'You're such a sweetheart!' Gréta giggled, and put out a hand to pinch her cheek. Then she handed Stella her phone.

'Could you call me a cab? The numbers are jumping all over the screen.'

It was no surprise that Gréta couldn't see straight; Stella felt dizzy just looking into her eyes.

'Are you going to another party?' she asked, booking a cab through the taxi app. 'Or are you going to meet *her*?'

'No, she's busy this weekend. I was going to get a lift up to the slope at Öskjuhlíð, or somewhere that's dark, so I can watch the Northern Lights,' Gréta said. 'I got a message from somewhere in space that they're fantastic right now. You know, something I have to see. It's the inner freedom I'm enjoying tonight.'

It was clear that Gréta's feet were some way off the ground, and Stella felt a surge of disquiet.

'Look, it's not smart to be going off somewhere in the dark with some taxi driver in the state you're in,' she said, taking Gréta's arm to try and get her attention, which seemed to flicker around the hallway as she stood with her coat half over her shoulders and a clownish smile on her face.

'I've never been in a better state,' Gréta whispered. 'More than likely I'm in the best state I've ever been in my whole life. Exactly at this moment right now.'

'Yeah, sure.' Stella rummaged through the pile of coats to find her jacket. 'I'll come with you on this Northern Lights expedition. There's no way you're going off around town in a taxi on your own.'

As she spoke, a horn beeped outside. Stella steered Gréta into the back seat as she complained about the light pollution that obscured her view of the sky.

When they stopped up on Öskjuhlíð, Stella asked the driver to wait in the car park outside the Perlan building. He made sure they paid before getting out of the car, and after retrieving a credit card from Gréta, who was hurrying off in search of Northern

Lights, Stella set off after her down the steps that led from the car park to the hollow below. Her eyes hadn't adjusted to the darkness and she slipped in the loose, ice-covered gravel that had been flattened underfoot. Tree branches whipped her face as she made her way forward in the darkness, then she suddenly walked into Gréta, who stood motionless, her eyes on the heavens.

'It makes you wonder what they want from us,' Gréta whispered in the darkness.

Stella gazed at the sky, and the green and pink lights that danced, jerking and swaying, unlike any she had seen before. It was as if the whole sky had been electrified by the gentle interplay of the lights, which seemed to exude an energy that she could feel rush across her skin.

'Are they really that wonderful?' she said. 'Or is it just the pills that are making them look so beautiful?'

'Does it matter?' Gréta asked, and Stella felt her warm hand on her cheek. 'Isn't all that matters what we sense here and now?'

Stella turned her head and met Greta's heavy lips with her own – a searing kiss that sent sparks of desire through her whole body. And while she had taken herself by surprise, ignoring good sense and under the influence of the lights, she knew this was where she ought to be.

59

The doors to the balcony stood open and through the stillness Gunnar could hear the pulsing bass notes from the bars on Laugavegur. This was the heartbeat of the night, which would end with shouts, shrieks and song out on the street, just before the tourists appeared, pulling their suitcases, which would rattle through the ice up the slope towards the waiting airport buses. He was the last Icelander left in the apartment block; every other flat was now rented out to tourists. He had been offered ridiculous money for this tiny place, but this was where he wanted to be. From the window he could see the district where all the ministries were clustered, less than a three-minute jog away, making it the perfect place if one of them needed him.

Íris had called; she was on her way to a night out with some of her friends, and he expected that she would go back to her place afterwards, so he decided to use the evening to look more closely at the emails that Úrsúla had received. He shook a protein drink hard and sat down with it at the coffee table, then began to line up Fossi's emails in front of him. He put them in the order in which they had arrived, both those that had been sent to the minister and those he had received after he had succumbed to the temptation to try and talk some sense into this idiot. It wasn't exactly his job to check the contents of the abusive emails that came to the minister, so he ignored all but the ones that came from Fossi. It was up to the chief of police's department to assess whether the more lukewarm hate-merchants, who felt a need to write to the minister and tell her how to do her job, dress or behave, posed any real threat. But there was something about these messages from Fossi, their virulence and hatred, that he couldn't leave alone.

The contents of the emails varied little between the first and the last. The sentences were short and angry, and Gunnar had the feeling that they had been written in a rush. There had been no softening in the tone either, although that first one had easily been the most revolting, describing how 'bitches who stick their noses where they're not wanted' would be rewarded with torture. The latest had come from Fossi last night; he offered to think again about raping Úrsúla if only she would resign from her post as minister. Aside from the language and the violent imagery, the contents of the messages revolved around his desire for Úrsúla to keep clear of something that was not her affair, and to step down. If she didn't do that, then she'd be abused and raped.

What was it that Fossi was so keen Úrsúla didn't interfere with?

Gunnar opened the state TV's website and scrolled back and forth through the domestic news items covering the minister and the ministry. The first of Fossi's messages had arrived less than a week after Úrsúla's first day in office, and over those six days the media had mainly focused on which of her predecessor's issues Úrsúla intended to pursue. First there had been the Coast Guard's complaints and the reminders that Rúnar had pledged to allocate them additional funding. Úrsúla had said in one interview that she intended to meet the Coast Guard's representatives to discuss the matter. She hadn't given a direct answer as to whether or not she would honour Rúnar's promise.

Then there was the naming committee that most people regarded as being almost a joke. It was clear from the social-media comments that there was a considerable generational difference in people's attitudes. Rúnar had been preparing a bill proposing changes to the legislation governing names, which would have included disbanding the naming committee, and it was obvious that many people were disappointed that Úrsúla intended to pursue this, while others welcomed it.

Then there had been the coverage of that old rape accusation in Selfoss. Gunnar stared at the first news item reporting that the ministry had been forced to announce exactly where in the system the case was. The date coincided exactly with that first revolting email, and those that followed seem to have been sent the same day, or the day after, there had been prominent coverage of the rape case and the ministry of the interior's investigation into the matter.

Could Fossi be from Selfoss?

Sunday

60

At some time during the night Stella woke up by Gréta's side. Her eyes were still playing tricks on her and she couldn't make out the numbers on the bedside clock clearly, but she thought it had to be around three. When she moved her head there was no sign of the pounding headache she had expected to wake up to, so she went to the kitchen and let the cold water run.

Their clothes were scattered around the living-room floor, and she found her shirt on the sofa where Gréta had straddled her, letting her heavy breasts tumble into Stella's face as she unclipped her bra, while Stella lay back in a daze of satisfaction, allowing the endless softness to envelop her.

She returned to the bedroom with the shirt flapping and a full glass of water in her hand, sipping it cautiously as she wasn't yet thirsty, and saw an old woman standing by the dressing table, staring at her, a twig broom in her hands. Stella knew this had to be her imagination at work; there was an electric glow to the old lady, as if the Northern Lights had taken up residence in her elderly body.

'Grandmother,' Stella said. '*Abuelita*.'

'Happy birthday,' her grandmother said, looking around her with a quizzical expression.

'Thank you,' Stella said, buttoning her shirt before embracing her grandmother. As always, there was a warmth to her, and the aroma that clung to her was a welcome blend of cocoa and burning candles. Stella's heart beat faster as her grandmother squeezed her as hard as she always did whenever they met.

'Do you want me to sing your birthday song, my little one?' her grandmother asked.

Stella shook her head, pointing at Gréta asleep in the bed.

'It's best if we don't wake her.'

'Is this something serious?' her grandmother asked, inspecting a pale leg that extended from under the duvet.

Stella shook her head.

'I can work a charm so that she'll be yours for ever,' she added.

Stella placed a hand lightly on Gréta's leg, and could feel that last night's rush of passion between them was still there, even as Gréta slept. Either there were a few too many drugs in her system that were skewing her senses, or this was love. But this couldn't be love. Gréta wasn't exactly her type.

'No, thank you, grandmother,' she said. 'This was just a moment's craziness.'

'She's plump and sweet,' her grandmother said with a sly smile. 'You must enjoy cuddling up with her.'

'Grandmother, really! Shh.'

Stella was shocked. This wasn't how her birthday night was supposed to be. She was meant to be alone at home, wide awake and with a clear mind as she waited for her birthday visit.

Her grandmother held her hand, stroking it with her thumb.

'Your father will die soon. So you'll be able to come home again,' she said. 'You can come home to me so I can look after you properly.'

Stella felt the tears begin to prick at her eyes. Nothing in the world would be as wonderful as being able to sit on the veranda of her grandmother's house in the warm shade, just as she had when she had been a girl, sipping sweet coffee with cardamom, scratching the monkey behind the ears while Grandmother prepared to teach her another spell.

'I look forward to it, Grandmother,' she said. 'I look forward to coming home to you, and I'll bring Mother as well. She sends her best wishes and loves you with all her heart.'

'Darling soul,' her grandmother said. 'Poor, beloved soul.'

She pulled Stella back in to her arms and squeezed her tight.

'Here's your birthday gift, baby-*bruja*, little witch,' Grand-mother said, blowing hard into Stella's ear so that her head was filled with a hot light.

Then Grandmother opened the balcony door, stepped outside and climbed, agile as any cat, onto the railing. She placed the broom between her legs and stepped off. Stella followed so she could see her fly away, but the old lady had already vanished into the silent night. The Northern Lights were still fluttering in the sky, but were dimmer now, and Stella felt she could hear the echo of a Mexican birthday song fade into the distance somewhere above the roofs.

Estas son las mañanitas...

61

It had taken Mum a whole weekend to finish the traditional woollen sweater Úrsúla had begged her to knit for her father. She had run into him downtown, shivering in an old padded boiler suit, its lining worn too thin to be of any real use against the piercing December chill. Her mother had flatly refused to invite Dad home for Christ-mas dinner, and said he'd be better off having a meal at the Salvation Army hostel with his friends. But she agreed to knit a sweater.

Úrsúla had watched in fascination as the eight-leaved rosette took shape in her skilled hands, and she felt a warm feeling inside as she saw how much effort her mother put into the pattern. She could have understood if she had simply rattled off a sweater with a straightforward design, or even something with just a single colour – it wasn't as if her father deserved anything better. But Úrsúla had looked forward to being able to bring him this beauti-ful Christmas gift. Her father had wept tears of delight. He had stroked the sweater with his scarred, grubby hands, and shed tears.

'This has been made with love,' he sniffed.

He wanted to hug and kiss Úrsúla, but he smelled so rank that she turned away, telling him to try the sweater for size. He pulled it on, and it fitted him perfectly. He strutted around in circles, calling out to everyone in the community canteen that his daughter had brought him this fine sweater, made by his old lady.

Everyone at the canteen was like her father, so this time Úrsúla didn't feel awkward when he crowed that he had the finest and most beautiful daughter in the whole world, before bursting into song.

Úrsúla sighed. These days her father was on her mind all the time.

She slowly ascended the stairs at the Social Democrat Party's central office and tried to shake off the angst that was so firmly attached to those memories. For the last few years she had followed the advice given her by a psychologist: to think back to positive memories of her father, from the days when he'd smell of aftershave and would plant a kiss on her neck, and the times he read to her from the sagas until she fell asleep.

That was before he walked out.

There was a crowd at the central office, and she knew that she'd have to pull herself smartly away from those memories and concentrate so that she could be congratulated on becoming a minister, and cope with the smiles, the pats on the back and the kisses that were showered on her. Also present were representatives of the affiliated groups; the morning was supposed to be spent giving them the opportunity to ask her about the work of the ministry of the interior. She had been looking forward to the opportunity of meeting party members in a more relaxed atmosphere than at the ministry or in the parliament's coffee room, but now she had a sharp sense of her lack of experience in party matters. She didn't know most of the people present, but she was anxious to clear the air over the media storm that had erupted around the request for Pétur's medical records. The party chairman brought her coffee and showed her to an armchair at one end of the hall. The party's brightest young hopeful, Edvard Thórsson, approached her with a smile on his face.

'It obviously pays to drop to your knees for the prime minister,' he said and took a seat in the front row, directly in front of her.

Had he really said that? She could have misheard him over the loud mutter of voices in the hall, but that was wishful thinking. She understood perfectly that his ego had been bruised, as Edvard and many others had been certain that he would be the one who would get the call when Rúnar stepped down. Was that what people thought – that she had fucked the PM to get a ministerial appointment? Did they imagine that her experience of social affairs and with UNHCR weren't the reason for her appointment, and a sordid transaction was? It wasn't as if she had any political ambitions. She had taken the job because of the opportunity it would give her to push immigration as an issue, and because taking on something new was the kind of challenge she enjoyed. It was true that having a spell as a government minister would do her CV good, for the future, when she'd go back to working for international organisations.

She looked out over the hall and hoped that people would take their time sitting down so she could get her heartbeat under control before the meeting began. The same regrets seemed to come at her from every direction. Everything, even her own memories, appeared to be telling her that she was in fact no use at all, that anything she could do would have no value – at least, no more value than a bottle of booze.

The next time she had met her father after bringing him the sweater, in the week between Christmas and New Year, she had found him shivering with cold, wearing the padded boiler suit and a cotton singlet under it.

'I'm no good,' he said, shedding tears of remorse for having swapped the sweater for a bottle.

62

Stella sat on a barstool in Gréta's kitchen and watched absently as she dipped slices of bread in whipped-egg and fried them in a pan. Her head was still filled with the hot light, and she was grateful to her grandmother for her gift. Each birthday brought her a greater understanding of her mysterious inheritance and her growing power to use it.

'I had the weirdest dream last night,' Gréta said. 'I dreamed there was an old woman in the bedroom with us and you were speaking to her in some other language. It was an unbelievably clear dream and spookily strange.'

'Yes,' Stella said, and smiled. 'Strange dream.'

It was the first time she had seen Gréta looking the worse for wear, standing in the kitchen in a dressing gown and fussing over the stove. Partying had finally caught up with her, which was no surprise considering how high she had been flying the night before.

'French toast,' Gréta said, as she placed the stack of fried bread on the table in front of her, took a seat by the corner and slopped coffee into cups. She poured a generous helping of syrup over the bread on her plate and added cream to her coffee. There was no way that Gréta was going to get any slimmer if she was going to carry on like this, Stella thought as she watched. All the same, she knew well the insatiable hunger that was the legacy of popping pills.

'Hey ... You know that yesterday was all about the pills?' she said. Gréta stopped chewing and looked at her enquiringly. 'If it hadn't been for the pills we wouldn't have ended up in the sack,' she continued.

Gréta looked away, and then down at her plate. She put down her knife and fork, and took a gulp of creamy coffee.

'Of course not,' she said, looking up and smiling as if in apology.

'It won't happen again,' Stella said.

It was as well to make that plain right away, as considering the vibes Gréta was giving off the previous night and how long she had chased after her with her tongue hanging out, it was worth making sure there were no misunderstandings.

'No, no. I agree entirely,' Gréta said, picking up her knife and fork again and proceeding to cut her fried bread into small pieces. 'I'm chasing this woman I met on Tinder, so anything else isn't on my radar either.'

Stella was grateful for how well she took it, making the whole thing easier.

'Yes, definitely. And I reckon it's best for both of us if we keep quiet. You know, no kiss-and-tell? All right?'

That had to be clear as well. Stella didn't want to make a spectacle of herself. The gossip among Reykjavík's lesbians was bad enough as it was. Now it looked like Gréta had lost her appetite; she pushed her plate away. She forced a smile, nodding to indicate that she understood. Stella could see that she had hurt Gréta and she felt sick at the thought; it was the usual sympathy that she felt for Gréta, but now there was something more – something about her forced smile and her tousled mop of hair that stuck out in all directions that gnawed at Stella's conscience. She felt so sorry for her. Or maybe she simply felt sorry for herself for being such a morning-after-bitch.

63

Íris was still in bed and had gone back to sleep. If she hadn't been so hung over, she would undoubtedly have stormed out by now, banging the door behind her. She had crawled into his bed in the middle of the night, feeling frisky and looking for some fun, but when she woke in the morning she was feeling rough and wanted him to tell her he loved her.

'I like you a lot,' he had said. 'I find you sexy and beautiful, and most of the time you're fun to be with.'

'Tell me you love me,' she wheedled.

'I like you a lot, little mouse,' he repeated. 'But I'll hold off going further than that until I'm sure I mean it, and that'll be when I've made my mind up for myself.'

She rolled over to face the wall, while he went into the other room and perched on the edge of the sofa, which was the only way to sit on it without falling through it onto the floor.

Gunnar finished putting together the week's security report relating to Úrsúla. There was plenty that needed to be recorded in detail now that they had both spent a week in a new job. First there had been the notes from the homeless man, Pétur Pétursson; it had been necessary to take measures to reduce the likelihood of these and similar messages getting through the front door and being found by the minister's family. On Friday, cameras had been installed at her home and a police patrol now drove past every hour. This was a temporary measure, just while Pétur was still at large with his cryptic notes. Gunnar checked the photographs the police had sent of other people who'd sent threatening messages to the minister. There had been three this week: one had come through doctors at a psychiatric ward, from a patient who had an obsession with Úrsúla; another was a troublemaker who repeatedly called the ministry; and the third had made some colourful online comments. Gunnar inspected the faces, closed his eyes and tried to visualise them, implanting them in his memory. Two of these reports included car registrations, so Gunnar wrote both of them on his wrist, using an indelible marker that wouldn't easily be washed off.

Then there was Fossi's hate mail. Gunnar opened a new message, attached a copy of the entire conversation with Fossi to it, along with news of the rape case in Selfoss, and addressed it to Boris at the commissioner's office.

Take a look at the dates of the news reports about this case being examined by the ministry and compare them to when the first message was received. Coincidence? I don't think so. Fossi is more than likely from Selfoss. Maybe it's worth getting a warrant to check the computer owned by that policeman who was charged?

Maybe it was just that simple, that the redneck cop who had raped the babysitter was sending death threats to the minister in the hope that she'd call off the investigation. It was a childish approach and unlikely to bear fruit, but maybe the wretched man was letting off steam over the rape furore.

He reached for the kale smoothie he had made in the blender. It tasted foul, but he forced it down as today was a fasting day. He had a day like this every once in a while, sticking to liquidised vegetables and water to clean his body and give him a chance to renew himself. Fasting always left him feeling good. The evenings were difficult, when he longed for food, and right now he'd have been glad to exchange this green gloop for something solid, but tomorrow he would wake up cheerful and refreshed, grateful that he had faith in himself. This was a mental exercise as much as a physical one. Just as Íris was his training ground in keeping his temper, fasting was his way of demonstrating his own strength of will: he could deny himself what his body craved; he was in control of his own body; he was his own master.

There was no way he was going to be like his father, who caved in to every weakness, whether that was food, drink, or the force of his own temper.

64

Marita couldn't sleep. There was a hard knot in her belly that she couldn't get rid of, even though she had taken long, slow breaths and spent a whole hour in a hot bath before going to bed. Now that Jónatan had been away so much, it was strange to have him there by her side in bed, as if she had become accustomed to his absence even though she had missed him.

She rolled onto her side and draped an arm over him. He slept soundly. She had always envied him this. He seemed to be able to fall asleep anywhere and at any time, almost like a child. There was something so innocent about how he could stretch out on the sofa or in an armchair and doze off, as if the whole world stood guard over his security and his rest. Marita could never sleep among strangers as Jónatan could, neither in an aeroplane nor in her own living room when they all gathered at Christmas. Now she was unable to sleep in her own bed in the middle of the night.

The knot in her belly twitched with its own rhythm, as if it had its own heartbeat that pumped regular doses of fear into her veins. She lay pressed against Jónatan's back and breathed in the warm scent of him. He was a big man, so she had always felt small and feminine next to him, even though she was quite tall and had put on a few kilos after Klemmi's birth. She had always seen him as some kind of protector. He was the big, strong man, the cop who protected her from anything evil, the foundation of her security. But all that had changed, and perhaps that was the deepest damage that had been done as she no longer had that sense of security that he had provided. This wasn't because she was in doubt about his innocence; far from it. Of course he hadn't raped that girl. Her doubts were about his judgement and the fact that he had placed the family's security in jeopardy. What had he been thinking, giving beer to a kid of fifteen? He would never have given Kiddi booze, that was for sure, and he and Katrín Eva were the same age – although girls tended to be more mature at that age. And why hadn't he taken more care, knowing that Katrín Eva had a crush on him? According to what Kiddi had said yesterday, Jónatan was very much aware of this, but had still exchanged flirty messages with her on Facebook, asking if she thought he was better looking than his sons. For a grown man, this had to be a complete failure of judgement.

Marita turned over, so they lay back to back, and continued to take deep, slow, long breaths all the way down to her core. She was about to fall asleep when doubt pounced on her again, like a predator from the shadows, taking her by surprise with a stab of pain. There was something she had seen in the newspaper, in the interview with Rósa that hadn't registered on her consciousness until now. In the interview, Rósa said that after Jónatan had raped her daughter, he had rolled onto his back and thanked her, just as if she had given him something of her own free will.

'Thanks very much', it had said in the newspaper. That was what he habitually did after he and Marita made love. He always said 'thanks, darling', sometimes adding how good it had been.

Thanks, darling, that was great.

Then Marita would giggle and be happy. She would be glad and satisfied with him, and satisfied with herself, their relationship and their life together. But how could Katrín Eva have decided to say that he had said those words to her? How could she know that was the kind of thing he'd say after sex? Had Jónatan had sex with her? Judging by what Kiddi said, the girl was already sexually experienced. Had she done it with Jónatan, regretted it and then gone home to tell her mother that she had been raped? Were there samples from him in the rape kit that the newspapers had reported?

Marita stared into the darkness. Her eyes were dry and sore, but she was so shocked that she was unable to blink. Could Jónatan have been unfaithful to her? With this teenage girl? With a child?

Monday

65

Edvard's vile comment had been a slap in the face – hurtful and humiliating; but somehow it had shaken her out of the dejection she'd felt after all this Pétur business. This new attack had somehow reinforced the armour that Thorbjörn had found his way inside, and which she now found she badly needed to keep in place. She had gulped a cup of coffee while people attending the meeting found their seats, then got to her feet. She had briefly introduced herself, for the benefit of those who didn't know who she was, and after listing her work experience and the main projects she had worked on, she moved on.

'Just to clear the air, I'd like to make it clear that I'm not a minister because I dropped to my knees for the PM, as someone suggested to me just now.'

A mutter had passed through the hall, and she could see that Edvard sank deeper into his seat in front of her, as if he longed to drop through the floor. She took care not to look directly at him, or anyone else, as she had no intention of letting anyone know who had made the offending remark. He had every reason to be relieved that she didn't mention his name, which would have opened him up to the fury of the party members. After the coffee break, his seat had been empty.

Now, at the morning meeting with Eva to organise the week ahead, she was bursting with energy and enthusiasm.

'First of all,' she said. 'I'd like you to organise a short press call so I can make a statement about this Pétur matter.'

The Sunday papers had certainly spun out of all proportion her ill-considered request for information on whether Pétur might be dangerous, raking over the death of her father and weaving webs of intrigue about why she had wanted Pétur's medical records.

'Wouldn't it be better to let the media know that you'll make a statement, rather than have a formal press conference?' Eva suggested. 'And we can do it outside. They'll be less inclined to hang around asking questions in the cold,' she added.

Úrsúla laughed and nodded her agreement. Eva had a talent for brilliant ideas.

'Then I'd like you to take the formal route and request a meeting with the prime minister,' Úrsúla said. 'I've been trying to reach him on his mobile all weekend and he won't pick up.'

This had worried her, but she had held on to the thought that he was busy with something else, and not intentionally blanking her. She needed to speak to him, both to explain the furore in the press and to discuss the South Coast Highway. She wanted to suggest the option of finding another source of financing, instead of these foreign funds that were owned by Ingimar the Terrorist.

'Would you make sure there's space in the schedule this week for me to show my face in parliament every day, and can you knock up a draft of an article about the immigration situation that I can finish off?'

'Is that it?' Eva asked, getting to her feet. She looked Úrsúla up and down for a moment. 'I'll get something for you to wear before you meet the hacks,' she added.

'What's wrong with what I'm wearing?' Úrsúla asked. 'You chose this blouse.'

'A shirt with a collar is too blokey,' Eva said. 'This time you need to appear more feminine, gentler. But not too lightweight. It's not a problem. I'll fix it.'

With a dazzling smile, she was gone. The last week had convinced Úrsúla that choosing Eva had been absolutely right. She worked with the smooth efficiency of a machine, plus she was fun to be around.

With a few minutes before the next meeting, Úrsúla helped herself to an espresso from the machine Eva had installed in the corner and scrolled through the contacts in her phone to find Rúnar, the former minister of the interior. She hardly knew him, but she'd attended his classes for a semester at university. He had been a good teacher. He was intelligent and had a particular talent for seeing things from an external viewpoint, giving him the big picture.

'I've been thinking of you, my dear,' Rúnar said as he answered the phone.

'Likewise,' Úrsúla replied. 'I haven't wanted to disturb you, what with you being unwell. I hope I'm not intruding now.'

She couldn't bring herself to mention what the prime minister had said about Rúnar's health issues; that in reality there was nothing at all wrong with him beyond losing his nerve for the job.

'That's all right,' Rúnar said. 'I started to feel better the moment I left the ministry behind me.'

He laughed hoarsely.

'I'd like to ask for your advice on this South Coast Highway,' she said.

'Hmm. I only wish I could give you some. What does the PM have to say about it?'

'He hasn't been answering his phone since he called on Saturday to pile on the pressure to cancel the whole thing.'

'Ah. Oh, well.'

'Well, what?'

Rúnar sighed and cleared his throat. 'To tell you the truth, I was surprised that you were picked for the ministry. I imagined that Edvard would be next in line, but the more I think it over, the clearer the reason gets.'

'They needed a woman in government...' Úrsúla began.

Rúnar snorted. 'It's convenient that you're a woman, but I don't think that's the heart of the matter. I have the feeling – I'm not saying I'm right; this is more a hunch on my part – that you were chosen because you have no particular political ambitions.'

'So I get to be the sacrificial lamb – the minister who cancels the South Coast Highway – because I wouldn't stay in politics anyway? I can afford to be unpopular?'

'That's it. It's about sparing Edvard and the other golden boys, who are supposed to be the face of the party when elections come around next year. Of course the Independence Party also has its golden boys and they're protected carefully.'

This was far from what the prime minister had said when he had offered her the job, and not exactly in line with the praise he had heaped on her for her previous roles.

'Thanks for confirming my suspicions, but I wish you'd have dropped me a line and warned me off,' Úrsúla said.

'I've more faith in you than I have in myself,' Rúnar replied. 'And that's been my opinion since you graduated with excellent grades, as well as leading the student debating team to victory and organising a national fundraising effort for ... what was it – the Red Cross?'

'All the same. You could have warned me,' she said.

Rúnar sighed.

'Would you have taken any notice, Úrsúla?'

She laughed. Of course not. She would have ignored every piece of advice; just the same as she always had.

66

'I have a special assignment for you,' Úrsúla said as soon as Gunnar appeared in her office. She gestured for him to take a seat and sat in a chair opposite him, leaning forward and looking him in the eye. 'I'd completely understand if you don't want or don't trust yourself to do it. OK?'

Gunnar nodded. His curiosity had already been piqued; he guessed it was something to do with her lover, the journalist she sneaked off to meet.

'I know that everything about your job is bound by confidence, but I'm still asking you not to breathe a single word of this to anyone.'

'Of course I won't.'

'I'm dropping a state secret into your lap, if we can put it that way,' she said, fixing Gunnar with an intense stare as he sat a little straighter in his chair. 'The prime minister has asked me to find a way to knock the South Coast Highway on the head, because it turns out that one of the individuals behind the financing is Ingimar Magnússon. And nobody wants to have anything to do with that gentleman.'

'Ingimar the Terrorist?' Gunnar asked, and shivered at the thought. There was something sinister about the name, and while Ingimar hadn't killed anyone, blowing up a radio station wasn't something that Icelanders were used to.

'That's right. Ingimar the Terrorist. This absolutely must not be allowed to leak. The whole government would become a joke overnight. But it would be worse if anyone were to find out that a contract that would make Ingimar even richer is about to be signed. The government would look corrupt. So it seems that the only option left is to ditch the South Coast Highway, as the original tender becomes invalid if the financing package is altered.'

'Oh,' Gunnar said involuntarily. He had been looking forward to driving along that road.

'The thing is this,' Úrsúla said. 'I need to be certain there's no other way to fix this mess before I call the project off, because, as you can imagine, it's going to do nothing for my popularity. This is an initiative that people have supported.'

Gunnar nodded. He could already imagine the furious hate mail that would cascade down on her.

'So what do you want me to do?' he said.

'I want you to go to the prison at Hólmsheiði and talk to Ingimar Magnússon in person, on my behalf.'

67

'Hæ, Gunni!'

He looked at the girl who greeted him so cheerfully, and saw that while her mass of curls had been tamed with something that made her hair shine, and the sides of her head had been clippered short, there was no doubt that this was Stella.

'Hey, Curlytop! What are you doing here?'

'I'm a cleaner,' she said. 'And you?'

'I'm the minister's driver,' he replied. 'Started exactly a week ago.'

He moved aside so that people making their way through the lobby could pass them. A crowd of media types had gathered outside, waiting for Úrsúla to appear and make her statement.

'I heard what happened to your mother,' he said.

Their eyes met, and he felt himself sinking into the endless depths of those dark eyes. They seemed somehow to have more darkness in them than any other eyes.

'Yeah, she's in care now, and she has to be medicated up to the eyeballs so she doesn't go crazy. There was some damage to her frontal lobe, and other injuries.'

'I'm sorry to hear it,' he said. 'I had the feeling that it wouldn't end well when you both moved back in with him.'

He remembered his own desperate dismay, standing by the window and watching the two of them get in the man's car. The guy was a powerfully built giant, and they were so delicate and small, like a pair of elves from another world. The girls who worked at the refuge had tried to comfort him with tales of re-unions that had worked out well, when the dad had forsaken the bottle, stopped beating his family and everyone lived happily ever after. But he could see in their faces that no one expected to see that kind of happy ending this time.

'She was so frightened we'd be deported if she left him,' Stella said. 'Anyway, what about your parents?'

'They divorced,' he said. 'Which is just as well. Mum lives in Tenerife with her cousin, and I don't know about the old man. We're not in touch.'

Gunnar looked her up and down, struggling to see her as a young woman. She had been such a cute child, and even though he had little patience with children when he had been a teenager, there had been something about the two of them shipwrecked together in the refuge that brought them together. He had called her his Curlytop, and they had played endless hands of cards. He just couldn't see her as a grown woman; all he could see was the strange, delicate child who had leaped from chair to chair in the refuge in endless attempts to fly.

'You're still casting spells?' he asked with a wink.

'Yeah!' she laughed.

Most of the little girls he had encountered had wanted to be princesses, or Pippi Longstocking, but this one had definitely aspired to become a witch.

68

Marita hadn't slept at all. But now, well into the morning, with daylight ready to assert itself before too long, everything seemed better. She set the percolator to run a second time and cleared the breakfast things away, while Jónatan sat at the kitchen table, reading the weekend papers with interest.

Every now and again he'd chuckle with satisfaction, before heaving a sigh and getting to his feet. She glanced at the spread he had been reading and saw it was something about the minister of the interior and that homeless guy, but she couldn't be bothered to read more and wondered why Jónatan had found it so amusing.

The percolator had done its work so she switched it off, pouring the coffee into a Thermos. This was the last of the coffee, so there would be no choice but to go to the shop. She would either get dressed and drive to Hveragerði to go shopping, or else send Jónatan down to the shop with a list. He didn't seem to notice the whispers and people gawping.

'What?' she called out when she heard him saying something in the bedroom. He didn't reply, but she could hear his voice. 'What did you say?' she called again. She opened the door out into the corridor so she could hear him more clearly, and realised he was on the phone.

'Just take a look at what's in the newspapers, and don't forget that you owe me one,' he was saying. Then he turned around, pocketed the phone and looked at her with a smile. 'Everything all right, love?' he asked.

'Yes. I thought you were saying something to me,' Marita said.

'No, just on the phone,' he said and smiled again.

She looked at him enquiringly. He looked cheerful, as if he had something to be happy, even optimistic, about. She hadn't seen him like that for a long time; not since this terrible business had begun. He gave her a wink and went into the bathroom where she heard him turn the tap on full blast. He always did that to get hot water to shave. Before long he would reappear, freshly shaved and sweet-smelling, with that cheerful look on his face. and Marita suddenly felt an urge to hit him. She wanted to slap that shaven, silky-smooth face, to knock the happy look from it, to beat it until he could understand, completely and with all his heart, that she would in all likelihood never again be happy.

69

Bergmundur, the specialist in Icelandic language and folklore, lived in the Grjótathorp district, in a pretty timber-framed house that had obviously been recently renovated, as the silvery sheen of its corrugated steel cladding hadn't yet succumbed to the weather and the salt to the extent that it needed a coat of paint.

On the house's gable end, red lights flashed at a speed that was out of keeping with the generally relaxed feel of the neighbourhood, which was otherwise like a village in the heart of the city. Gunnar opened the gate and walked up to the house, surprised that the folklore expert had seen fit to put up Christmas decorations in early November.

Úrsúla had pointed the man out to him, as he had stood at the back of the press pack that afternoon to hear her statement on the ministry steps. She told Gunnar that she had run into him at the Árbær Museum at the weekend, and that he had been disagreeable. He had looked sour, and even angry, as he listened to Úrsúla explain to the assembled journalists that she had not asked for any law to be broken, nor had she any intention of snooping into medical records; all she had been seeking to establish was whether or not Pétur Pétursson posed any danger to her or her family.

The journalists fired questions at her as soon as she finished reading the statement, then, as her assistant, Eva, brought things to a close, Gunnar saw the man leave with a long face.

According to Úrsúla, Bergmundur was not connected to any media organisation so had no business being there. Gunnar had to admit that this was suspicious, and also typical of stalker behaviour.

He stood in front of the door to the little house and peered at the nameplates in the flashing light.

These announced the names of Bergmundur, a woman – presumably his wife – and a number of associations, all of them concerned with folkloric studies of nature. At the bottom of the brass plate he made out *Foss Friends – The Association for the Protection of Waterfalls*. It was a name he had heard before: this association fought for the protection of the numerous waterfalls threatened by hydro-electric power projects.

Gunnar waited for a moment and thought things over before knocking. Could it be that inside this mild academic lurked a violent misogynist? Could he be Fossi?

Tuesday

70

'This cannot be allowed to continue!' Óðinn thundered as he strode into Úrsúla's office with the slip of paper in his hand.

It had been delivered to reception downstairs in a neat white envelope stamped with the words 'by hand', so someone had clearly delivered it. The receptionists said that it had been handed over by a perfectly normal-looking man who didn't appear to be a homeless type; they assumed he must have been a taxi driver or a courier. Freyja had innocently opened it, expecting some standard official letter to drop out of the clean, white envelope, and had been taken by surprise.

The letter itself looked like something Pétur Pétursson would have sent; a piece of greasy paper, the kind used to wrap chips at fast-food places, with a message written in shaky letters:

The Devil's accomplice guilty of her father's death

'So you've seen what was waiting to brighten up my day?' Úrsúla said and grimaced at the sight of it.

'Freyja handed it to me as I was on my way up to see you. I'm terribly sorry, my dear,' he said, easing himself into the chair opposite her. His voice trembled and Úrsúla stared at him in surprise. He took a handkerchief from his pocket and mopped pearls of perspiration from his forehead. Úrsúla thought he looked exhausted. It was as if the grey in his hair had somehow spread to his face, making him appear colourless and drained.

'It's not your fault, Óðinn. This person is clearly not right in the head,' she said.

This note hadn't given her as much of a shock as the previous ones had. It was as if the initial shock of Pétur's persecution had now worn off, and had been replaced in her mind by a cool clarity that allowed her to shake off any discomfort. If anything, these notes had begun to spark her curiosity. What did this person mean by sending her these semi-poetic lines, and who was this devil he always referred to?

'It's completely unacceptable that the ministry can't shield you from this kind of thing, especially here, inside the building!'

He raised his voice for the last few words, and as the door was open, Úrsúla figured that this was intended for Freyja.

'Óðinn,' Úrsúla said gently. 'It's all right. It may sound strange, but both these notes and the foul emails I've been receiving, on top of the miserable media attention, don't hurt my feelings anymore. I think I'm becoming immune to this.'

Óðinn sighed.

'It's bizarre that anyone would have to get used to this kind of thing,' he said, and held up the greasy scrap of paper, shaking it as if he was drying fresh ink. 'But this man has to be taken out of circulation. This can't go on.'

71

Gunnar could feel only sympathy for Úrsúla as he scanned the day's media coverage. He had been at the press conference when she explained her reasons for enquiring about Pétur, and at the meeting with Boris and Óðinn that had triggered the whole thing, so he failed to understand how this could be twisted into a suggestion that the minister couldn't trust her own ministry to handle the situation – the conclusion most newspapers had managed to reach.

Úrsúla had called him in, and as he waited outside her office, looking through the newspapers, he wondered how anyone could be tempted to go into public life. The public had to be the world's worst employer, and it included individuals like Fossi, whose main aim was to achieve maximum hurt and distress.

'There was another letter,' Freyja whispered to him as he headed for the minister's office.

Úrsúla handed him the crumpled fast-food wrapper on which had been scrawled a threat in the form of a riddle.

'We don't need to look too hard for the sender,' he said, examining the misshapen lettering.

'No, it's pretty obvious that this is from Pétur,' she said, busy at the coffee machine in the corner. 'Would you like an espresso, or something else?' she asked.

He shook his head. People continued to offer him coffee, even though he always said no, and he wondered how long it would take Úrsúla to realise that he always declined.

'I'll take this to Boris,' he said. 'The commissioner will soon be able to hold an exhibition of Pétur's artworks.'

Úrsúla laughed. She seemed relaxed, less tense than she had been.

'Ingimar the Terrorist has agreed to a prison visit at Hólm-sheiði,' she said. 'He's there because there's no room for him at Litla-Hraun. I don't know how Eva managed to arrange this so quickly, but he's expecting to see you at visiting time today.'

Gunnar swallowed, This wasn't a job he was looking forward to.

'I noted down a few questions that I'd like you to ask him,' she added, handing him a handwritten note. 'Is there anything to report on that other matter – the folklore specialist who seems to show up everywhere?'

'I don't think Bergmundur is Fossi,' he said. 'He's just a sour old guy who's struggling to accept that the world around him is chang-ing. He's part of the naming committee, and he obviously revels in it, and sincerely believes that everything that's Icelandic will turn to dust if people are free to christen their kids Barbie or Boris.'

They both laughed. Gunnar had looked Boris up in the national registry after his conversation with Bergmundur, and had found that his full name, as the naming committee required, included an Icelandic name as well: Boris Thór.

'So what was he doing there yesterday with the journos?' Úrsúla asked, now sitting at her desk, shuffling through the papers in what seemed an aimless manner.

'He said that he'd just happened to be passing when you came out of the ministry and started addressing the journalists, so he stopped to listen.'

The old man had been astonished to find that Gunnar thought this behaviour strange, and had embarked on a long lecture about Iceland being a free country. Gunnar bit his cheek and held back a comment to the effect that freedom clearly didn't extend as far as the naming committee. But the man's account had been convincing, and Gunnar didn't have the feeling that he was someone who would make rape threats.

'So he's just an eccentric?' Úrsúla asked.

'That's it. I passed all the information to Boris, just to be on the safe side. I mean, Boris Thór,' he added, and Úrsúla laughed out loud.

72

Gunnar parked in the practically deserted car park in front of the prison. He had come in his own car so as to minimise the risk of the staff or anyone passing by making the link between the ministry of the interior and this secret visit. A smiling prison warder came up to him in the reception area, checked his identification papers and allocated him a locker for his coat, watch and phone. Then Gunnar followed him into the next room and stepped through the metal detector, and the warder quickly passed a drug detector wand over him, including Úrsúla's folded note.

'How do you and Ingimar know each other?' he asked. Gunnar wasn't sure if this was some kind of interrogation, and his answer would decide whether he would be allowed in or not, but the warder looked as if he was just chatting.

'Just old friends,' he muttered.

The warder nodded.

'At sea together?'

'Hmm.' Gunnar nodded as he hummed. It wasn't exactly a lie. At least, not as much of a lie as an outright 'yes' would have been.

The warder smiled amiably and opened a door to a long corridor, set with many doors, and told Gunnar to go to room three and to ring the bell if he needed anything.

Gunnar gingerly opened the door and slowly stepped into the little room. There was a bench at the back, and a chair by a glass partition. Gunnar sat and waited. On the other side of the glass was a tiny room, so small that it was hardly more than a cell. The only thing in there was a chair. He unfolded Úrsúla's list and read through it again, hoping to imprint some of the questions on his memory, but he had hardly begun before the door of the tiny room opened. Ingimar Magnússon walked in and sat in the chair.

'Hello,' he said, sounding rather cheerful, almost friendly. His voice was low and slightly hoarse, and Gunnar was surprised at how harmless he seemed, considering the man was a bomber. He had expected some indication of inner madness, something in his eyes or a fury of some kind – an underlying reason why someone would set off a bomb in a public place. On the contrary, this Ingimar came across as relaxed. He was grey, with hair cut short, no more than a trace of stubble to be seen, and somehow it seemed odd that he was dressed in a carefully pressed shirt in prison. Gunnar had imagined that everyone in prison had to wear a track suit.

'I'm a driver—' Gunnar began.

Ingimar interrupted him. 'I know who you are,' he said. 'We don't need to mention that again.'

He lifted a finger and circled it in the air, indicating that they were being watched, maybe being listened to as well. Gunnar felt the sweat break out everywhere. How was he supposed to ask questions without giving away who he was? He hadn't expected that their conversation would be monitored.

'I have some questions,' he said, holding up Úrsúla's note, and Ingimar nodded.

'Hold the paper up to the glass,' he said to Gunnar's relief.

Gunnar decided not to challenge Ingimar's suspicions. He thought it was unlikely that anyone would listen in to prisoners' conversations. But that might not apply to Ingimar. Maybe the police were still keeping tabs on him. After all, this man was Iceland's only terrorist. Gunnar held the paper flat against the glass, and Ingimar peered at it. He squinted slightly, as if he wasn't able to see clearly, or it could be because Úrsúla's handwriting was not particularly clear.

'The answer to the first question is no,' Ingimar said. Gunnar recalled that this concerned Ingimar's willingness to back out of the contract for the road and for another investor to be brought in. 'In answer to the next four questions, I would tell them not to hesitate. The ownership of the investment funds behind this will never be revealed. When people are as satisfied with something as they will be with this road, they won't start looking for problems.'

He continued to read from the sheet of paper and then sat back in the chair, arms folded over his broad chest as he looked directly at Gunnar.

'You can tell your boss,' he said, 'that if I'm kicked off the project, then the pension funds will be out as well. It's all or nothing. I have friends in the right places.'

The last few words were accompanied by a faint smile that for some reason irritated Gunnar. There was something infuriating about this man behind the prison glass, getting on his high horse with Úrsúla. He wasn't looking forward to bringing her the bad news. As he saw it, she would have no choice but to end the South Coast Highway initiative.

'So you still have strong connections?' Gunnar said, angry at the sight of the man's self-satisfied smile. 'In spite of being a terrorist?'

Ingimar got to his feet.

'Those who have money will always have friends,' he said, pressing the button to summon the warder. 'And those with a lot of money have very good friends.'

73

The astonishment on the man's face was entirely genuine. Nonni had answered the knock on the door and the man had asked for Úrsúla, so Nonni had called her and disappeared back into the kitchen to finish preparing lasagne. Úrsúla had asked the man if there was something she could help him with and now they stood in the doorway, staring at each other.

The man was middle-aged, with thinning hair and wearing a very thick, orange down jacket.

'Didn't you send me a message?' he asked.

Úrsúla shook her head.

'Do we know each other?' she asked, looking the man in the face.

Now he shook his head. 'I'm sorry. This must be some misunderstanding,' he said, turning to leave.

But Úrsúla stopped him. 'Could I see this message that I'm supposed to have sent you?'.

The man looked awkward. 'Well, you see ... actually, no,' he said. 'If it wasn't from you, then, well, it's embarrassing.'

He went down the steps, but when he placed a foot on the icy pavement, he slipped. He managed to regain his balance without falling, and glanced at Úrsúla and apologised again.

'It's a misunderstanding,' he said, plunging his hands deep into his coat pockets.

'Where did you see this message?' she called after him. 'On Facebook, or an email, or what?'

He didn't stop making his way carefully over the icy pavement, but he half turned to reply, 'On Tinder.'

Úrsúla stood speechless on the steps and watched him disappear. She went inside, shut the door and dug in the hall cupboard for her coat. It was furthest in, behind the children's coats, as for once she had been home before them. She dug out the mobile phone that she had intended to leave there, on silent, for the evening and found Gunnar's number.

'A small problem,' she said as soon as he answered. 'There was a man here just now who said he had received a message from me on Tinder. He was very surprised when he saw Nonni and even more surprised when I had no idea what he was talking about. I guess he was expecting he was coming over for sex.'

'Are you all right?' Gunnar asked.

'Yes, yes. I'm fine. But this is just so weird. I don't really want to be on Tinder, sending messages to men all over town that I know nothing about.'

She tried and failed to force a laugh. She wished she could see a funny side to this, that she could snigger and tell everyone the story of the stranger who had come to her door with something particular on his mind, but it felt too humiliating.

The thought that someone was sending strange men messages in her name that were, as the man had said, embarrassing, was deeply disquieting. She felt a stab of apprehension: she would have to tell Nonni. There was no way that he would see a funny side to this.

Wednesday

74

'You're joking, surely?' Úrsúla said for what must have been the tenth time since Gunnar had appeared in her office to hand her an envelope of printouts of the Tinder profile that someone had set up in her name.

'Someone put a lot of effort into this, setting up a Facebook page that looks like your personal page, and then using that to set up the Tinder profile.'

'And no prizes for stylish prose,' Úrsúla said.

'No,' Gunnar agreed. 'The use of language is very similar to what we've seen in the rape-threat emails from Fossi. It doesn't need much sleuthing needed to figure out it's the same individual.'

'What do we do about this?' Úrsúla asked. She was less than keen on more awkward visits from hopeful men knocking at her door.

'I've already had the accounts closed, both on Facebook and Tinder, and I'll do my best to keep track of any new profiles that are set up in your name. But the only solution is to find the person responsible for all this, to find Fossi. Boris and co. have all the information, and hopefully they'll get some results soon.'

'The Coast Guard's waiting for you,' Eva said, her face appearing in the doorway.

Úrsúla got up from the sofa.

'Thank you, Gunnar,' she said. 'I don't know how I'd manage without you.' She had often meant to tell him how much she appreciated having him at her beck and call, considering her initial doubts about whether she would need him.

Gunnar smiled and went to fetch the car, and she weighed the envelope of Tinder profile printouts in her hand, wondering whether or not to take it home to show it to Nonni. She decided against it. He would take it personally, and he had already been through enough, so Úrsúla dropped the envelope in the bin, grabbed her coat from its hook and went to find Eva.

'I'm all ready for the Coast Guard,' she said, and they set off together. As the lift doors shut behind them, Eva handed her a sheet of paper.

'It's the report on the rape case that you wanted checked. You might want to call the mother yourself with the bad news, as you made a personal promise to look into it. The police have decided to drop the investigation.'

75

Despite the dry suit, the cold enveloped Úrsúla and her senses were swamped by the sea so that she felt she was sinking, even though she knew that the lifejacket and flotation suit would keep her afloat. The salt water had made its way inside the mask and stung her eyes, so she had to fight to keep them open and pay attention to what was happening around her. Somewhere in the water close by was one of the Coast Guard crew, who had jumped out of the boat ahead of her; and above them hovered a helicopter, which was preparing to winch them both to safety.

The downdraught whipped up the waves, turning them into a mist so that sea water rained all around them. Úrsúla had not been fully able to take on board what she was experiencing, her thoughts still dulled by the phone call she had forced herself to make to Rósa, the mother of the girl who had made the rape accusation. So only part of her attention had been on the Coast

Guard team as they explained the rescue procedure and helped her into the dry suit.

The girl's mother had wept while Úrsúla read out the report the ministry had received, stating that due to numerous shortcomings, the investigation would be dropped.

'How can the rape kit get lost between Selfoss and Reykjavík,' she had sobbed. 'How can they be so careless with something that's so important?'

Úrsúla had only been able to reply that she was deeply sorry.

'You promised me that you'd bring that horrible man to law,' the mother had said, and Úrsúla felt as if she had been punched in the belly. It was completely true that she had made a promise. She had pledged that she'd ensure justice was done. It went without saying that there could hardly be justice when the case would not even be investigated.

'I'm truly sorry,' she repeated.

She said the same words again before the conversation ended, and now she muttered them again as she lay on her back, clad in a dry suit under the salty rain whipped up by the helicopter's rotor blades, and waited for this demonstration, clearly intended to impress the minister, to come to an end.

The diver was winched down from the helicopter, which was deafening as it hovered directly above them. He dropped into the water next to Úrsúla, swam over to her, fastened the two of them together with some sort of harness and waved to the helicopter. They were instantly lifted into the air above the sea. The harness strapped around her pressed so tight that she felt she could not fill her lungs properly, and there, in the weightlessness between sea and sky, she allowed herself to yell as loudly as she could with the little air left in her chest. But her screams were drowned out by the thunderous din of the helicopter and as she was pulled on board, she was exhausted.

Someone strapped her into a seat, took off her helmet and mask, and handed her a towel, which she used to massage her chilled face and hair. She was startled by a sudden flash of light. She didn't feel this was the ideal moment to be photographed, her face stiff with cold, eyes red from the salt water and her hair left in a mess by the helmet.

She blinked a few times before her vision returned and saw that the flash had come from the smartphone in Adolf's hand, as he sat, wearing an overcoat and a scarf, in the seat opposite her, a malevolent smirk on his face.

76

'It's fucking creepy, buying trash,' she said to the guy, who just grinned and took the bags, chucked them onto the back seat of his wreck of a car and gave her a couple of one-thousand-krónur notes.

Stella stuffed the cash in her pocket and set off determinedly towards the bus. She would use the time she'd have to wait between buses at Mjódd to buy a snack of some kind for her mother. She could scoff down a whole bag of paprika chips before dinner without denting her appetite, and another one after. This seemed to be one of the few things that genuinely brought her pleasure. She neither thanked Stella, nor offered to share, just as if she had become a small child. Stella liked to watch her work her way through the chips, every now and again pausing to lick the paprika dust from her fingers and lips.

Half an hour later she had bought the chips and smoked a cigarette outside the bus shelter at Mjódd. It would be another ten minutes before the bus showed up. It was too cold to wait outside, so she ambled around the waiting area, checking out the people waiting to be carried hither and thither. In Iceland only kids, old people and the poor used buses. Everyone else travelled around in their cars – the smarter the car, the better.

'It's the car that makes the man,' Guðmundur had said. She and her mother had thought that funny, but it was something special to be driven around the city in such a cool car. That had only lasted until she had accidentally spilled a carton of juice over the back seat. She shook the memory off. Visits to her mother inevitably brought back thoughts of Guðmundur, even though she would have preferred to erase him completely from her memory, along with the screams, the scoldings and the beatings.

She noticed the television in one corner. Gréta had just appeared on the screen. The news had begun so Stella went closer so she could hear. The volume was set so low that she could hear no more than a murmur over the loud chatter of the teenagers on the far side of the waiting room and the hiss of the automatic doors that endlessly opened and closed as people came in and went out.

She stood beside a blue-haired woman and peered at the screen. The woman was obviously trying to make out the content of the news programme, but Stella simply stared at Gréta, who appeared between news items, looking the viewer in the eye as she said something that Stella couldn't hear. Gréta's hair looked fantastic. She had been to the hairdresser and completely changed her look. Now her hair was short one side and almost down to her shoulder the other. It suited her.

Stella wouldn't have objected to sitting right now at Gréta's kitchen breakfast bar, knocking back French paté and beer, or any of the foreign delicacies that seemed to accumulate in Gréta's kitchen cupboards. She also wouldn't have minded another faceful of Gréta's tits. A jolt of excitement passed through her at the memory, although she knew the pills were what had made the experience so powerful. This wave of contentment was just fake. There was no magic there, just ordinary chemistry.

77

The last few days had been lost in the fog of forgetfulness, which to Pétur meant there had been enough to drink. He'd managed to wangle his way into this lovely house with Eddi, who had forgiven him; they had agreed that something neither of them could properly remember simply couldn't have happened. Eddi had wheedled his way into the terraced house where this woman lived, and there had been a stocked bar and a full fridge when they arrived. The woman was lonely and afraid, so for her it was a comfort to hear them singing when she emerged from her doped sleep. Eddi crawled into bed with her now and again, while Pétur lay in a hot bath and recited verses to himself. He wasn't sure how long they had been there, but everything that could be drunk had been finished and the fridge was empty, and now he was sitting, watching TV, absently munching on chocolate biscuits, long past their sell-by date, that he had found at the back of the cupboard.

His heart leaped as Úrsúla appeared on the screen wearing some kind of outdoor suit and with a huge helmet under one arm. There was a helicopter in the background and some smiling men wearing the same sort of overalls. He stared at her and felt the gnawing guilt creep up his throat like bile. He had completely forgotten his responsibility, his battle with the Devil, and judging by the look in Úrsúla's eyes, she had to be completely within his power. Her eyes were dull, tired and sad. The eyes never lie; even when the body is a slave and the soul in chains, the eyes always tell the true tale. It was obvious that the Devil had enslaved her soul.

'And what's next on the minister's agenda?' the reporter asked in a jovial voice. This was clearly one of those light-hearted items that were so important for every news bulletin.

'I'm going shopping, and then cooking for the family,' Úrsúla replied. 'It's not every day that I can tell my children about such an exciting day at the office.'

She smiled, and Pétur could see a trace of the original, unspoiled soul, the face of the child who laughed and shrieked when he and her father had joked with her or sung her a song. Then the news bulletin was over, and Pétur got to his feet. The item had been recorded in the afternoon darkness, so it hadn't been that long ago. If he was quick, he'd have a chance of catching her. Having spent so much time in the boot of her car, he knew exactly where she normally shopped for groceries.

78

'I was going to give you full marks for that piece of PR,' Eva said. 'And then it turns out you really are going to cook dinner for the children.'

Úrsúla laughed. 'I'm not always devious,' she said.

They walked together from the helicopter hangar and over to the car park. There was a bitter tang of fuel in the frosty air, and somewhere in the background the chug of heavy machinery at work could be heard; compared to the roaring dim she had endured for most of the day, it seemed like a mellow undertone.

'It's exactly that human side, or maybe we should say the feminine side, that you need to show,' Eva said. 'You need to let yourself laugh more often, show a milder side in television interviews, and put some emphasis on being a mother and a wife, not just a minister.'

Úrsúla sighed. 'So is that really how far we've come? The men are supposed to come across as decisive and women as mild? Is that it?'

'Well,' Eva began, and stood still, so Úrsúla knew that a long explanation was coming. 'Women in politics have to appear decisive to be respected. But if they fall short, and negativity appears, then that same decisiveness instead triggers hatred. Now you're in the position in which the media has tasted blood, so you'll have to work to overcome the general impression that's being formed that you're a harridan who tramples over everyone, including innocent street people. So you need to appear mild and smile more. A smile always disarms the opposition. That interview just now was perfect. Really, it was.'

'All right. I hear what you're saying and accept it. I'll bear it in mind.'

The ministerial car pulled up next to them, and Eva shook her head.

'I'll take a taxi home,' she said with an arch smile. 'You can go shopping for the family and be a perfect wife and mother for a change.'

Úrsúla laughed as she got into the car, and as she shut the door behind her, she remembered what she had meant to ask Eva, and rolled down the window.

'Eva,' she called after her; she turned and bent down to the window. 'Would you speak to Adolf and make sure he erases that picture he took of me in the helicopter. I was like a drowned rat when he took it; it would be just like him to spread it around.' Eva nodded. 'And maybe you could also find out why he was there at all?'

'I asked the Coast Guard guys and they said that he's been their main point of contact at the ministry, so they decided to invite him along. I'll tell him to erase the picture.'

Úrsúla lay back in the seat. She was exhausted, and all the exertion, and the hot cocoa the Coast Guard team had given her after, had left her with a feeling of relaxed wellbeing. If she were to close her eyes, she would be asleep immediately.

'Are you OK with stopping off at the shop on the way home?' she asked Gunnar. 'I have to cook tonight as Nonni's teaching a course until half past seven.'

79

Gunnar didn't even have time to curse himself for letting Úrsúla have her own way and walk from the car to the shop alone before he was hurrying after her. As he ran he pressed the button on the hands-free communicator that connected him to the car's emergency radio. She had wanted him to park some distance from the entrance, as she felt it would be odd to pull up right by the door in the gleaming-black ministerial car. In fact, he had agreed with her, as it could look out of place, but now, as he raced across the car park in the hope of reaching her ahead of Pétur, who had come running from the other direction, he bitterly reproached himself. What the hell had he been thinking?

'Úrsúla!' he called out, instinctively rather than because he had thought things through.

She turned towards him and his voice, her back to Pétur, who grabbed her from behind, lifted her off her feet and spun her round, just as Gunnar took hold of him. He caught Pétur in a headlock, gripping one arm and twisting it high behind his back to force him to crouch down. This pushed Úrsúla to her knees, as Pétur was still holding on to her with one hand. She managed to pull herself free and stood up.

The old man yelled an endless litany that could hardly be understood, about her father and the devil. In fact he seemed to be indicating that Úrsúla herself was the devil.

Gunnar clicked handcuffs onto Pétur's wrists and holding him in a restraint posture, he used the communicator to call for police assistance. Úrsúla's breath came shallow and fast, clouds of vapour formed in the cold air around her head and lit up like a halo in the glow from the shop's lights.

'What on earth do you want with me, Pétur?' she snapped. Several customers leaving the shop stopped to watch the spectacle. 'What the hell is all this about?' Úrsúla asked, her voice quieter now.

The old man stopped yelling and instead began to sob. He didn't reply, but simply repeated her name.

'Úrsúla,' he said. 'Úrsúla. Úrsúla Aradóttir.'

'You're not hurt?' Gunnar asked.

She shook her head as a police car came to a halt outside the shop and two police officers got out.

'Can we keep this low key?' Úrsúla asked, dusting off her coat. 'Can you have the police take him away, but keep this under the radar? Nonni's nerves are already shot to pieces. It's better for him and the children not to know about this.'

Gunnar nodded. He would need to give the police an explanation for the handcuffs and persuade them to take a flexible approach. Normal citizens, even those working as bodyguards, shouldn't carry handcuffs.

As the two police officers took Pétur away, he saw Úrsúla disappear into the shop, picking up a shopping basket on her way as she strode with determination between the aisles. Maybe it was his imagination, but he thought he saw she was trembling.

80

Úrsúla was jerked into wakefulness, the feeling of being choked so strong that she rolled out of bed and onto the floor, where she crouched for a moment while she regained her breath. Still half asleep, she passed a hand over her face, almost to convince herself that she wasn't wearing a plastic overall and a ski mask, even though neither the Ebola outbreak nor Liberia had featured in her dreams. Maybe it was something as simple as the duvet resting on her face and hindering her breathing. Nonni muttered in his sleep, and so as not to wake him, she left the room and closed the bedroom door quietly behind her. Kátur sleepily got up from his basket and padded over to her. He followed her downstairs, where she turned on the tap in the kitchen and held a finger under the rush of water until it was numb with cold. She filled a glass and drank it down in one long draught, the cold water making her chest ache on its way down.

'You want some water as well, Kátur?' she asked, then filled the glass again and poured the contents into his bowl. He clearly wasn't thirsty as he ignored it.

She was wide awake now and knew there was no point trying to get back to sleep, so she went to the living room, lay on the sofa and switched on the television. Kátur jumped up beside her and curled up at her feet, where he heaved a sigh so heavy it would have done a much larger dog credit.

She skipped between channels for a while. They had a long list of cable stations, but she had demanded satellite TV as well so that she could follow the news from anywhere in the world. This time she was lucky enough to find a report on the Ebola epidemic. She turned the sound down and took in the images as they rolled past on the screen. The sequences showed an emergency clinic in Sierra Leone that looked exactly like the one she had been at in Liberia. This one was also run by Médecins Sans Frontières; the hospital tent itself was the same and the staff putting on protective clothing outside used the same procedure as they had followed in Liberia. She watched them, and in her mind recited the regulations for dressing and undressing. Working with the doctors, she had ordered a dressing coach to be present for every shift, reading out the regulations while they prepared, and afterwards when they took off their protective gear, to minimise the possibility of a mistake that could cost someone's life. Taking a glove off out of sequence could lead to infection.

Úrsúla closed her eyes and for a moment was back at the staff hostel, where the infection specialist sat in a corner, sketching a diagram linking patients in the hope of finding patient zero, to trace the source of the epidemic. Jean-Pierre sat on the sofa, weeping, having stopped himself administering a lethal dose of morphine to a young woman to alleviate her suffering, while

Martina, the Spanish nurse, was on her knees, praying to God in his mercy not to let any of the patients survive. Úrsúla opened her eyes and watched the report continue. It was somehow strangely calming, some kind of confirmation that she hadn't dreamed it all, that the Ebola epidemic hadn't just been a horrendous nightmare of bodies glistening with fever as they were brought in, to be carried out later as twisted corpses, but that this had genuinely been her life for a few weeks.

Kátur shifted on the sofa, making himself comfortable on her chest as if he was trying to absorb the sorrow that he knew was deep in her heart, but which she couldn't feel.

Thursday

81

The last thing she expected to do was break down in tears in front of Thorbjörn. Maybe it was the shock of being attacked by Pétur the day before, which she had suppressed to prevent Nonni and the children becoming even more concerned about her, or it could have been the news Thorbjörn had given her – that the media had got wind of the Tinder profile. As it was Thorbjörn, she could hardly refute, with an aggrieved expression on her face, the suggestion that she could be unfaithful to her husband, so instead she burst into tears.

'Hey, don't cry,' he said, stroking her hair, which magnified her sadness so much that she wanted to throw herself into his arms and spend what was left of the day crying. His sympathy was tender and hugely comforting, but she was keenly aware of her betrayal. It wasn't right for her to accept solace from any man other than Nonni. It was no better than cuckolding him.

She got to her feet, reached for a tissue and wiped her face.

'It's a stalker who registered a profile under my name,' she said. 'The police are searching for him. This is supposed to be typical stalker behaviour.'

Thorbjörn's eyes followed her around the office. She wondered whether he had found her display of sensitivity embarrassing.

'I'm sorry,' she said, taking out a lipstick as she went over to the mirror. She applied a thick layer to her lips.

'There's nothing to apologise for, Úrsúla. I'll spike the story so we don't use it, and I'll see that it doesn't leak out to the rest of the media. And if it does get out somewhere, then we get a scoop about the stalker. OK? That would explain it all. "Stalker Puts Minister's Profile on Dating Site".'

Thorbjörn sketched quote marks in the air as if he was casting an invisible spell.

Úrsúla laughed. 'Thanks, Thorbjörn.'

'Not a problem,' he said sincerely, and again she saw the depth of sympathy in his eyes, knowing that if she were to throw herself into his arms now he would be good to her, love her with all the sympathy she desperately wanted, with no explanations needed. She felt a spark of heat inside her that grew until it flowed through her whole body.

82

He didn't notice Stella as he strode with rapid steps out of the minister's office, even though he looked in her direction and walked right past her, with only a few metres between them. There was something about pushing a cleaning trolley that made someone invisible to most people. A little later the minister herself came out of her office. She said something to her secretary then winked to Stella and nodded her head towards the corridor, indicating that it was time to go out onto the balcony for a smoke. Stella could feel the secretary's disgust follow her as she followed in Úrsúla's footsteps. It was the look she had become used to as a teenager when most of her friends' mothers decided that she wasn't ideal company for their daughters.

Outside, Stella buttoned her sweater while Úrsúla fished in her bag for a lighter. There was a bitter, dry frost that worked its way into your marrow, and even Esja, the mountain across the bay, seemed to be huddled down to shelter from the worst of it. They lit their cigarettes, each providing the other with shelter from the wind, and as Stella held the lighter up for Úrsúla, who made a bowl of her hands around the flame, she noticed the redness that spread from her jaw and down her neck.

'Hey,' she said in a low voice. 'You have a bit of, um, beard rash on your neck.'

Úrsúla stared for a moment at her, as if thunderstruck, and snatched the handbag hanging from her shoulder, cursing to herself in an undertone as she drew out a little packet of wet wipes. She opened it and pulled a few of them out, crunched them into a ball and dabbed at her neck as if this was something she had to wash off as fast as she could. She dropped her handbag and Stella stooped to pick it up, handing it to her. Úrsúla dropped the used wipes in it as if it was a bin, and then rummaged busily for a makeup compact. Her hands shook as she opened it and used a sponge to ladle tan concealer onto the lower half of her face and her neck without being able to see what she was doing. Stella pointed to some heavy marks, and Úrsúla blended them in as directed.

'It's not beard rash,' she said, without catching Stella's eye. 'It's an allergy to something that sometimes breaks out.'

Of course it could have been that, and there was every chance it was a coincidence that her allergy broke out just as the creepy guy strode out of her office. But it was her clumsy reaction with the wipes and the makeup that told Stella that there was no coincidence behind this: the creepy arsehole of a journalist who bought the bags of rubbish was also fucking the minister.

83

'Thanks for walking with me,' Úrsúla said from beneath the scarf wrapped around the lower half of her face. 'I needed to stretch my legs, get some fresh air.'

'No problem,' Gunnar said.

They had chosen to walk along the sea front, despite the biting onshore wind, as this seemed to be the only pavement in the district that had been properly cleared and gritted. They had walked almost as far as the Sun Voyager sculpture. Heavy grey cloud reached down to the middle of Esja's slopes, but there didn't seem to be a likelihood of more snow. It was too cold for that.

'How did he come across to you?' she asked, and Gunnar knew exactly what she meant. 'I'm curious.'

'He seemed to be strangely normal,' Gunnar said, 'considering he's a bomber.'

'Hmm,' Úrsúla said. 'More than likely what goes on inside most people just isn't visible on the surface.'

'But it's obvious he's the kind of guy who's used to having his own way. The sort who gets a kick out of power. When he said "it's all or nothing" he smiled a little bit, and he had this look on his face as if he was completely confident he would win. You know what I mean? I don't know how I can explain it more clearly...'

'I know what you mean,' Úrsúla said. 'I know precisely what you mean.'

They stopped by the Sun Voyager and watched weather-beaten tourists taking pictures of each other in front of the sculpture.

'A shame there's nothing in the background for them,' Gunnar said.

'That's true,' Úrsúla replied. 'I feel sorry for these poor things who come here in the depths of winter, expecting to see Northern Lights, and instead they get grey clouds and lousy weather the whole time.'

They turned and walked back towards the ministry.

'Do you think you'll call off the South Coast Highway renewal?' Gunnar asked, hoping deep inside that the answer would be no. He wanted her to say there was a new solution, some way to make the initiative possible. He couldn't imagine the storm that would break over her if she were to dash so many people's hopes – including his own. He had seen himself bowling along the broad, straight South Coast Highway, with slip roads on and off, like a proper motorway, instead of the narrow lanes running each way currently, cut through by country roads, each of which presented a hazard.

Úrsúla said something, but it was drowned out by the rattle of nail tyres on the jeeps hurtling by.

'What did you say?'

'I'm thinking it over,' she said, pressing the button for the lights on the Sæbraut crossing. 'I'm thinking it over as hard as I can.'

84

'Everything you're telling me says post-traumatic stress disorder,' the psychologist said thoughtfully. He was a young man, so youthful that Úrsúla had almost cancelled the appointment when she saw him. There was something laughable about a youngster hardly old enough to be confirmed giving her advice on life.

'I don't think I'm getting the symptoms that my colleagues in aid work have described. I never have flashbacks or find myself out of touch with reality, and I've never not known where I am or anything like that. A friend of mine who was with me in Syria threw himself on the floor in a smart restaurant in Stockholm because he heard a noise that reminded him of gunfire. His wife was devastated, and all the diners and waiters stared at them. I'm not on edge like that. In fact, I'm pretty laid back. Nightmares are rare, no panic attacks.'

Úrsúla realised that all this added up to a defence of some kind. She hadn't meant to be on the defensive. After all, she was the one who had booked the appointment with the psychologist.

'You told me you scare easily,' he said, tapping his pen against the notebook in which he had jotted things down as he took her through what he referred to as her back story. 'And you suffer from guilt,' he added, looking up at her with a questioning expression on his face.

'Maybe that's because of other things,' she said. 'I've been hounded since I stepped in as minister, and a week ago I freaked out because of something that turned out to be nothing at all. It was as if all that fear had collected inside me and it overflowed when an old man selling dried fish knocked on the door.'

'Was there something that led up to this? Was there anything else that day, or over the previous days, that upset you in any way?'

'I have a stalker – probably more than one. And I've been unfaithful to my husband.' She said the last words without meaning to. Somehow they fell out of her mouth. She immediately regretted them. She sincerely hoped this psychologist kept everything he heard confidential.

'I see,' he said slowly, and looked at her thoughtfully. 'Was that with an individual for whom you have feelings?'

'I don't know,' Úrsúla said. 'I don't know what emotions I do or don't feel. I'm aware of fear and irritation and boredom, and I seem to be able to burst into tears over something completely trivial. But this numbness I told you about appears to have swallowed up all the good emotions. I'm never glad, never pleased, and I have practically no positive feelings towards anyone but the dog. Even though we've been to a counsellor, nothing happens. I just yell at Nonni, my husband, because I'm angry at him for asking for something I can't give him. I know I'm supposed to love him and the children, and I know I used to, but those aren't feelings I have any longer. At least, I have them for just a fraction of a second at a time. But there's no way I could tell my husband that I love the dog more than him.'

'And the man you were unfaithful with,' the psychologist said. 'Do you have feelings towards him?'

'I do,' Úrsúla said. 'But it's not exactly love. It's more a kind of excitement that I don't understand myself. When he looks at me I get the feeling that he feels sorry for me. A bit like the dog.'

The psychologist snapped his notebook shut and placed it on the coffee table between then, laying the pen on top of it. He flexed his fingers, leaned forward and rested his elbows on the knees of his threadbare corduroy trousers.

'This confirms my diagnosis of post-traumatic stress disorder,' he said. 'It's normal to demonstrate stress responses after a traumatic event, but traumatic stress doesn't become a mental disorder unless it lasts more than a few weeks. It's more than a year now since you left aid work, and in that time you've moved home and taken on a highly demanding role.'

Úrsúla was about to make the point that in comparison with aid work there was nothing remotely demanding about being a minister, but the psychologist raised a finger like a strict teacher.

'Increased pressure can set off traumatic stress, and from what you've told me, it seems you have followed a pattern of numbing emotions so as to avoid having to deal with them. Then there's some kind of trigger, and you seek out behaviour that sparks emotion.'

'Compared to all the work I've done before, there's not much pressure on a minister,' Úrsúla said.

'Then maybe the reasons lie elsewhere,' the psychologist replied, clearly determined to stick to his guns. 'Stress disorders can manifest themselves in forgetfulness and numbness just as much as in panic attacks and nightmares. People bury deep inside themselves experiences and memories that are too painful to deal with, and doing this deadens their emotions. But the numbness works against them over time because having no feelings leads to depression, and people seek out behaviour that sparks emotion. Generally that tends to be behaviour that to some extent is self-harming, as I believe your unfaithfulness to your husband is.'

Úrsúla said nothing. All this was nothing new, but all the same, it was an indescribable relief to hear someone put into words what she had fought with for so long.

'Keep away from drugs or alcohol, and from this man you've been having an affair with, and I'll see you next Thursday. Then I'll go through a method of mental processing and we can assess whether or not it would suit you.'

'There's one more part of the back story that I ought to add,' Úrsúla said as she got to her feet. 'It's about my father.'

She was certain that the psychologist would have read about all this in the newspapers, but the expression on his face showed that he knew nothing.

'What about your father?' he asked.

'My father was murdered in a prison cell many years ago, and this whole matter has surfaced again. You can read about it in the papers.'

'Then that's the trigger we were talking about,' the psychologist said, jotting something down in his notebook.

85

Úrsúla had decided to go home after her appointment with the psychologist, telling Freyja that she would call her to pick up any messages. Now she stood on a chair in the kitchen so she could peer deep into the spice cupboard, and spied a glass jar they always used to mix the cinnamon and sugar the children liked to have on rice pudding. Kátur watched her with vigilant eyes, always hoping that something edible might come his way.

She stepped down from the chair, put two slices of bread in the toaster and turned up the setting so they would be properly dark. The bread had to be fully toasted, otherwise it wouldn't be right. This was one of the things that people who hadn't been brought up poor couldn't understand. There was a kind of victory to be had in toast with cinnamon sugar, and in enjoying it, even now when the fridge was full of the selection of brie, marmalade and other delicacies that Nonni made sure they had. There was a comfort in knowing, as a pampered westerner, that the secret of life simply came down to making sure your belly was full. There was a certain security that came with this knowledge.

As she scattered sugar onto the hot bread, it melted into it, releasing the cinnamon aroma. Úrsúla chewed the toast and wondered whether to make herself coffee – or even tea, as she had done as a child – but she didn't want to ruin the flavour of the cinnamon bread right away. This was the taste of the woollen sweaters that her mother knitted after work, the taste of the two of them delivering newspapers before school, the taste of the lies she had to invent to keep the school from knowing about the situation at home.

This background had made it easier for her to work in challenging conditions – where there were few comforts, where the food was bland and the demands were high. She had no problem with sacrificing sleep if there was work to be done, and didn't care if she had to live on rice alone for weeks at a time. Many of her colleagues in the aid sector had struggled with this, but for her it was straightforward not to think about what wasn't available.

The doorbell rang, and Kátur responded with a volley of barks. For a moment Úrsúla felt her heart sink, and contemplated not answering the door. Nonni wasn't at home to open it for her, as the police guidelines had laid down. But she shook off the fear. After all, Pétur was behind lock and key. Now she had the security camera and the emergency button, so what could go wrong?

A neat young man holding a box stood on the steps, or so the strange angle of the security camera showed her. He had to be a delivery driver, so she picked Kátur up and held him under one arm to prevent him greeting the man with a further barrage of barks.

The man handed her the box as soon as she opened the door.

'Do I need to sign for this?' she asked.

The man laughed. 'It's the chocolate you asked for,' he said, winking and smacking his lips twice as if she ought to know that she had requested chocolate.

'Who sent this?' she asked. 'I didn't ask for any chocolate.'

'Are you saying you weren't expecting me?' he said without waiting for an answer. Then shouldered her aside and forced his way in.

Úrsúla tightened her grip on Kátur and fumbled desperately for the emergency button.

86

'There you go,' Stella said to the creepy journalist as she handed him the bags of rubbish.

He smirked as he handed her notes, and now she wished she had planted something nastier than a banana skin in the middle of the minister's bag – or what he thought was the minister's bag. Today she had shredded the waste from the minister's office, as she was supposed to, along with the paper waste from the permanent secretary's office, and had handed the creep rubbish that had come from some other office, with no idea of what went on in there, but which had nothing to do with the minister. The guy deserved to spend time going through two bags of ordinary junk in the hope of finding some dirt on the minister. She couldn't stand men who slept with a woman and then treated her badly.

Stella stopped in her tracks in the middle of the ministry car park, her eyes drawn to that grey tower block that loomed over the city's Shadow District. Was that how she had treated Gréta? Slept with her and then let her down badly? Had she hurt her by suggesting unnecessarily that they shouldn't let anyone know what had gone on between them? She had made it glaringly obvious that she didn't want to be seen with her. Was she no better than that arsehole of a journalist?

She strode with determination across the car park and out into the street, then took a short-cut across Klapparstígur and between the white apartment blocks. She was going to apologise to Gréta. She could feel deep in her heart that it was the right thing to do. She wasn't going to be a bitch. She jogged through the playground that nestled between the high-rise buildings and was panting by the time she reached the lobby of the grey tower block. She punched in the number of Gréta's apartment and waited, but there was no reply. She tried the number a second time and pressed the bell icon, but before it had finished buzzing, the door opened and Gréta stepped out. Stella didn't have to glance twice at the tall fair-haired woman beside her to know that this was the one she had been so captivated by on Tinder. She was even more attractive than her profile picture had indicated. Stella wondered what this woman saw in Gréta. They looked an unlikely pair, but there was something about them, some glow that joined them together. Stella was certain that they had only just got out of bed.

'*Hæ*, I was wondering if I could have a word?' Stella said, the words tumbling out of her.

Gréta's reaction wasn't what she had expected. There was none of the usual delight in seeing her, not even a smile. Gréta seemed unusually reserved.

'Is this something to do with the ministry?' she asked, and Stella shook her head.

'No. Just a small private matter.'

'Well, we're going to dinner and we're already a little late, and after that we're going to the theatre.'

Gréta opened the outer door for her blonde companion, who stepped out like a princess and stood waiting on the pavement, looking Stella up and down. Stella followed them out.

'Could we meet for a coffee tomorrow evening?' she asked.

Gréta shook her head. 'I'm working tomorrow evening.'

'And Saturday?' Stella asked and Gréta hesitated.

The blonde sighed. 'On Saturday we're going to Harpa. Remember? The concert and then dinner.'

Gréta nodded and spread her hands theatrically, while Stella swallowed her annoyance and felt a growing disquiet in her belly. What was this stranger doing, interfering in her meeting Gréta? What the hell business was it of hers? All she wanted was to talk to Gréta, simply to make up for her own bad behaviour. But it was obvious there was no point. She wouldn't ask again. It was clear that Gréta didn't want to meet her.

87

'I just pressed the button and ran out into the street,' Úrsúla repeated, one more time, for Boris this time, as he had just made an appearance. 'I thought I had to get out right away or I'd be so frightened I wouldn't be able to move, so I ran for it and waited for the police.'

'You did exactly the right thing,' Boris said. 'Women are like songbirds – prone to freeze if they're attacked, so it's as well to escape while you can still make decisions.'

The man had been taken away by the police. To begin with they had taken him into the kitchen, and Úrsúla had been able to hear the special-unit officers who had been first on the scene talking to him. They had led him out through the living room, where she sat with the female officer who had been in the second car. The man had looked dejected and subdued, and for some reason it occurred to Úrsúla that she had made too much of the incident. Perhaps it had just been panic on her part, just as it had been a few days before when she had freaked out at the thought that the man delivering fish had been Pétur.

'Do you think this could be a misunderstanding on my part?' she asked.

Boris shook his head. He was about to say something when a plain-clothes officer appeared in the doorway and called him. Boris went over and they spoke in muted voices. Úrsúla saw him hand a phone to Boris, who looked through the contents. She heard no more as the female officer sitting at her side patted her hand, asking if she wanted some water or a blanket, and Úrsúla realised that she was shivering. That had to be either nerves, or else the cold draught blowing in through the open door along with the flashing blue lights of the police cars outside.

'Nobody has a right to push their way into your home against your will,' the officer said, still patting the back of Úrsúla's hand. 'You did precisely the right thing by pressing the alarm button. That's what it's for. It's better to use it once too often than to not use it at all.'

The officer's words were presumably intended to be encouraging, but Úrsúla couldn't help thinking this was a once-too-often occurrence; needless hysteria or panic, which could be symptoms of post-traumatic stress. She felt her face flush with discomfort and took a deep breath, preparing herself to stand up, tell the coppers to get out and pour herself a double brandy – her way of toughing things out.

But before she managed to stand up, Boris had returned with a perplexed look on his face. He perched on the coffee table opposite her and cleared his throat awkwardly.

'I'm going to recommend to Gunnar that we run twenty-four-hour security around you while we get to the bottom of this. I've already spoken to him and he's ready. We'll have a police presence outside as well. I know it's uncomfortable to have the police breathing down your neck the whole time and a member of staff staying in your house while we figure this out, but it's the best way.'

'Figure what out?' Úrsúla asked.

Boris cleared his throat again. 'There's ... err ... This Tinder account that someone has set up in your name.'

'I knew about that,' Úrsúla said. 'That's been closed down.'

Boris again cleared his throat and this time it was closer to a cough.

'What?' Úrsúla demanded.

'Well, there's a new account and...'

'And what?'

'It seems that the person in question has been in touch with the man who pushed his way in, encouraging this behaviour. While we don't know how many other men this lunatic has encouraged to do the same, it's best that Gunnar is at your side all the time.'

'Encourage what? Just what are you talking about?'

'The person in question, acting supposedly on your behalf, asks men to come to your home and fulfil – what shall we say? – certain fantasies of yours. The men are encouraged to ignore pro-tests or physical resistance as this is supposed to be part of the game. Some kind of role play, you see.'

Úrsúla felt her heart skip a beat, and the terror that she had kept under control since the man had pushed her aside in the doorway returned with full force. She felt her innards turn to a liquid that seeped down to her feet, leaving her unable to move.

Boris coughed again.

'The person in question supposedly speaks for you in saying that you fantasise about being raped.'

88

Gunnar picked up a toothbrush and clean underwear, and stuffed them in his bag along with his laptop.

'What do you mean, you're staying in her house?' Íris snapped.

She was already furious, even though he had explained it to her and apologised for ruining the evening they had expected to spend together.

'In *their* house,' he corrected. 'With her and her husband and their children.'

'What stupid shit is this?' she said. 'I've never heard that drivers get to stay with ministers. Are you fucking her, you idiot?'

Gunnar stopped and sighed. 'No Íris. I'm not sleeping with the minister. And don't call me an idiot.'

'I'll call you what you are,' she hissed. 'Not the sharpest chisel in the toolbox, are you? You think I haven't seen your profile on Tinder? You set it up the day before yesterday and you don't need to tell me you're staying with this Úrsúla just to keep her safe. If you're not fucking her, then you're fucking some cow you found on Tinder.'

'I set up a Tinder profile because of work,' he said. 'There's someone who registered a profile in the minister's name, some stalker. I did it so I can keep track.'

Tears flowed down Íris's face, her mascara forming two black stripes. He reached out and tried to pull her into his arms. He wanted to hold and reassure her. Normally he took deep breaths and took care not to let her furious outbursts affect his emotions, but now he felt sorry for her.

'Fucking liar,' she whispered, and sniffed.

'I know it looks weird, but it's the truth,' he said. 'There's someone out there stalking the minister, sending her disgusting messages, and now he's put up a Tinder profile in her name and invited some guys to her house. I'm responsible for her safety, so I do what the police ask me to do. That includes staying in her house.'

'You're telling lies,' she sniffed, and he felt a stab of pain in his belly. She was so miserable and helpless in her anger that he wanted to find something he could say that would comfort her. Her jealousy was so painful.

'I swear it, Íris. I've never two-timed women. I'd never be un-faithful. I'm not that kind of person.'

The blow was unexpected and was too fast for him to dodge. The sting of pain in his cheek where her ring burst open the skin sent a rush of adrenaline through him. He put a hand to his face and looked at his palm. It didn't appear to be bleeding much, but his cheek was left as numb as if a dentist had anaesthetised it. She had slapped harder than he could have imagined. He felt the stress hormones set loose in his body. He was angry, and also deeply hurt. This assault on his temple, the body he worked so hard to look after, came with a set of associations different to the old man's beatings in the old days. Íris's hands were the ones that should stroke his cheek, hold his hand and play with his fingers, leave scratches down his back when they made love. He felt the tears filling his eyes and he could see Íris staring at him in wonder, the fear building up in her face. He knew that look from his father. After the fear came more anger, then repentance and finally passion.

'Now it's over between us,' he said, and he could feel the subsiding adrenaline rush leave his legs weak.

He took his bag and left, gently closing the door behind him. There was a good chance she would trash the place, but there wasn't all that much there to trash. He could always buy new crockery and a new TV, and he'd have to get the lock changed.

He wiped the tears and the blood from his face as he jogged down the stairs. Later he would shed proper tears, when he started to miss her. But right now he was going to allow himself to feel the relief that streamed through his veins like a celebration. He had just graduated from his very own school of serenity. He had proved to himself that he was nothing like his father. He hadn't returned Íris's blow. What was more, he hadn't even wanted to. Maybe the time would come when he could allow himself to love someone.

89

'It's good news, Kiddi,' Marita said, glancing from father to son across the dinner table where the two of them sat without speaking. 'It's good news for us that the police are dropping the investigation.'

'I know that,' Kiddi said, without looking up. Instead he speared chunks of sausage with his fork, stuffing them into his mouth as fast as he could.

Jónatan was hunched over his plate, eating at a leisurely pace. He cut slices of sausage, speared them with his fork, piled mashed potato on top with his knife, and put it in his mouth. Neither of them touched the salad any more than they usually did, so there would be leftovers of that tomorrow.

She and Jónatan had been delighted when the lawyer had called. They had fallen into each other's arms and Marita had burst into tears.

'There, there,' Jónatan had said, brushing a tear from her cheek. 'You see? I told you I'd be proved innocent.'

Marita nodded and buried her face in his chest while her whole frame trembled with relief. She had read enough about rape cases over the last few months to know that a case being dropped didn't mean innocence, but simply that the police did not believe there was enough evidence to support a prosecution. But that didn't matter. Of course Jónatan had to be innocent, and the conclusion bore that out. But now it seemed that Jónatan's elation had faded away. The petulant look on Kiddi's face had been enough to spoil his happiness. The boy had been unusually moody since all this had begun, which was understandable, but now this was all over so he could be a little more cheerful.

'Maybe we should do something to celebrate this all being over,' Marita said. 'Maybe a holiday, somewhere warm. The Canaries, or Tenerife.'

'Tenerife is part of the Canaries,' Kiddi pointed out sulkily.

Marita shrugged. She had long since given up taking any notice when she was corrected or told what to do. As a Faroese, she would never have been able to thrive in Iceland otherwise. But as he entered his teens, Kiddi seemed to have formed the impression that his mother was less than smart.

'The weather should be good there,' she said and smiled. 'What do you two think? A week on a sunny beach?'

Kiddi stood up and dropped his plate in the sink.

'You two can go with Klemmi,' he said from the kitchen doorway. 'I'm not going anywhere on holiday with him.' He pointed at his father.

90

Pétur sat on the mattress, his mind on steadying his breathing. His body was so used to the cold that by now he was literally over-heating, even though he had stripped down to underwear. He knew from experience that if he were to get up, pace the cell, yelling and hammering at the door as he shouted that he was suf-focating, then he'd only get even hotter. It was better to sit still and breathe deep. That way his body would gradually cool down and adapt to the temperature in the police station.

Inside, he was still boiling with frustration after yesterday's al-tercation, and that was why he overheated when he thought about the incident. He had only meant to take Úrsúla to one side to talk to her; somewhere out of sight, maybe behind the shop where the Devil couldn't watch them through some security camera, some-where he could hand her the newspaper clipping of her and the Devil so he could ask her straight out if she had chosen to follow the path of evil.

Pétur lay down on the mattress. It was plastic and his hot skin stuck to it, so he rolled onto the floor and lay there with his back against the cool stone. He had often spent time here – sometimes alone, sometimes with others. There had been times when he felt good here and had been grateful for the shelter and the shower and breakfast; at other times he had been sick, injured and hu-miliated. And there had been that one time he had seen a man die in just such a cell. That had been his friend Ari.

Now he had failed yet again to speak to Ari's daughter, Úrsúla, to tell her about how it had all happened. It was impossible to get close to her now that the Devil was at her heels every step of the way. When she had been small he had often picked her up and spun around with her in his arms. He had picked her up as if she had been as light as a feather, showing off his own strength. She had laughed and made fun of him, and he had replied that lifting such a little child high in the air was nothing. It wouldn't have been hard to lift her now, either, if only she hadn't struggled. Of course it had been damned stupid of him to try and abduct a grown woman, but he was desperate. Úrsúla needed to know the truth.

He ran a hand over the roughness of his face. That black-clad agent of the Devil hadn't been gentle as he jumped him from behind to get him away from Úrsúla. He had rubbed Pétur's nose in the dirt, and as he lay manacled and face-down he had tasted the blood mingled with the salt on the ground and been grateful that his handling hadn't been rougher.

The man in black could easily have knocked Pétur's head hard on the pavement if he had wanted to. He could have landed a kick to his head. He could have stamped on his head in fury. But he had done none of these things, because even though he was clearly an agent sent by the Devil, he wasn't the Devil himself.

Pétur sighed. It was taking him a long time to cool down. The sweat ran from his armpits and soaked his vest. Maybe he'd wake up in the night in a wet shirt and with a chill. If that happened, he'd crawl onto the mattress and pull the blanket over himself.

He had managed to get the note into Úrsúla's pocket. He had stuffed the slip of paper into her coat while she struggled, as soon as he realised that there was no possibility that he would be able to take her to one side to explain things quietly. And this scrap of paper, this message, would have to suffice, because he had now given her the evidence, the picture of her from the newspaper in which she stood holding the Devil's hand.

91

Lying on the sofa downstairs, Gunnar couldn't make out what was being said above his head, but it was obvious there was an argument going on. It was like an echo from his childhood, lying alone in the darkness, nerves stretched taut, waiting for it to boil over.

That was when the first blow was struck. He tried to take deep breaths and calm his mind. There was no danger of that here. Nonni wasn't a man given to violence.

Gunnar scrolled through Tinder on his phone, swiping all the women left, as he wasn't looking for a date but simply checking to see if Úrsúla would appear. The first couple of profiles had been deleted, but there was no telling if this crazy Fossi would decide to register her yet again. He was relieved that the police had decided to investigate the Tinder thing. He thought Boris hadn't taken Fossi's emails seriously enough; it looked like they had gone into the pile with all the other oddball messages to ministers. But now that there was a clear threat of physical violence to the minister while she was under their protection, they had knuckled down and set the cyber-security department to work on it.

Gunnar sat up as he heard footsteps on the stairs. Úrsúla had come down, so he got to his feet and followed her into the kitchen.

'Everything all right?' he asked.

She sighed. 'I was going to get myself a beer. Would you like one?'

He shook his head, but she handed him a bottle all the same, so he took it and went with her into the living room.

'I'm sorry. The racket we're making must be keeping you awake.'

She sat in an armchair, tucking her feet under her. She wore tracksuit bottoms and a T-shirt. Gunnar found it odd to be here, in her space, inside her private life; somehow it made her appear smaller and slimmer than he had seen her before.

'It's all right,' he said, taking a seat in his nest on the sofa – he had made a bed with the duvet Úrsúla had given him. He always kept a sleeping bag in the car, but she had insisted that if he was going to bed down on the sofa, he should have a decent duvet. He had told her more than once that it wasn't a problem; part of the job.

'I feel a lot happier keeping an eye on you here than being at

home worrying that there's some idiot banging on your door,' he
added.

She looked up, caught his eye and smiled.

'I'm absolutely in agreement with everyone who told me at the
start that the best thing about being a minister is having a driver.'
She sipped her beer, woke her phone from sleep and handed it to
him. 'In fact, I think the only good thing about being a minister
is the driver,' she added as Gunnar read the text on the screen:

'Pétur Pétursson Detained Without Charge', the headline read,
and the article beneath it hinted that Úrsúla was using her privilege as a minister to persecute an aged homeless man as a way of
settling old scores. Under the article was a link to a petition that
people could sign, demanding her resignation.

Friday

92

Úrsúla hadn't slept much; one beer with Gunnar had turned into three. Nonni had been asleep when she went upstairs and was still sleeping when she got up, or else he was pretending to sleep so he didn't have to talk to her. She seemed to have managed to get everything in their relationship wrong since becoming a minister, and as they had argued the evening before, he seemed to have found an outlet for an anger that she had underestimated. She had known that there were many things that irritated him about the changes to their life, and she regretted having kept a few things back from him, such as the incident at the shop, but the depth of his dissatisfaction had taken her by surprise. Maybe he sensed the gulf that had formed between them, felt something that couldn't be put into words, and knew that she wasn't completely there even though she played the part well. Perhaps it was for these reasons that he took trivial things so much to heart.

The guilt weighed on her shoulders as she thought of Thorbjörn and what had gone on between them over the last week, and she felt herself helpless and drained of energy. She stared out of her office window at the double-decker tourist coach that had stopped outside the Harpa concert hall and was swallowing up a whole queue of travellers who had been shivering for some time in the cold gusts that came off the sea. Something inside told her that everything would be fine if only she could be honest with Nonni and share with him even a fraction of the horrors that were buried deep in her soul. But she had no desire to do so. She felt she had no right to wreck his happy outlook on life by telling him that it was a stormy biological process that a single kiss or an explosion could in an instant reduce to a foul-smelling pool of blood, or a puff of smoke and steam.

The psychologist Médecins Sans Frontières had sent her to after she returned from Liberia had told her that she needed to reinvest in life all over again. She had to believe that she would recover. For a few weeks she had thought it over, but then had pushed the idea away as she pounced with relief on the next assignment. That was overseeing the movement of two thousand people and their refugee camp from Syria, across the frontier into Jordan.

Úrsúla pushed away her coffee cup. When Freyja appeared she would ask her to fetch breakfast. She wouldn't be pleased, and on top of that she would have to put up with the presence of the police officer who was there to stand guard outside Úrsúla's office all day long. She heard sounds out in the hallway, so it seemed the ministry was coming to life. She sighed deeply, stretched as if she had just woken up and clicked on the online news to see what the day's headlines were. Aside from the conspiracy theories that suggested she was engaged in some Monte Cristo-style vendetta against the wretched homeless man who had murdered her father, most of the newspapers led with the rape charge against the Selfoss police officer. As she scrolled through the comments she could see people beside themselves with anger that the charges had been dropped, alongside the sincere delight of others who equated the investigation being halted with the accused man being innocent. Úrsúla suppressed the longing to add a furious lecture of her own to the comments, or to call Thorbjörn and ask him to underline the words 'investigation halted due to technical mishandling of evidence' in his paper. She felt a second wave of guilt engulf her as she thought of the mother of the young woman and the promise she had made on her very first day in office. She had promised to see justice done. There was no shred of justice in this outcome: the case would not even be investigated.

There was a knock at the door and Óðinn came in.

'Well,' he said, 'we don't need to concern ourselves any longer with that rape charge.'

He seemed cheerful, and despite Úrsúla understanding perfectly well that his role was to protect both her and the ministry from anything potentially uncomfortable, this wasn't how she had imagined that a department under her charge would operate.

'Tell me the truth, my dear Óðinn,' she said. 'Did you bring any pressure to bear to make sure the charges would be dropped?'

Óðinn smiled awkwardly and cleared his throat, as if buying himself time as he thought through what he could reply. His bulky body seemed to shrink, and he appeared to stoop, as if trying to make as little as he could of his own presence. He drew a handkerchief from his trouser pocket and dabbed at his upper lip.

'I do my job,' he said slowly, taking a seat in the chair opposite her.

Úrsúla took the sheet of paper with the following week's schedule on it, staring at it as she pretended to read while she swallowed her disappointment. The feeling that she had become some kind of pawn in a system that chugged along according to its own rules had become overwhelming.

93

Pétur had the feeling that he was being watched, and that it had been going on for a while. He walked at his habitual pace along Laugavegur and didn't need to turn round to know that the car slowly driving behind was shadowing him. He acted as if he'd noticed nothing and carried on until he was right by the underpass that led to the steps up to Grettisgata. This was the classic way of shaking the cops off, as they could rarely be bothered to continue the chase on foot. But it could hardly be the cops after him now; they had only just let him out, with a stern warning that he ought to keep out of trouble. He turned and saw that the car that had followed him was a large, black, gleaming 4x4. The windows were tinted, but the moment the car stopped beside him, the driver's window hissed down and the face of the Devil himself appeared.

'Jump in and we'll have a quick chat, Pétur,' he said.

But Pétur didn't stand still long enough even to refuse; he had already taken to his heels, through the underpass and up the steps. He hurried straight across the car park and over Grettisgata, into the playground outside the nursery, through the gardens and up onto Njálsgata before he dared look back. The Devil hadn't followed him. He would hardly leave that beautiful shiny car in the middle of Laugavegur. Pétur's heart hammered and he panted with exertion. It had been a long time since he had looked into the Devil's eyes. The last time he had escaped he had sworn that he would never again let himself be caught in his clutches. But now the Devil was on his tail, and that had to mean he knew Pétur's message had reached Úrsúla, that he knew he had warned her about him, that he had told the truth. Now the Devil knew everything. Pétur felt the fear take hold of him. The Devil's voice had been friendly enough as he had invited him into the car, but he wasn't going to let that fool him, knowing what the man was capable of.

In the old days the police boys had sometimes been downright offensive, especially the young ones, giving them an earful and calling them a waste of space. But it was worst when the Devil was on duty. He was the meanest of all of them, and quick to use his fists. That night he had lost his temper with Ari, who had dropped a tab of acid, was disobedient and smelled pretty foul because he had been sick down his front. When the Devil had punched him to force him into the cell with Pétur, Ari had spat at him and called him by his right name: Devil. He had spat a second time, this time right in the face of the Devil, who reacted furiously. Pétur never knew if it was the spit or the fact that Ari had known his true name that turned him into such a personification of fury, but he didn't stop punching and kicking, even when Pétur tried to put himself between them, receiving such a heavy punch on the jaw that he had been thrown back against the wall and knocked unconscious. He had come to his senses again to see the Devil with his boot on Ari's throat. There was no life in his face, as if he had already forsaken himself and left behind that vomit-smelling, blue-faced bag of blood that didn't move, but lay on the floor of the cell, groaning at intervals. As Pétur sat up, he was aware of a lad of a part-time policeman hauling the Devil out of the cell.

'That's enough,' the youngster had said, catching hold of both of the Devil's hands to stop him. 'That'll do.'

The cell door slammed shut and the lights went out, and he could hear the young policeman yelling at the Devil, demanding to know what the hell he was thinking and if he had lost his mind.

Pétur knew then and there that the Devil didn't think. He simply roamed the world and whatever was in his way would suffer the heat of his anger.

When the cell door had opened again, it was the young lad who threw a pair of shoes in to him.

'Your shoes,' he said, shutting the door again and switching off the light so that Pétur had to fumble in the darkness.

He found the shoes and put them on, ready to run the moment they'd let him out. He wanted to flee from the terror, to save himself from the Devil. He laced the shoes tightly but it wasn't until he had them on that he realised they didn't fit. Although these were police-issue boots, like the ones he usually wore, these weren't his.

Pétur had felt a trickle of blood run down his face from where his scalp had grazed against the wall as he had fallen. He put his hand to the wound to stop the bleeding as he sat in the darkness and snivelled, while Ari took his last few difficult breaths.

94

The hot light that Stella's grandmother had given her on her birthday would burn in her head for a while, but then fade away, and she hadn't yet worked out what it meant. She would figure it out. She would learn to understand what it meant when her head was filled with the hot, blue-green brightness. So far she wasn't sure whether she was being warned of something when it lit up, or whether it was an indicator that she was doing the right thing.

Mostly it came on when she thought of Gréta. Now, as she stacked packs of toilet paper on the shelves of the cleaners' storeroom, remembering how Gréta and the blonde had walked away from her outside the grey apartment block, practically in step, hand-in-hand, her head blazed like a broken gas burner.

She growled in irritation as one stack of toilet paper toppled off the shelf and the packets bounced across the floor. She picked one up and hurled it against the wall, but it gave her no relief, and instead she found herself suddenly choking, so she snatched up the two bags of rubbish that came from some office that dealt with finance, banged the door shut behind her and hurried out and down the steps to the rear staff entrance.

Outside she drew the air deep into her lungs several times to bring some oxygen to her overheating head. The creepy journalist's car was parked behind the rubbish skip in the lower car park. She hurried over to it. She was about to put her hand on the door handle when she realised that there was someone in the car with him. She was about to quietly back away, back to the ministry building, but was startled as the car's door opened and Óðinn, the permanent secretary, stepped out.

'That wasn't what I asked you to do!' he yelled into the car, just as he saw Stella.

He was clearly taken by surprise. He stared at her for a moment, and Stella felt a strong urge to run away. At the same time the fire in her head cooled so that the cold wind chilled her through to the bone, blew in her ear and down her neck, so that she shivered.

'Not a single word about that to anyone,' Óðinn hissed at her, his anger as cold as the wind. 'Otherwise you'll get what you deserve for what you've done!'

It took Stella a moment's thought before she worked out what the permanent secretary had meant; he clearly knew that she had been selling the ministry's rubbish, but he hadn't been sitting in the creep's car to trap her. He had been there because he had an errand of his own with the journalist. He had been berating the creep, venting his displeasure because the man hadn't done as he had been asked.

Stella threw the bags into the car and snatched the proffered notes from the journalist's hand. She felt tears running down her cheeks as she walked back across the car park and down to Sæbraut, taking care not to look in the direction of the grey tower that loomed over the district.

She licked her lips, tasted the salt, and wiped her face, growling to herself at her own feebleness. Had the permanent secretary's rebuke triggered the tears, or was she crying with relief that she hadn't been sacked on the spot? Her eyes finally strayed to the grey tower. Was she crying over Gréta? The blue-green flame burst into life in her head, so hot that it almost hurt. Was that it? Was she really in tears over the fat newsreader?

95

'I'll find another photo of me that you can have,' Úrsúla said with sarcasm. 'Looking ministerial in front of the flag. I could even sign it for you.'

There seemed to be some kind of karma that repeatedly brought them together, as this was the third time she had found herself going from floor to floor in the lift with Adolf. As before, his bulky frame seemed to fill more than half of the space. He had begun by complaining that Eva had made him delete the picture he had taken of Úrsúla in the helicopter, which he decided was tantamount to censorship.

'It was just a bit of fun,' he grumbled.

'If it's fun, then it would have to be funny,' she retorted, not bothering even to try to hide the irritation in her voice. She might have been overstepping the mark, but everything seemed to leak from the ministry to the media, and she had no desire to see the picture Adolf had taken of her, chilled through and soaked, on the front page of a newspaper.

'You people – feminists – are completely humourless,' he said and squeezed out something that was undoubtedly supposed to be a grin but which turned into a scowl.

The lift halted, and Úrsúla stood in the opening as she turned to face Adolf.

'The Coast Guard will get its additional funding,' she said. 'That's because of me, and not you. If anything, it's your pushiness and lack of manners that have made it harder for them. You people – men who can't accept a female minister – are completely tactless.'

She turned and stormed away, and instantly began to wonder if she had been too hard on him. She shook the feeling off. It had been a hard day, on top of which she had slept badly the night before, which had left her irritable. Right now she had no patience with men who tried to blame their own inappropriate behaviour on a woman's poor sense of humour.

Gunnar was waiting for her right by the door, with the car already warm. She was set on using the ministry's front door from now on, convinced that there was no reason to sneak in and out of the back door as if she preferred not to be seen. She was going to use the same strategies as she had in Syria. She was going to hold her head up high, crank up her determination, even though it might be at the expense of a little courtesy, and look straight in the eye those who seemed to relish reminding her of her every minor shortcoming – something that seemed to be an inevitable part of this job.

'Home, please,' she said to Gunnar and pulled off her leather gloves to put them in her coat.

As she did so, she found a scrap of paper in her pocket. She opened the glove compartment, where Gunnar kept a small bag for rubbish, but as she was about to drop the paper into it, she saw it bore her own face. She smoothed it out and inspected it.

It was a cutting from a newspaper; less a cutting than something that had been torn out, leaving the edges ragged and tattered. It was from the day she had taken over as minister. For a moment it seemed that it had been long ago, even though hardly two weeks had passed. Lettering in a hand she had come to recognise had been scrawled on the paper, the letters misshapen and the lines wavering, as if the fingers holding the red pen had trembled.

'Look,' she said to Gunnar, who slowed the car and stopped by the side of the road as he took the scrap of paper from her hand.

'Where did you find this?' he asked in surprise.

'It was in my coat. I found it when I put my hand in my pocket.'

Gunnar looked at it for a long moment.

'Pétur must have slipped it into your pocket,' he said.

Úrsúla took it from Gunnar's fingers and read the shaky script on the clipping.

'Little Úrsúla' had been scrawled by her face, which was smiling for the cameras as she took the keys to the ministry from Óðinn, who was handing them over to her. Over his head had been drawn a pair of red horns, and the words 'Devil-cop, Ari's killer'.

96

'Here it is,' Úrsúla said, passing to Gunnar the laptop that rested on her knees, still logged in to the ministry intranet. 'There's the article about Óðinn's appointment eight years ago as permanent secretary. And look, underneath it details his whole career.'

Úrsúla leaned back in her seat and breathed a couple of heavy sighs.

The tension had left Gunnar sweating, so his fingers slipped on the screen of his phone as he had searched for information about Óðinn. But now Úrsúla had found what they were looking for.

'Óðinn was on the Reykjavík police force from 1979 to 1989, and was an inspector from 1986 onward.' Gunnar leaned back in his seat, and his heavy sigh echoed Úrsúla's. 'That means he was a serving police officer at the time your father died.'

'Fuck,' she spat, punching the plastic dashboard in front of her. 'I don't know what to make of this.' She shook the scrap of paper that had been in her pocket. 'I don't know what the hell to think.'

'Do you have any of the court documents from Pétur's trial?' he asked.

Úrsúla sighed again. 'I know them practically off by heart,' she said. 'But the names of the officers on duty that night aren't mentioned. They're just Police Officer A and Police Officer B. I've never even wondered about their names. It never occurred to me that there was any kind of doubt about the events of that night. I was a child at the time, and everyone accepted it as fact that Pétur had beaten Dad to death.'

'I know who could help us,' Gunnar said, and tapped a message to Boris into his phone:

Who were the cops on duty the night Pétur P was supposed to have murdered Úrsúla's dad?

He knew the wording would spark Boris's curiosity. He had deliberately said 'supposed to have murdered' instead of 'murdered'. Boris would be intrigued and he'd definitely check it out. His phone pinged an alert almost immediately. He opened Boris's reply:

Is Monday OK? We're having a weekend out of town.

Gunnar swallowed his disappointment. Pétur's scrawled note

wasn't grounds for wrecking Boris's cosy weekend in his summer cottage. Maybe it was just something the old man had dreamed up.

'There's only one way to find out what he means,' Gunnar said, starting the engine. Úrsúla seem to understand instantly what he had in mind.

'We'll have to find a way to keep him calm so we can talk to him,' she said, staring straight ahead.

The engine had been switched off, and in their excitement, their breath had clouded the car's windscreen, and even with the heater turned up to maximum, it still hadn't cleared by the time Gunnar brought the car to a stop outside the police station at Hlemmur. Úrsúla opened her door, but Gunnar placed a hand on her arm.

'I'll go inside,' he said. She nodded as she clicked her door closed again. It wasn't ideal for the minister of the interior to march into the police station, asking about a particular prisoner.

She sat and stared ahead with empty eyes, and it occurred to Gunnar that as far as this matter was concerned, she was no longer a minister, or even a grown woman, but a little girl; a frightened little girl who missed her dad.

97

The police officers who searched the house wouldn't answer Marita's questions, other than with questions of their own. The one who was in charge had handed her a sheet of paper that he told her was a search warrant, but she was so upset, for all she knew it could have been a recipe from a cookbook.

'Where's your husband?' he asked as he handed another of the uniformed officers the family computer.

'He went back east last night to finish his shifts there. He comes home, back to his old job, next week,' she said. 'What's all this about? And why are you taking the computers?'

The man finally stopped.

'There's a suspicion that your husband has been sending threats to the minister of the interior, Úrsúla Aradóttir,' he said and looked at her with searching eyes, as if she might know something about the matter.

'What kind of threats? What do you mean?'

'Threats of violence and more, if she doesn't resign. He came to our attention as there was a charge already against him that was being reviewed.'

Marita shook her head in disbelief. She couldn't understand any of this. Now a second uniformed officer appeared with Kiddi's laptop in his hands. Kiddi followed with a sour expression on his face. Marita was surprised that he wasn't erupting with rage. Maybe he was holding back until the police had gone. Normally he yelled at her when only the two of them were at home.

'Did your husband take a computer with him when he went to the east?' the policeman in charge asked.

'No. Or yes,' Marita said. 'He has one of those little tablets that he reads the news on. This has to be some misunderstanding,' she added. 'Jónatan would never make threats against anyone, let alone a minister...'

She fell silent as the image came to mind of Jónatan in the bedroom with the phone to his ear the previous Monday. *You owe me,* he had said to the phone. *You owe me.*

Could he have been speaking to the minister then? Could she owe him something? Marita couldn't understand all this.

'This has to be some kind of misunderstanding,' she repeated, maybe more to convince herself than the police.

98

As Úrsúla waited in the car while Gunnar was inside the police station, the question Boris had asked at the meeting last week came back to mind. Who was this Devil Pétur seemed desperate to warn her against? Could there be anything in the accusation scrawled on the scrap of paper? Could Óðinn, the permanent secretary himself, be her father's murderer? It was too crazy to be real. Her thoughts whirled around in circles; Pétur and all the notes he had left, and then the two occasions he had physically attacked her, which now seemed strange in this new context. Why had he attacked her if all he had wanted to do was warn her against Óðinn? She had to find an explanation. There was nothing for it but to speak to Pétur quietly.

'He's not here anymore,' Gunnar said as he got back into the car.

'Then where is he?'

'He was released. They couldn't keep him any longer. They said to check the shelter on Lindargata. That's where the street people stay.'

'This really is completely crazy, isn't it?' she asked, hoping that Gunnar would agree, that this was just the confused mind of a mad old drunk dreaming up something to excuse his own guilt.

But Gunnar shrugged. 'If you think it through, nobody's going to believe someone who's on the street, especially if he comes across as not all there. He makes the ideal scapegoat.'

They sat in silence for the rest of the way to the shelter. Gunnar parked on the corner and hurried inside to ask about Pétur. Úrsúla stayed in the car, her feet restless with impatience. She longed to run inside after him, to find Pétur and question him about every detail of the whole affair. She wanted to know what he meant by all those notes he had left for her, why he had jumped her outside the shop, and why he had spent all that time in the boot of her car. But most of all she wanted to know what had happened in that cell the night her father died.

'He hasn't been seen here for days,' Gunnar said as soon as he returned. 'Not since he beat the crap out of his pal, another homeless bum, who was staying here as well.'

Saturday

99

The children lay in the big double bed with Úrsúla, their eyes wide and fastened on her. Tears flooded down Herdís's cheeks as she listened to her mother's account, and the expression on Ari's face showed that he had discovered a completely new side to her. Of course he had. She had never told them much about her upbringing, just a few vague words to say that her father had died and her mother had worked hard to make ends meet. But Nonni had told her that the time had now come: they were already hearing about the story from the media. He was right, of course. It went without saying that she should have told them long ago how her father, their grandfather, had lost his life.

She stroked their cheeks tenderly, and for the first time in far too long she felt herself properly close to them, and enjoyed the feeling. This time Ari didn't shrink from her touch, and there was none of the usual 'oh, Mum' or 'duh' from Herdís. They both sat watching her intently while she tried to find neutral or pleasant words to describe the misery and the violence for them. Kátur lay on her lap and snored quietly, and Nonni sat at the foot of the bed with a cup of coffee in his hand, occasionally offering a word or a comment. For the moment there was nothing outside this little world of theirs: no ministry, and certainly no Thorbjörn. Nothing but the four of them was of any importance, there in the light of the lamp that cast its gentle glow over them that dark midwinter morning, packed close together and snug in soft bedclothes. It was now, right now, that Úrsúla rediscovered her clear love for them all. She felt her heart swell with an emotion she had not experienced for a long time. Maybe the session with the psychologist was starting to work already.

'Why didn't he want to come home, if he could have?' Ari asked. 'If he had, he wouldn't have ended up in prison and died.'

'Maybe not,' Úrsúla said. 'When I was young I couldn't understand it either. I often went downtown to look for him and ask him to come home. But he was an alcoholic so he wasn't really able to make his own decisions.'

'Can you be an alcoholic suddenly?' Ari asked, eyes wide with horror. 'Could Dad become an alcoholic?'

'Of course not, you idiot,' Herdís hissed, giving what had become the standard answer to her brother's questions.

'Talk nicely to each other, please,' Úrsúla said, brushing a stray lock of hair away from her face. 'Your dad's not an alcoholic,' she told Ari. 'If anything, it's a struggle to get him to have a drink.'

She winked at Nonni and he laughed. She was about to embark on a longer explanation of alcoholism when Ari steered the conversation in another direction.

'Was there a lot of blood on him?' he asked.

Úrsúla nodded. 'Yes,' she said. 'I didn't see for myself, which is just as well, but I read all the court documents and they said there was a lot of blood because he was so badly hurt. The reason he died was because there was bleeding in his brain where he was hit so hard.'

'But why isn't this Pétur in prison?' Herdís asked. 'Why's he on the street?'

'He was in hospital for a long time after that, in a secure unit, because he wasn't right in the head and the judge decided that he hadn't known what he was doing. So when he recovered, he was allowed out.'

Herdís looked thoughtful, and Ari closed his eyes and curled himself up deep in the duvet, as if he wanted to give his mind a rest.

'But it's not a hundred per cent certain that Pétur was the one who beat my father so badly,' Úrsúla added. 'There were also two police officers on duty who...' She saw from the expression on Nonni's face that she had ventured onto dangerous ground, so she pulled back. 'Maybe we'll never know exactly how your grand-father lost his life. We might have to accept that it was some kind of mishap, some sort of terrible accident. Perhaps we'll have to live with the uncertainty.'

The children were silent. She kissed the top of Herdís's head, and then reached for Ari's hand, planting a kiss on his palm as she had done since he had been tiny. It could well be that she was telling the children the truth, that they would have to accept living with this uncertainty. But the more she thought about the news-paper clipping that Pétur had slipped into her pocket, the more her doubts grew.

100

'Hello there, old man,' said the amiable young fellow behind the counter in the kiosk at Hlemmur. 'What do gentlemen of the road have to say today?'

'Things look bleak,' Pétur replied. 'The Devil's at my heels.'

He stood by the door and peered through the glass to see if he could make out the black car.

'That's quite something!' the boy said, and he sounded amused. 'The Devil himself in person? You really do have the Devil on your tail.'

'He drives a big black car,' Pétur muttered, moving closer to the counter. 'If a man driving a big black car comes in here looking for me, then you mustn't breathe a word to him that I've been in.'

'No chance,' the lad said. 'I'll be as silent as the grave.'

'He knows I warned Úrsúla,' he said, more to himself than to the youngster. 'He has the minister in his power, the bastard. But I warned her, and now he's after me.'

He glanced at the doorway, but everything was quiet.

'Úrsúla? You mean the minister of the interior? Is that who you're talking about?' The lad seemed astonished. 'Hold on. Aren't you the guy whose medical records she asked for? Are you *that* Pétur?'

'And what's your name?' he asked in reply.

'My name's Steinn,' the lad said. 'You don't have much of a memory, do you?'

'I always forget everything,' Pétur replied. 'The Devil told me to forget everything. So you'd best keep your mouth shut and forget everything too. Otherwise I'll end up like Ari.'

'Who's Ari?'

'Keep your mouth shut and forget everything, was what he said, before he let me out.'

'And what do you think about the minister demanding your medical records? Aren't you angry about that?'

'I'm furious. I'm angry with the Devil. I'm angry with Úrsúla for letting herself be fooled.'

The lad opened the till, took a handful of change and handed it to Pétur.

'Here you are, old man,' he said. 'Go and get yourself something to eat.'

Pétur bowed, but forgot to thank him. His mind was on the Devil. He wondered if he should leave through the kiosk's back door, but he couldn't see any sign of the black car nearby. At least, not until he was outside.

101

She saw Gunnar hesitate before handing her the green folder, and when she opened it she saw why. It was the post-mortem report on her father. She stared at the diagrams of the front and back of a body, and the injuries that had been marked on it; the injuries to her father. These were almost all to his head and throat. She closed the folder and handed it back.

'I can't read this,' she said. 'Tell me what it says.'

She swallowed the bitter bile that rose in her throat and took deep breaths, all the way down to her belly, to loosen the hard knot that had formed down there. Gunnar took the folder back but didn't open it.

'The cause of death was bleeding to the brain,' he said, and Úrsúla nodded. She already knew that. 'There was a great deal of bruising to the whole body, but chiefly to the head and neck, consistent with being kicked while lying on the floor.'

None of this was new. She had either heard it all before, or read it in news reports.

'What is strange,' Gunnar said, 'is that there were several clear boot marks on his face, which the report says match the boots Pétur was wearing.'

'They don't get to wear shoes in the cells,' Úrsúla said.

'Exactly,' Gunnar said, putting aside the pathology report and picking up another folder. 'The police report – Boris got hold of it for me,' he said. 'It says that Pétur wasn't made to hand over his shoes. It was an error, probably because Ari, who had been picked up at the same time, was making himself difficult. It doesn't go into any more detail, but according to the court documents, these were police boots, the same as the police used at that time. The investigation found that Pétur had spent a night in the cells some months before, and a police officer had seen how bad his shoes were and had given him a pair of boots.'

'OK. So the weird part of this is that they forgot to make Pétur hand over his shoes,' Úrsúla said, lifting her feet onto the coffee table.

Nonni had taken the children to his mother's so she and Gunnar had peace and quiet to talk, but she missed them and hoped they wouldn't be long. She could well imagine spending the rest of the day as they had the morning, the four of them nestled together in one bed, where they could hug and whisper about anything that came to mind, and she could feel the warmth in her heart that had been absent for so long.

'That's right,' Gunnar said. 'It's an odd mistake to make. What's more, it seems to have been so busy that they didn't manage the routine twenty-minute check on each cell that they're supposed to carry out. So it was probably more like two hours that nobody looked in on them. But the really strange thing is that one of the officers on duty that night was Óðinn Th. Jónsson.'

Úrsúla's throat felt very dry.

'We have to speak to Pétur,' she said. 'We must be clear about what he meant when he called Óðinn Ari's killer. We have to find out if there's anything to all this, or if it's just a wild accusation from a completely crazy man who may simply be trying to clear his name.'

Gunnar swept the documents together into a stack and stood up.

'I'll go for a drive and see if I can track him down,' he said.

102

Marita sat in shock next to Kiddi on the sofa. The police officers from Reykjavík, a man and a woman, were both young and had serious expressions on their faces. The representative of the Agency for Child Protection, a heavily built local man – someone Marita felt it was just as well she didn't know – sat on a kitchen chair to one side of them with a blank look on his face. It didn't seem to be these strangers who were making Kiddi nervous, though; rather it was her own presence.

'Does my mum need to be here?' he asked the police officers at regular intervals throughout the interview. As time passed, Marita came to understand why. The male police officer did most of the talking, while his female colleague sat and watched mother and son, and jotted things down in a notebook. Kiddi had started by denying everything, until the police officer told him that they had evidence. They had found what they had been looking for on his computer's hard drive.

'You're not as smart as you think,' the policeman said. 'It's a lot harder than most people think to erase your trail from a computer. We have the IP addresses, and it's clear that it had to be someone in this house. The family computer is clean; your father's iPad is clean; and you're the only one who uses your computer, aren't you?'

Kiddi hung his head and Marita nodded. Kiddi always kept his computer in his room, and the one time that Marita had tried to use it, she had found it locked with a password.

As the interview continued, Marita found herself becoming increasingly numb. She sank into the sofa. She would have stood up and beaten the boy if only she had the energy; even with the police in the room. The anger inside her seethed and boiled, but it was a feeble fury, almost a hopelessness, and although she wanted to cry, she found that was also beyond her.

'I wasn't going to hurt her,' Kiddi said. 'I just wanted her to be frightened. For her to...'

He stopped and for a moment there was a deathly silence in the room. The police sat opposite them, waiting for them to break the silence. Marita took a deep breath and the words tumbled out of her in a confused order, her Faroese accent strong. The police officers watched her with their blank expressions.

'You know that Jónatan, my husband ... erm, Kiddi's dad, was charged with rape. And it has to be because of that ... Yes, that was earlier this year. And then somehow that went away. Or it was stuck in the system or something. Then this new minister picked the case up again, and it was in all the newspapers all over again, like the whole thing being raked over. And a lot that the papers said just wasn't true. But Kiddi threatening the minister and wanting her to resign, that's obviously just ... Yeah. He must have thought he was doing something to help his dad,' Marita said.

Kiddi leaped up from the sofa as if he had been hauled to his feet by an invisible wire that had been stretched to its limit.

'Help him? I wouldn't help him if I was paid for it! You're always so fucking clueless, aren't you? I was trying to help *you*. So the whole thing would be over, and you could go back to work, and people would stop judging you because of that arsehole you're married to!'

103

The needle stung like hell as it pricked her nipples, but the best spells always demanded sacrifice. She had taken three drops of blood each from the index finger of her left hand and the ring finger of her right hand, and a drop of blood from each nipple. She mixed them together into a red ink in a disposable plastic sushi dish and dipped the point of her knife in it to carve a Helm of Disguise into the piece of charcoal. She had bought barbecue charcoal, the only kind she had been able to find. Now she just had to wait and see if the spell would work. It also called for blood from the brain of a living raven, but that was an extra ingredient to protect her from enemies. This girl from Tinder wasn't exactly her enemy, even though she now wished she hadn't helped Gréta reel her in.

She covered her nipples with toilet paper so blood wouldn't stain her bra and examined the photocopy of the Helm of Disguise to remind herself of the lines. This was a more than usually complex rune, made up of eight circular runes, so she wasn't certain that this little piece of charcoal was big enough for it. She also didn't know what to do if the blood ran out. She didn't have that much to work with. She had no idea how long the spell would work, and for that reason she had decided to prepare it in the toilets in the basement of the Harpa concert hall, so as to not waste valuable invisibility time walking there.

She would have needed a magnifying glass to see the rune clearly in the piece of charcoal, as by the time she had finished carving it into the surface, the rune's delicate, complex lines seemed to have become a network of illegible scratches. But that didn't matter, so long as it worked. Stella pressed the piece of charcoal against her forehead, then she left the cubicle and looked at herself in a mirror. Instead of being printed neatly, the rune had left a mess of blood on her forehead. She could see herself in the mirror, but more than likely you'd always see yourself. The only way to be sure the magic had worked was to find out if other people could see her.

As she went up the stairs and towards the lower restaurant, a little man with a bald head almost walked into her. That might indicate that she couldn't be seen, but she couldn't be sure. There were so many men who expected women to make way for them. She continued up the broad staircase. Most of the events taking place in the building had to be over by now, so if Gréta and the blonde had attended any of them, they had to be having dinner by now. The blonde had said something about a concert and dinner at Harpa, and Stella hadn't seen them in the buffet downstairs, so they had to be in the restaurant on the top floor. Gréta was classy, so nothing less than a pricy dinner would do, now that she had finally got herself a date.

The narrow staircase from the middle level up to the restaurant was closed off, so she jumped into the lift, where a smartly dressed couple were waiting to go up. The doors almost closed on her and Stella just made it inside; she wondered if the lift's sensors maybe didn't register invisible people. She checked out the couple on the way up, but they paid her no attention, either because they couldn't see her or because they were so engrossed in each other.

She walked fast into the restaurant, and neither the waiter at reception nor the one who came towards her with a tray of drinks seemed to notice her. She dodged the one with the tray, went over to the buffet, which looked to have a Christmas theme to it, snapped off a piece of snowflake bread and munched it. If she were visible, someone would have stopped her by now. She took a piece of cold smoked lamb, which lay neatly sliced on a salver, dipped it in mustard sauce, and ate it. Her mouth watered at the sight of ceviche in the chiller, but she decided not to bother with it as all the ceviche she had tasted in Iceland had turned out bland in comparison to her mother's. Instead she took a slice of reindeer paté, popped it in her mouth and went into the dining room.

Gréta and the blonde were at a table in the furthest corner. They weren't facing each other, but had taken seats almost side by side, their backs to the room as they looked out over the harbour. As Stella approached, the intensity of the hot light in her head grew and she suddenly wanted to cry. She longed to turn and run, but steeled herself to continue. She had come here to see for herself what their relationship was like, to see if this was something serious or just a passing fling. She stood behind them and saw Gréta slip a hand under the table and place it on the thigh of the blonde, who leaned closer to her and whispered something Stella wasn't close enough to hear. Gréta withdrew her hand and fidgeted somehow with it in front of her, and as Stella came right up to the table she could see the blonde leaning close to Gréta and gazing into her blouse. She had told Gréta to undo a button to give her a better view of her breasts. Stella edged slowly around the table and examined them. Gréta's eyes glistened as she looked at the blonde, who had a dazed expression on her face, her eyes fastened on Gréta's impressive cleavage.

'I'm besotted with you,' Gréta said to the blonde in a low voice.

Stella wanted to shake her head in disgust that she should say something so mawkish and stupid, after knowing the woman for only a few days, but there was a sincerity on Gréta's face that stabbed deep into Stella's heart. She was suddenly no longer able to hold back, and knocked their champagne glasses over, so that the bubbling contents spilled over the table, and mostly over the blonde.

'What on earth...?' she heard Gréta say, and saw her snatch up a serviette to dab at the blonde's front.

Stella rushed away, out of the restaurant, down the closed-off staircase, then the broad staircase, down to Harpa's ground floor, where she took to her heels. The frost had hardened so that her lungs were seared by the first breath of cold air, and now she finally allowed herself to weep. She could have been in the blonde's place, sipping champagne and sampling the Christmas-themed buffet, in between basking in Gréta's adoration and admiring her cleavage in anticipation. But instead she was alone and shivering in the bitter cold outside Harpa, badly dressed, invisible and with sore nipples.

104

Pétur had managed to lose the black car outside the kiosk that morning, and since then he'd kept away from the main streets. He'd lost it by setting off along Laugavegur, sauntering as if he was unaware the car was following him, then once he had crossed Snorrabraut and was sure that there was another car behind the black one in the narrow street, he had doubled back against the direction of the traffic, leaving the Devil unable to turn around and follow him.

Since then he had kept to the shadows as much as he could, sticking to pedestrian streets and narrow roads, sometimes clambering through snow-filled gardens to avoid the main traffic routes where the Devil could be waiting in his big jeep.

He felt pretty good as he ambled along the waste ground by the harbour, a Bæjarins Besta hot dog warming his belly along with most of a half-bottle of booze he had been able to cadge from some tourists, who seemed to hold on to their cash less tightly than the locals, who were themselves undoubtedly more giving when they went abroad. There was something about travel that made people generous. He remembered that from his own time in Denmark. He wished the city library would stay open longer in the evenings, as he wanted to go straight there and find a book of pictures of Denmark so he could recall that time of his life. Denmark was just one big garden where everything that sprouted from the ground was edible. The delightful girl he had followed there lived in the countryside, where she taught him to pick apples from the trees and find roots called artichokes that they cooked with the fish he pulled effortlessly from the stream every morning. What was odd was that he had been about to be on his way back to Denmark ever since he had returned from there, so many years ago he had given up counting.

Somehow or other he had found himself living from one moment to another; time became a roundabout on which one day was like the next one, which always felt the same as the one before. He and Ari had always been on their way back, about to escape the temporal roundabout. He was on his way to Denmark, and Ari on his way back home.

He had now made his way all the way down to the Grandi district. There was an acquaintance down here who had an old net store where he was sure he'd be allowed to take a nap. He walked along the quayside, looking down at the boats and the still water, in which the lights of the city on the far side of the harbour were reflected. The street lights seemed sharply defined in the frosty air, while the Harpa concert hall looked gloomy and forbidding, its lights facing the other way, towards the city. The light in the glass that faced Grandi was a reflection, as if the building was part of the sea, a kind of iceberg that had just broken free from the land. Through the dark mirror of the glass, though, he could make out the line of yellow light at the top of the restaurant where the smart set dined and drank.

Pétur glanced behind him as he heard a car approach, but it wasn't the black car so he didn't worry about it. His leg was killing him after all that walking, running and climbing over fences. He'd find a box or a bale of net to support it when he reached his pal's store. He took out the half-bottle and was about to glug down what was left, but decided against it as it could be payment for shelter. Those who had a place to lay your head were normally more willing if there was a drop of something to share.

'Pétur!'

The call came from behind him, and he felt the chill along his whole spine, like snow down your neck that melts and slithers all the way down your back. He turned and found himself looking into the eyes of the Devil himself. It hadn't been enough to watch out for a black car, and he hadn't realised that the Devil could wear a disguise. He had popped up from one of those little rental cars that tourists ran around in. This one was an innocent pearl white.

The Grandi quayside was dark and there wasn't much life in the district at this time of day, so there was no point calling for help. His leg wasn't going to let him run anymore; at any rate, not quickly enough to escape the Devil's clutches.

Sunday

105

While he never touched coffee himself, he knew how to make it good and strong. A spoonful for each cup and one for the pot, as his mother had taught him. By now the coffee had probably been in the jug too long, even though it wasn't yet seven o'clock, as he hadn't been able to find a Thermos and hadn't wanted to disturb the family upstairs by rooting through the kitchen cupboards. He hadn't been able to get back to sleep after the message from the police had reached him, and he had decided that Úrsúla would need a decent cup of coffee once he had given her the news.

He felt a stab in his guts when he heard footsteps on the stairs. He took a deep breath and focused his mind on the flow of hot air from his nostrils and over his upper lip. This calmed him, and he stood up as Úrsúla appeared in the kitchen. He poured coffee into a cup and handed it to her.

'I have bad news,' he said. 'Pétur was found dead in the harbour last night.'

Úrsúla swayed, putting out a hand to the worktop to support herself, and dropped onto a barstool. She still had the cup in her hand, and she didn't seem to have noticed that some of the contents had spilled onto the table. Gunnar picked up a cloth and wiped the surface clean.

'At the moment it's not known if he drowned, or died of other causes. There are marks on his body consistent with having been in a fight.'

Úrsúla nodded and looked thoughtfully down at the worktop.

'So it's too late to try and get hold of him,' she muttered.

There was a depth of regret in her voice, and Gunnar understood how significant this had to be for her. The man who had been with her father when he died, finally silenced and gone, and with him the knowledge of what had really taken place in that cell all those years ago.

'Isn't it strange that he should lose his life right now?' she added, subdued and slumped on the stool.

'I don't know,' Gunnar said. 'I don't know what to think. The cops said that he was well known for getting into all kinds of rucks with people, so maybe it was an accident. Maybe he fell into the water. Maybe the marks on the body are from before last night. Maybe he was in a fight earlier in the day and took his own life by jumping in the water. It's difficult to tell.'

Úrsúla made no reply, but slumped even further down on the stool. Gunnar didn't know what he ought to do or say. He placed a cautious hand on her back and muttered something about how sorry he was. His insignificant words of sympathy seemed to break the dam, as she suddenly broke into loud sobs.

He had the feeling that her tears weren't for the dead homeless man, but more for his lot in life; and not just for his life but for another that had been similar. He felt that Úrsúla wept for her father.

106

Marita had read through the paperwork the police had left with her three times, and some of it a fourth time, but she still failed to understand how her sweet boy could have put such vile things into words. Where had this shocking loathing for a woman's body come from? Along the corridor she heard Kiddi's bedroom door open and then the bathroom door open and shut. She got up and fetched breakfast cereal and milk, placing them on the table with a bowl and a spoon. She poured coffee into her mug and waited for the coming conflict.

'Breakfast!' she called when she heard the bathroom door open, and before long Kiddi stood in the kitchen doorway. She had expected to see angry truculence, but instead he stood there, his face puffy with tears.

'I'm sorry, Mum,' he wailed.

She went over and wrapped her arms around him. He shook as he sobbed on her shoulder, and she wondered how long it had been since she had held him like this. His frame, which had so recently been boyish and slim, had bulked out as his shoulders had broadened and his muscles had built up. Physically he was a fully grown man, but this was still her little boy crying on her shoulder.

'I'm not angry,' she said gently, leading him to the kitchen table and sitting him down. 'I'm just shocked at how you were able to fool those men into intending to harm that woman. I can't understand how you could think of doing such a thing. I'm not sure you comprehend what could have happened.'

Kiddi said nothing, but filled his bowl with a generous helping of cereal.

'The woman could have been raped. She could have suffered all sorts of violence,' she continued. 'And those disgusting messages...'

'I was just trying to scare her,' Kiddi said, pouring milk over his cereal.

He began to spoon food into his mouth, and Marita sat and watched as he shovelled it up with a warm feeling of fondness that filled her whole body. In spite of his size, regardless of the fear he had inflicted on a complete stranger, despite the danger he had conjured up, he was still a child. He was still a boy who shovelled breakfast cereal into his mouth as he waited humbly for his mother to scold him.

'I know that in your own way you were trying to help me and your dad,' she said. 'But trying to scare people into not investigating a case is absolutely not the right way to do it. The right thing is to make efforts to prove your innocence...'

Kiddi shoved his bowl away so that milk spilled onto the table.

'Dad isn't as innocent as you think,' he snarled. 'Maybe it's time you figured that out. Even though that fucking whore Katrín Eva isn't telling the truth, Dad isn't the angel you always seem to think he is.'

He bolted from the kitchen and Marita heard the bedroom door slam behind him, as she stood up, feeling her own rage finally boiling over.

All the inner terror that she had again and again gulped down, the anger that had smouldered so long deep in her belly, erupted with a force that took control of her body. She rushed along the corridor after Kiddi and wrenched open the door to his bedroom. A red mist had formed in front of her eyes and the blood pumped through the veins in her head at a fearsome pace.

'Tell me what you mean!' she yelled. 'What do you think you know that I don't? Tell me, everything, all of it. Tell me every fucking thing!'

107

Úrsúla had waited in front of the television for the last ten minutes, as if she could will time to move faster to six-thirty and the news. She had been on edge the whole afternoon, since the announcement of the discovery of the body in the harbour on the three o'clock bulletin. She would have liked to have had Nonni by her side – she missed his composure and comfort – but she was also relieved that he had made sandwiches and taken the children up to the Blue Mountains to go skiing. Up there they would be away from all the media and away from their mother's tension. This was the first time since Thursday that she had been alone in the house. Gunnar had gone home, as the twenty-four-hour guard duty had been lifted because the stalker who had sent the emails had been found. It turned out to have been a youngster – the son of the police officer in Selfoss who had been charged with raping a young girl.

Úrsúla glanced yet again at her watch and turned up the television, even though the adverts were still running. She wasn't able to stay still, so she stood behind the sofa where Kátur had curled up to sleep, her hands on the back, her fingers squeezing the upholstery to ease the tension. Finally, a chubby female newsreader in a pastel outfit began by reading out the main headlines.

'The man found dead in Reykjavík harbour last night was Pétur Pétursson who was homeless. His death is believed to be suspicious. The police are searching for a white Suzuki Swift that was seen on CCTV in the harbour area.'

The newsreader continued with the headlines, something about greenhouse-gas emissions and the Kyoto Protocol, but Úrsúla dropped onto the sofa and stared at the screen without seeing it, and listened without hearing. She was stiff with shock and her nervous energy had vanished. She felt drained, unable to move. At last she took her phone from her trouser pocket.

'I'm on the way back to your place, toothbrush and everything,' Gunnar said as he answered.

'What?'

'Yes, I'm staying with you until Boris has organised security in the street. There's a call out for a protest to be held outside your house tonight.'

Úrsúla felt herself floating on the fringes of consciousness, her mind locked on to the news bulletin playing out in the background.

'What?'

'I'll send you a link to the Facebook group that you can take a look at. I'll be with you in ten minutes.'

His voice sounded flustered, and he ended the call before she was able to answer. She was relieved that he would be there shortly.

That would ease the loneliness and the longing for the security of Nonni's presence. Her phone pinged to announce Gunnar's message. She opened it and tapped on the web link.

It took her to a Facebook group announcing a protest outside her house, with people encouraged to take part and demand her resignation as minister. More than thirty people had confirmed that they would join in, and some had left comments on the page. One of the comments included a picture. It had clearly been taken in the dark, but the ministry car could be easily made out, with her in the front seat:

This picture was taken outside the homeless shelter on Friday, the comment read. *What was she doing there? Time to get that witch out of the Minister's office! #notmyministerofjustice*

Monday

108

'This stuff's supposed to be good for your hair, isn't it?' Úrsúla asked as she leaned over the wash basin to rinse the mess of raw egg from it. Her feeble attempt at humour seemed to bypass Eva, who stood behind her, concern plain on her face.

'Won't you take a shower?' Eva asked, a towel in her hand.

'No. That'll do. Could you look in the cupboard and see if there's a clean blouse in there?'

'Of course there are clean blouses in your cupboard! What kind of an assistant do you think I am?' said Eva as she turned and left the room.

Úrsúla laughed, but as she began to towel her hair dry, she felt her hands tremble. A second before the egg had hit her head someone among the gaggle of protestors outside her house had yelled 'murderer!'

Gunnar had walked her through the crowd and those few steps to the car had felt endless.

Murderer. She had wanted to stop, to look the person who had said it in the eye, to explain; to tell them that she and Gunnar had searched for Pétur at the police station and then at the homeless shelter on Friday so they could talk to him. But this desire gave way to the fear of this throng of angry men, who wanted nothing but the worst for her, and she let Gunnar push her into the back seat. They had sped away from the echoing shouts, Gunnar muttering something under his breath about it being hopeless to try and talk to people under these circumstances, as if he had sensed what she had been thinking.

'Here you are,' said Eva, reappearing in the bathroom with a blouse that Úrsúla was sure she hadn't seen before. She had become used to wearing whatever Eva told her to put on. She would miss it when she was no longer there at her side to deal with all those little daily matters.

'Will you please call a press conference for tomorrow,' she said to Eva. 'And put together a draft of my resignation from office?'

Eva stared at her, her mouth open in surprise.

'You're sure?'

'Yes,' Úrsúla replied. 'I can't remain in office as long as I'm under some kind of suspicion of having murdered Pétur.'

'That's just a few idiots,' she said.

Úrsúla shook her head. 'I have to stand down while an investigation takes place. This photo of me outside the homeless hostel seems to have become a real bone of contention, and there's no point trying to explain that Gunnar and I were looking for Pétur so we could talk to him. It all looks very suspicious, considering the man was found dead shortly afterwards. The neatest thing is for me to step aside so the police have a free hand to pursue an investigation.'

Eva looked at her questioningly, took out her phone and tapped notes into it.

'OK,' she said. 'You'll need to speak to the prime minister, and there are all sorts of issues that need to be dealt with. Where do you want to start?'

'First of all I need to speak to Óðinn,' Úrsúla said. 'Would you send him along to me? But first I'm going outside for a smoke.'

She knew she needed a dose of nicotine to stop her hands from shaking.

*

Stella the cleaner was already on the balcony, finishing a cigarette. But when she saw Úrsúla approaching, she took another one from her pocket and lit up. The temperature had risen above zero and the snow had begun to melt. Water dripped from the roof, pattering on the handrail, which rang like a bell under the beating drops.

'Thanks for your company out here,' Úrsúla said. 'This is my last day. I'll be resigning tomorrow.'

It was as well to practise her speech out here. In the morning she would have to gather the ministry staff in the central meeting area and repeat it.

'What?' Stella said. 'Because of the homeless guy and all that?'

'Yes,' Úrsúla confirmed. 'First I was accused of trying to get hold of his medical records without permission, then of having him locked up without reason, and now it's being insinuated that I've actually killed him. You hear that?'

She held a finger to her ear, indicating that Stella should listen. The mutter of protestors' chants could be heard by the main entrance around the corner.

'But that's crazy!' Stella said, her vehemence taking Úrsúla by surprise. 'Nobody believes that. That's just bullshit. You mustn't resign.'

'I don't have a choice,' she said. 'It's pretty much impossible to be in a worse position than having the insinuation of murder hanging over you.'

'But you can't resign!' Stella said in desperation. 'I can help you. I'll do everything I can.'

Úrsúla stubbed out her cigarette and dropped the butt into the can they used as an ashtray. The young woman's earnestness genuinely took her by surprise, and it warmed her heart. She spread her arms and hugged her close.

'You've already helped me a lot,' she said. 'It's been lovely to share smoke breaks with you.'

She planted a kiss on Stella's cheek and stepped back inside. She hoped the rest of the staff wouldn't take her departure so personally.

'Is Óðinn here?' she asked Freyja on the way back to her office.

'No,' Freyja replied. 'He's on holiday in Spain.'

Úrsúla was brought up short.

'I wasn't told he was taking any holiday,' she said.

Freyja coughed gently, and Úrsúla knew there was no point applying any pressure to her. Undoubtedly it made little difference that ministers came and went. Freyja would always be first and foremost one of Óðinn's staff. The permanent secretary was just that – permanent – while ministers stayed for a little while, or, as in her case, a very little while.

'He must have forgotten to let you know,' Freya said. 'It was booked ages ago.'

She put her hand cautiously under her carefully lacquered hair and adjusted it upwards, as if the lie had displaced it. This was at least one member of the ministry's staff who would hardly miss her – and who she wouldn't miss either.

109

Stella didn't bother to clock out as she left, but that didn't matter. She wasn't going back to work there. She was too upset to figure out which bus routes would take her to the TV station, so she ran up to Hverfisgata and flagged down a taxi.

Once she arrived at the studio, she asked for Gréta at reception and was shown into the station's newsroom. It wasn't lunchtime yet, but it looked like Gréta was already working her way through a packed lunch at her desk while she peered distractedly at the screen in front of her.

'*Hæ*,' she said in surprise as Stella greeted her, and seemed even more surprised when Stella asked if they could talk somewhere private. 'I'm drowning in work—' she began to explain, but Stella interrupted.

'This is a work thing. Big news,' she said. 'The minister of the interior is resigning tomorrow.'

Gréta quickly got to her feet and motioned for her to follow her into a room with a long conference table and chairs.

'What did you say?' Gréta asked as she sat down. 'How do you know?'

Stella began to recount her story, but then decided that she would need some assurance that she would be able to get out into the open what needed to be said.

'I'm not saying any more unless I'm interviewed and can tell the truth in my own words,' she said.

'What do you mean by that?' Gréta asked and gazed at her with interest.

Stella felt the glow flow through her. She felt a kind of warmth when Gréta looked at her in that way, as if right now she was important. This was the look of concentrated energy that Gréta sent out to TV screens across the whole country when she looked into the camera and read the news.

Stella couldn't help opening up to her and was barely halfway through the tale of the creepy journalist who had bought the bags of ministry rubbish, and how the permanent secretary had been in his car, when Gréta stood up and asked her to wait a moment. She left briefly and returned with a grey-haired man she introduced as the news editor.

'I want to try to save the minister by admitting my part in all this,' Stella said.

But he shook his head. 'I think she's beyond saving,' he said, but sat down nevertheless.

'Úrsúla is having an affair with a creep of a journalist called Thorbjörn, but he buys her waste paper from me so he can write about all kinds of stuff that's taken out of context. And I believe the permanent secretary asked him to do it – or at least is controlling all this – because I saw him get out of Thorbjörn's car. He was yelling at him, telling him that he hadn't done as he had asked.'

Stella was desolate, struggling to pull together what she wanted to say.

'You mean Óðinn Jónsson, the permanent secretary?' Gréta asked.

Stella nodded. 'Yes,' she said. 'Don't you think all this sounds like some sort of conspiracy?'

Gréta and the news editor went out into the corridor and stood there for a while, whispering. Then Stella heard him say 'OK' in a loud voice before walking away.

While the sound technician fitted her with a microphone for the interview, Gréta brought her a cup of coffee.

'You know this is going to cost you your job, don't you?' she said, and Stella nodded. She knew, but hoped that her confession would do something to help Úrsúla avoid having to resign.

Stella had no great understanding of politics, but a journalist buying the contents of the minister's waste paper bin had to have some significance, especially when the website he worked for began publishing reports about the homeless guy, which seemed to be a sensitive subject. Plus there had to be a reason the permanent secretary had been talking to the very same journalist.

She would have preferred to be elsewhere. But if her story could do anything to make up for the damage she had done to Úrsúla by selling her waste paper, then it was worth the shame and the loss of her job.

She drank her coffee while the makeup artist finished her work, and noticed Gréta watching her closely. Maybe she was watching her being made up, but Stella felt that behind her piercing gaze was some kind of disdain. Somehow their roles had been reversed. She had a fantasy of Gréta fixed in her mind, made up of her bulky body, heavy perfume and weighty breasts. But now it seemed that for the first time Gréta saw Stella for what she really was: unremarkable scum.

110

For the first time in many months Marita felt she could see clearly. The mist that had clouded her mind when the whole matter had begun, and which she had hardly noticed, had now lifted. Maybe she had just needed to do all that crying to clear her mind. She needed to cry and scream. She had screamed in the living room and the kitchen. She had screamed at Kiddi, and later on she had screamed into her pillow long into the night.

She had packed for Klemmi. He had a whole suitcase of clothes that had gone with him to the Faroes, but now she had filled another case with clothes that had been on the large size for him when he had left, along with some toys and books. She had packed many of her own belongings in the two largest cases they had, as she also needed to take outdoor clothing and shoes with her. She went over to Kiddi's door and tapped gently.

'How's it going?' she asked, and he sighed. He sat hunched over the desk with a hand holding his chin and stared at a sheet of paper that looked to Marita to still be blank.

'Can you help me with this?' he asked yet again.

She shook her head. 'I'm not the one who needs to apologise to Úrsúla Aradóttir,' she said. 'I haven't done her any harm. You're the one who has frightened and threatened her, not me. And that's why you're going to send her a written apology, even if it takes you a month.' Kiddi sighed deeply and scratched his tousled head. 'It's not just so that she's more likely to accept a settlement and you get away without a sentence, but because it's good for your soul. It's so you recognise what you've done,' she said, placing her hands on his shoulders, bending over and kissing his cheek. 'It's simply not acceptable for my sons to be women-haters,' she added.

Kiddi snorted. 'They're called misogynists, Mum,' he said.

She smiled, left his room and went over to her own. It was as if the previous day had also brought Kiddi some relief. Maybe the screams and the tears had lifted a stone from his heart; and he had plenty to shed tears over. Marita hadn't known that he had been so fond of Katrín Eva. In love with her, he had said, head over heels. But all Katrín Eva saw was his father.

Marita looked around the bedroom and wondered which of the things in there she would want to keep. She came to the conclusion that there was nothing she wanted, neither the vase on the chest of drawers that she had paid far too much for, nor the painting Jónatan had given her for her fortieth birthday. All these things were bound up with the bedroom where Jónatan had lain beside her, whispered sweet words to her, and acted as if a few months ago he hadn't done something that had snatched away the foundations of her existence. It could all be left behind in the past. The whole room smelled of betrayal, or rather, some kind of revulsion, because betrayal alone would have been easier to bear. In reality, she wished that he had simply betrayed her, as men do. That would have been normal, almost to be expected, and at least something that she could have coped with.

'I came home that evening,' Kiddi had said. 'I came home and went into the living room. I saw the old man on top of Katrín Eva, and he was fucking her. And the whore was crying because she already regretted it, she should have known fucking better...'

That was as far as he had got before Marita slapped him, hard.

'Women shouldn't cry when they fuck,' she yelled, not knowing whether she should speak in Icelandic or Faroese to make herself clear, so that he would understand without question and the message would be imprinted on his consciousness for the rest of his life.

'Really what you're telling me is that your father raped Katrín Eva.'

111

Úrsúla switched on the lamp and scanned her desk. This would be her last afternoon here, as in the morning she would collect the few personal items she had brought to her office during her time at the ministry. A draft of the press release that Eva had written, outlining her resignation, was contained in a couple of neat sheets of paper in front of her, along with notes for what she would say at tomorrow's press conference. She had also put yellow sticky notes on some of the files she would be leaving behind.

On the folder of South Coast Highway documents she had written *This is lethal! Call me. Best, Úrsúla*. She was going to be here for her successor, to warn him or her of the hazards. There was just one folder left on her desk and this was the one she wanted to finish herself.

'Hello, Rósa,' Úrsúla said as the girl's mother answered the phone. 'I have an idea that I'd like you and your daughter to consider. It states in the report that Jónatan gave Katrín Eva an unusually large amount of money that night, much more than he normally paid for babysitting. Even his wife corroborates that.'

'That's right.'

'I'd like to point out that buying sexual services from a minor is a punishable offence.'

There was silence. Úrsúla waited for a while, listening, and coughed gently to remind the woman that she was still on the line.

'You mean that I should have my daughter be branded the town whore?'

There was a resignation in her voice, a flatness that had replaced the usual burning anger.

'It's something to consider. Sexual offences that seem most likely to make their way through the justice system concern purchasing sex. So there's at least a probability that the man would receive a sentence. If it works out, it wouldn't exactly be justice.

But it would go some way towards it. At any rate, he wouldn't be able to serve any longer as a police officer.'

Úrsúla ended the call by telling the girl's mother once again how painful it was that she had not been able to keep the promise she had made to her on her first day in office.

Her desk was now clear, except for the slim green folder she had brought with her to work, and which she would take home with her. This was the folder Gunnar had given her containing all the documents related to her father's death. She had eyed it, and held it in her hands for some time, but hadn't trusted herself to open it. But now, as she finally did so, she was astonished. Her heart skipped a beat and she gasped.

Could it be true? She stared at the sheet of paper in front of her with a cold flash of understanding. In her life, she had experienced only a few such moments, when all the threads came together, leading to a conclusion that had previously evaded her. This piece of paper would explain so much, and maybe lead to some kind of justice after all. She took a picture of the report and sent it to Boris with a message. She was considering calling him to follow this up when Eva swept into her office, a look of something approaching desperation on her face.

'Úrsúla, evening news!'

She said nothing more, but fussed with the little television on the wall, her hands trembling as she handled the remote control.

'That's our cleaner, isn't it?' Úrsúla said in surprise as the picture finally appeared.

Her understanding was even slower to take shape. It seemed that time had suddenly slowed down. Úrsúla noticed that darkness had fallen outside and that her office was dim; she hadn't switched on the main lights, only the desk lamp. These were the details that registered on her consciousness as her heart began to hammer in her chest.

'It's Stella isn't it – who cleans?' Úrsúla asked again.

'Úrsúla, she...' Eva was clearly in distress. 'She's saying that a journalist, clearly Thorbjörn from *Vefpressan*, has been buying the ministry's waste paper from her, and that she saw Óðinn talking to him in a car outside the building, and that she believes that this journalist has had ... an intimate relationship with you.'

The question was there in Eva's voice, but Úrsúla was unable to give her an answer. She was unable to explain, unable to remain there any longer. She had to get home, to Nonni.

112

Eva had sent Gunnar a message, asking him to drive Úrsúla home, but instead she had ignored Eva's calls, run through the ministry building, down to the entrance and rushed out and across Arnarhóll. Úrsúla hurried along, her coat flapping, but she didn't feel cold as a thaw had set in and the streets were awash with treacherous slush. She made her way through the centre of the city without registering her surroundings, her thoughts too disturbed to see the details as she hurried along Hólatorg, beside the graveyard, and tried again to call Nonni. He didn't answer. She hoped he hadn't seen the news, that he had taken the children swimming or that he was watching some comedy with them with his phone switched off, or that he was cooking and the music in the kitchen drowned out the sound of his phone ringing. There was nothing unusual about him not answering the phone, so it didn't have to be a bad sign. How often had she desperately tried to call home to let Nonni know that she was fine – to let him know that she wasn't the Médecins Sans Frontières member of staff who had been in isolation after being infected with Ebola? That she was unhurt after the shells had hit the ground just outside the refugee camp in Syria? Now she could feel the hot tears running down her cheeks at the thought that he might have heard on the news that she had betrayed him, that she had broken the single most important promise she had ever made; the promise she had made to him.

The pavement along their street was packed with a deep layer of ice that made it impassable, so there was no choice but to step out into the road and walk along the tyre tracks where the rising temperature had sliced through the ice and exposed the road surface below. This groove in the ice had become a river of melt-water running down the street and she could feel the icy water leaking into her shoes. She paid it no attention; those shoes could go to hell and her toes could freeze from her feet for all she cared, as long as she could get home to Nonni before he could hear the news somewhere else of what she had done.

She stumbled over the bank of solid snow and onto the path outside their house, which was clear because Gunnar always carefully shovelled and salted it. Her fingers trembled with a mixture of confusion and cold as she fumbled to slot the key into the lock, unwilling to use the doorbell in case the children were at home. She needed to go directly to Nonni, to shut the two of them away, to try and find the right words to explain this to him. She had to find words to tell him that she loved him, and only him; that she knew this now, and that she felt more clearly than ever before that he and the children meant more to her than anything. Thorbjörn had been some kind of terrorist attack on herself, a horrible mistake.

The lights were on in the kitchen but nobody was there. Everything was quiet. A fillet of fish lay on the worktop, still in its packet, and next to a chopping board, a knife and some chopped onion stood half a glass of white wine. She went up the stairs and looked into the empty rooms. Ari must have been playing with Lego, judging by the bricks that were scattered across the floor, and in Herdís's bedroom a pile of clothes lay on the bed, as if she had been in the middle of one of her occasional sessions of trying everything on, and had left in a hurry. In the bathroom the children's toothglasses were empty, and only her toothbrush stood in the glass that she and Nonni shared.

She went back downstairs, went into the living room and sat

on the sofa in the darkness. Nonni had undoubtedly taken the children with him to his mother's, or even to a hotel if the humiliation had been too crushing. He had even taken Kátur with them. She missed the dog terribly. If he had been at home, by now he would have been in her arms or sitting at her feet, gazing at her with love in his eyes and waiting for her to pick him up. Her mind was numb, and if she hadn't known better she would have said that her heart was bleeding, as if a hole had been ripped in it. She kicked off her shoes and a pool of water formed on the floor around them. This was the beautiful, polished wooden floor on which Nonni had strictly forbidden shoes or playing with a ball. All of a sudden, that insignificant detail took on a new importance. She had dirtied what had been clean. She had desecrated what they had built up. She couldn't understand what had been going on in her mind. What had she been looking for with Thorbjörn? The Thorbjörn who had used her; the Thorbjörn who had triggered a passion in her, and then betrayed her.

She blinked, trying to force tears, needing to unburden herself and seeking the clarity of thought that would follow weeping. But she couldn't allow herself that. She had no right to cry. She had given up that privilege. It was more painful to betray than to be betrayed.

She was startled by movement behind her, and leaped to her feet.

'What are you doing here?' she gasped, her thoughts swinging between astonishment and terror.

113

'What's the matter?' Gunnar asked. Eva spoke so fast into the phone that he wasn't able to piece together what she was saying.

'Didn't you see the evening news?' she asked, and he said that he hadn't. He was bathed in sweat in the changing room at the gym, and had noticed four missed calls from Eva when he checked his phone. He'd immediately called her back.

'Úrsúla rushed out in a terrible state. I'm sure she was going home on foot to see Nonni, but she's not picking up the phone. And now I don't know if she's at home or not. I went to her place and the lights are on, but nobody's answering the door. I'm really worried. You have a key, don't you?'

'Yes,' Gunnar said. He held the phone to his ear as he pulled off his training gear. He'd have to stay sweaty. 'I'll check on her.'

'Please. And go inside. I hope everything's all right. I'm sure they're having a row and that's why nobody's answering the door, so if that's the way it is you'll just have to back out again.'

'Why do you think they're arguing?' Gunnar asked.

'Ach ... shit. The evening news pretty much accused her of having an affair with that Thorbjörn who works for *Vefpressan*, the one who was all over the rape case. Do you know anything about that?'

'No comment,' Gunnar said. 'I'll check up on her.'

He tugged the sweat-damp singlet over his head, dried his armpits and chest with a towel, pulled on his trousers and shirt, threw his training gear in his bag and hurried out. It wasn't until he was in the gym's lobby that he decided against going outside barefoot. He paused to pull on his shoes. The melting slush in the car park was filthy and had to be full of salt after months of ice on the roads.

The car hurtled along Sæbraut towards the city centre, and as most of the evening rush-hour traffic was over, he made good time. He took the most direct route past the East Quay at the harbour, up along Vesturgata, put his foot down along Garðastræti and headed into the western part of town. He parked on the pavement next to the hydrant below Úrsúla's house, hoping that no smart passer-by would decide to snap a picture of the badly parked ministry car and post it on the internet.

He rang the bell and hammered hard on the door. When

nobody answered he took out his key, gently opened it and stepped inside, listening for any sound. The house was silent, so he called out.

'Hello! Úrsúla!' He slipped off his shoes, shut the door behind him and went towards the kitchen. 'Úrsúla? It's Gunnar. Just checking you got home safely.'

There was no reply.

'Hello? Anyone home?' he called as he went into the living room. It was deserted, so he continued to the kitchen, where it looked as if someone had been interrupted in the middle of preparing a meal.

Úrsúla sat there on a tall stool at the breakfast bar, fear etched deeply into her face. It took Gunnar a moment to wrench his eyes from her and to realise that she wasn't the only one in the kitchen.

114

Marita's phone began to ring the moment she switched it on outside the airport at Vágur. There were at least five missed calls from Jónatan. She hadn't wanted to answer him until she had arrived back home in the Faroe Islands. Kiddi and her mother were stacking cases in the back of the car, so she took a few paces away from them before she hit the reply button. She put the phone to her ear, but she couldn't make out what Jónatan was saying. His furious gabble was no more understandable than the fuzzy sound of a badly tuned radio. She looked up at the hillsides and then down at the flat land by the airport building and felt a relief to be rid of the snow. A fall of snow never lasts long in the Faroes.

'Kiddi saw you,' she said to stop Jónatan's tirade in mid-flow, as he demanded to know what she was doing travelling to the Faroes in the middle of winter without letting him know. 'Kiddi came home, saw you, and left.'

No further explanation was needed about what, where or when. He knew exactly what she meant.

'I'm going to stay here for a few weeks while I think things over,' she said, although that wasn't true. She had no intention of returning.

'We could make a new start,' he said. The irritation over her sudden departure had vanished from his voice, replaced by a desperate tone. 'All that legal stuff is over now, so we could put a real effort into sorting out our problems.'

'I don't need to sort out problems,' she said, not even trying to hide the coldness in her voice. 'But you definitely have stuff you need to work on.'

'Don't be like that,' he said, and Marita couldn't make out whether the touch of impatience she could hear in his voice was anger or frustration. 'Are you talking about whatever it was that Kiddi *thought* he saw? I was teasing the girl; we were just playing the fool. He must have just misunderstood things.'

'Katrín Eva's lawyer called me today before I got on the flight. She asked if I would be sticking to my testimony that Katrín Eva had an unusually large amount of money when she left that evening, and I said I would. I remember thinking at the time that you certainly paid her generously.'

'What are you talking about? What's this bullshit, Marita?'

'Rósa is bringing a case against you: purchasing sexual services from a minor,' Marita said.

There was a silence on the line, and then Jónatan sighed deeply.

'You have to be joking...' he said.

'No,' Marita said. 'This is a long way from being over, and I don't want to be anywhere near when the next storm breaks. You can pay the price of your own misdeeds.'

'Marita,' Jónatan said, and now his voice was beseeching. 'Marita, this will all be sorted out. I have a guy on the inside at the ministry. It's someone who was with me when I joined the police. It'll blow over soon enough, woman. Then we can start all over again, bring Klemmi home, and maybe we can have that trip to the sunshine that you were talking about.'

Marita cleared her throat to stop him, and so that she could get a word in.

'Jónatan.'

'Yes?'

'You can go to hell.'

She ended the call, set her phone to silent and walked over to the car, where Kiddi had squeezed himself into the back seat with the luggage and her mother sat behind the wheel, ready to drive them to Tórshavn.

Marita took a deep breath of the damp air, absorbing the green-ness around her that warmed her heart. It was remarkable that despite being only a little further south than Iceland, the Faroe Islands were always dressed in green: light green in summer, grey-green in winter.

115

The relief at the sound of Gunnar's voice calling her name was so overwhelming that she almost called out. But Óðinn, who towered over her like a giant as she sat on the stool, put a finger to his lips to tell her to keep quiet.

'Shh,' he whispered, and backed into a corner of the kitchen, seeming to hope that if they kept quiet, Gunnar would retreat. But Úrsúla knew him better than that. If Gunnar had come looking for her, then he wouldn't leave until he had searched the house from top to bottom.

Óðinn stood as still as stone, and she saw his eyes flicker from side to side as he listened to Gunnar's footsteps go from the en-trance hall, along the corridor and into the living room. Her heart began to race as she heard him approach the kitchen, and when she saw his face appear in the doorway, she let out a loud, instinctive sigh that forced itself out of her throat. She felt herself trembling, but when she looked down at her hand on the kitchen worktop, it seemed motionless.

'What's going on?' Gunnar asked.

Úrsúla sniggered hysterically, her voice strangled. She hardly recognised it herself – the laugh seemed so at odds with the palpable tension in the air. Úrsúla coughed and regained her voice.

'Óðinn came here to ask me to do certain things,' she said slowly, searching for words that would explain things to Gunnar without provoking Óðinn, who seemed about to erupt. 'I told Óðinn that I wanted him to go now, that we could talk things over later, but he wasn't agreeable and that's why I'm sitting here.'

Gunnar quickly grasped the situation and nodded, just as slowly. It was as if they were both held back, so that their movements were hampered and speech had been slowed right down.

'I understand,' Gunnar said in a relaxed voice that had an everyday tone, as if he was listening with one ear to something else that was mildly interesting.

He took one step into the kitchen, and then another, so that it was clear he was placing himself between Óðinn and Úrsúla.

'I think you should go out to the car, Úrsúla,' he said, still in the same measured voice as he took one more step.

Óðinn seemed to realise what was happening, as determination replaced the indecision in his eyes and he leaped forward, pushing Gunnar aside so that he lost his balance for a moment. Before Úrsúla could move from the stool Óðinn had snatched a handful of her hair, making her wince, and a strong smell of onion filled her senses as she saw the carving knife had vanished from the chopping board, leaving the pile of chopped onion that Nonni had obviously intended to have with the fish that still lay on the table.

Óðinn stood behind Úrsúla, and she felt the cold blade of the knife against her neck. She wondered if death would come quickly if he cut her throat, or if the blade would have to be higher up to open an artery. It was sharp, regularly and carefully steeled, like all Nonni's kitchen knives.

Óðinn loosened his grip on her hair and took hold of her head, but his hands were so slippery with sweat that they slipped from her forehead as he tried to hold her at the same time as he wielded the knife.

'Relax, Óðinn,' Gunnar whispered. 'Let's not get carried away, eh? Let's calm down and think things over? OK?'

Gunnar stood perfectly still opposite them, and Úrsúla found herself thinking that even if Óðinn were to cut her throat, he wouldn't get Gunnar as well. He would hardly be a match for someone so powerful. She felt some relief at the thought that someone would be left to tell her children how she had lost her life, to recount exactly what had happened in her last few moments. Gunnar would be the witness who accompanied her in those final seconds of life. It was odd that she had never before thought this through. She had never considered that the children could be left with the same deep-felt uncertainty, the same gap left by the loss of a parent in circumstances that could not be accounted for. In Liberia she had only thought that Nonni would be devastated if she were to die of Ebola; she had never imagined that it would make much of a difference to the children.

They had become so accustomed to being alone with Nonni, she had always imagined that their lives would hardly change much without her. But now she suddenly saw everything in a new light. Her father had been absent from home for so long before he died, but all the same, the sorrow of his passing had been the single most momentous event of her life. Her compulsion and desire to create order where there had been chaos, to do what she could to help people in need, more than likely had its roots in her father's death. Because she couldn't save her father, she had spent her life giving aid to others.

Probably this was what the proximity of death did to people. It opened up an understanding of the law of cause and effect, so that they saw their lives pass by as if projected on a screen. She opened her eyes and little by little emerged from her own deep thoughts as Gunnar's voice purred, slowly and reassuringly.

116

'We want the same thing, Óðinn,' Gunnar said calmly. 'We both want Úrsúla unharmed. I know you didn't come here to do her harm, did you?'

Úrsúla felt a shiver pass through Óðinn's body as he stood close behind her, and she could hear his fast, shallow breaths.

'It won't be long before they find out that the car seen by the harbour was rented by the ministry,' he hissed, his voice taut and his breaths strained, as if coming with an effort. 'Úrsúla either needs to stop the investigation or say that she asked me to rent the car for her, that she had been searching for Pétur so she could talk to him, and he fell into the water. That way it can be explained as accidental. He's just as dead either way.'

Gunnar stepped to one side and Óðinn stiffened.

'Stay still!' he snapped, and Úrsúla could feel the blade sting as it grazed her skin. A drop of blood ran down her neck to her chest.

Gunnar raised his hands. 'I won't move an inch,' he said. 'I'll stay perfectly still. I'm sure there's a way to stop the investigation. Don't you think so, Úrsúla?'

Gunnar winked, indicating that she should lie – play along and say what Óðinn wanted to hear, so as to not infuriate him.

The cut to her neck stung like a burn, and the pain of it sent a wave of anger through her. She bit her lip to stop herself from shouting out loud. But then a moment of thankfulness seized her – the knife hadn't gone deeper – and with that she took her decision. She wasn't going to play along and take part in Óðinn's fantasy.

'It's over, Óðinn. Whatever happens now, it's over.'

'That's right,' Gunnar added. 'It's only going to make things worse if Úrsúla is hurt...'

He was clearly still working on keeping Óðinn calm, but Úrsúla interrupted him. The burst of adrenaline rushing through her demanded a release.

'You won't be working at the ministry ever again, Óðinn! I've already seen through you. I saw something today that made everything clear. Jónatan: does that name ring any bells?'

A look of shocked terror appeared on Gunnar's face, and Úrsúla could feel Óðinn's anguish as the knife pressed harder against her neck.

'What do you think you know?' he hissed.

'I think I know that you beat my father to death in a cell at the police station all those years ago and you got a young colleague, Jónatan Kristjánsson, to cover it up for you.'

'I ought to shut you up—' Óðinn began, until Gunnar yelled at him.

'Then you need to shut me up as well!'

'And Boris,' Úrsúla said. 'I sent him a memo today instructing him to look into all communication between you and Jónatan going back to when the rape charge was raised. I've no doubt he'll find a trail of messages and calls between you.'

Úrsúla felt Óðinn's body sag behind her and the hand holding the knife dropped so that the blade now hovered over her chest.

'I've known for years this would come back to haunt me,' he said, his voice slow and dark. Úrsúla thought she caught a sob as he spoke. 'You can do the right thing your whole life, work hard and try to do better. But when the past catches up with you, all that's worth nothing.'

'You mean when Jónatan raised his head after so long and started blackmailing you into suppressing the rape charge against him,' Úrsúla said.

'He was calling in an old debt, as he had every right to,' Óðinn said. 'But when you started digging into all this and demanding it be followed up, he was scared stiff. He started calling all the time, going wild, and expecting me to work some kind of miracle.'

'It's over, Óðinn. Now it's time for you to let me go,' Úrsúla said, hoping that the tension she could feel draining out of him was an indication that he was about to capitulate.

But instead Óðinn stiffened and moved his arm to hold Úrsúla in a headlock. Her chin rested in the crook of his arm and the smell of onion from the blade gave way to the stronger odour of sweat.

'You have influence with Thorbjörn,' he whispered. 'You can call him and let him spin a story on all this. *Vefpressan* takes the lead and all the other media follow.'

'You mean the Thorbjörn you were seen talking to outside the ministry? Didn't you see the news earlier? The cleaner, Stella, saw you getting out of his car and said it was obvious you had been arguing. What were you and Thorbjörn plotting?'

'We've both been plotting with Thorbjörn – each in our own way. Don't think I haven't noticed,' Óðinn snarled, but before Úrsúla could formulate a reply, she saw Gunnar step towards them. Óðinn shouted something, and then Gunnar leaped and all three of them fell to the floor.

She heard the men struggling beside her as she fought to catch her breath, but she was unable to because of the pain of the knife deep in her chest.

She didn't feel fear, but as she lost consciousness she was thankful that Nonni and the children were elsewhere, somewhere safe.

117

The knife clattered out of Óðinn's grasp as he fought back, and as he tried to reach for it, Gunnar landed a punch to his face. The blow left Óðinn dazed. He looked around, gathering his wits, so Gunnar made to pin him down, but he twisted away and was on his feet with surprising agility and looked ready to make a break for the door. Gunnar threw himself into a tackle that brought Óðinn to his knees and a moment later Gunnar had him in an arm lock. Óðinn was heavily built and a powerful man, but was left helpless as Gunnar held him, putting his weight behind him so that Óðinn fell to the floor. With one arm holding Óðinn down, Gunnar felt for his belt and the handcuffs that should have been there – but they had been taken from him by the police after the altercation with Pétur.

He fumbled for his phone, but it had fallen out of his pocket during the struggle, and he hadn't put on the hands-free set after leaving the gym to hurry to Úrsúla's house. For a moment there was silence in the kitchen, and Gunnar wondered how he could keep Óðinn in check while also finding a phone to call for help. He wasn't sure if it was a moment or longer, as time flashed past with the rush of adrenaline, but gradually his attention was drawn to Úrsúla's regular gasps. *Úrsúla!*

She lay motionless on the floor, silent apart from her unnerving gasps as she fought for breath. He was caught in a quandary. He would either have to release Óðinn to look after Úrsúla, in the hope that he would make a run for it instead of attacking her a second time, or else hold Óðinn down and hope for some miracle that would bring help. He released his grip on Óðinn, who scrambled to his feet and vanished through the door, and a second later Gunnar heard the front door slam shut behind him.

The holder for the home phone was empty, so the phone itself had to be somewhere else. He wasn't going to waste valuable time searching for his mobile. So, dizzy with the exertion, he supported himself against the furniture and the door frame and found his way to the front door and pressed the red alarm button. The special unit would be there any minute, armed to the teeth, but Úrsúla also needed an ambulance as soon as possible, so he went outside and ran a few steps along the street to the ministry car. He opened the door, and on his knees in the passenger seat, made a call using the emergency radio.

'Help, now!' he called. 'Ambulance! The minister is injured. I think she has a knife wound and is losing blood.'

He hurried back, fighting to keep his footing on the ice. The GPS locator in the ministry car would ensure that the ambulance would come right to them.

In the kitchen he dropped to his knees beside Úrsúla, looking for the source of the pooling blood that had turned most of her blouse dark red. He found the wound on the right side of her chest. He put his palm over it and pressed. The hissing sound stopped as he closed the wound, but her breathing was irregular and her eyes closed.

The next few minutes passed in fits and starts. He heard the wail of a siren, and before he knew it a paramedic was loosening his hands from Úrsúla's body. He dropped back and sat on the floor, while another of the ambulance crew fixed a drip into her arm and placed an oxygen mask on her face, before they slipped her onto a stretcher and quickly wheeled her out. Then he was sitting on the sofa, telling a detective about what Óðinn had done, and a moment later Boris was there, asking if he knew where Óðinn had gone.

'He's not right in the head,' Gunnar said. 'He's crazy and desperate. If he's not on his way to the airport to get out of the country, then he could be heading for Selfoss.'

'Selfoss?'

'That's right. He might well try and attack a man called Jónatan Kristjánsson. He's the only living witness to a murder that was committed many years ago.'

'We need the hospital to check you out as well,' Boris said.

'The worst of it was having to let the bastard go,' Gunnar muttered.

Boris laughed. 'You did the right thing,' he said. 'You were the perfect person, in the right place at the right time. You saved her life.'

Gunnar smiled, and in spite of the thundering headache that pounded in his head, he felt the satisfaction of having done right. He had done what he was supposed to do. He had made a difference between life and death.

Tuesday

118

Gunnar was more cheerful when he woke up, but he'd had a troubled sleep. Úrsúla had undergone an operation, and Gunnar hadn't been able to relax during the night until he'd found out she was in what the healthcare professionals called a stable condition. He had only minor injuries himself and had come home late in the night from Accident & Emergency, where they had been treated.

He took a shower, put on clean clothes and picked up a box of chocolates for Úrsúla on his way back to the hospital. She was on a general ward, having been discharged from intensive care. The police officer outside her door sat reading a magazine. He was there primarily to keep the media at bay; Óðinn had been picked up the previous evening as he had driven into Selfoss.

Gunnar leaned over Úrsúla in her bed and gave her as much of a hug as he could. There was a drip in her arm and an oxygen feed in her nose, but otherwise she seemed buoyant. She put her arms around him and held him for a long time, patting his back and whispering that it was good to see him. He straightened up and sat down at her bedside, and they looked into each other's eyes for a long, serious, thoughtful moment, until Úrsúla finally smiled.

'It's pretty wonderful to be alive,' she said, and he laughed.

'Has Nonni been in?' he asked.

Úrsúla shook her head. 'He was here last night when I came round after the operation, and I had a call from him earlier. He's not delighted with me right now. With good reason.'

Gunnar reached out and placed a hand on her arm.

'It'll sort itself out,' he said, and Úrsúla was about to reply when there was a knock on the door frame.

'Am I interrupting?' Boris asked, and they both said no at the same time. 'It's luxurious being a minister,' he said. 'Private room and everything. Poor old granny's in the corridor downstairs because there's no room to be found for her anywhere in the hospital.'

'Oh,' Úrsúla said. 'Can't you bring her up here to me?'

Boris grinned and planted a kiss on her cheek.

'Good to see you're all right,' he said in a low voice. 'That was a terrible thing to happen.'

Úrsúla nodded, and Gunnar realised that he had never seen Boris so agreeable. He had always been dry, stiff, decisive, resourceful. But there had never been any warmth to him, until now.

'The situation...' Boris said. 'Óðinn is in custody and will be charged with kidnap and your attempted murder.'

'And what about my father's case?' Úrsúla asked, making an attempt to sit up, as if her interest pivoted on events in the distant past and not her narrow escape the night before.

'Jónatan Kristjánsson has been called in for an interview at the police station tomorrow. That's something I'll be listening in on.'

'Apart from Jónatan apparently making efforts to get important evidence to disappear,' Gunnar said, 'he also put pressure on Óðinn to derail the rape investigation. Óðinn admitted as much last night.'

Úrsúla nodded her agreement. 'And he said he had known for years that this would come back to haunt him,' she said. 'By that he meant my father's death.'

Boris fetched a chair from the corner of the room, dragged it across the bed and sat at Úrsúla's side.

'According to data from the phone companies, Óðinn and Jónatan had been in touch a lot, beginning around six months ago, or shortly after Jónatan was charged with rape. That gives us certain indications, but if neither of them admit it, it'll be difficult to prove. And I'll warn you that opening an old case isn't a simple matter; it's one of the most difficult things to do. More than likely, for your father's case to be reopened, they would both need to admit guilt.'

'And Pétur?' Úrsúla asked. Gunnar heard the note of desperation in her voice. 'Won't Pétur's death be investigated in view of the new information?'

Boris patted the duvet as if to reassure Úrsúla. 'The whole matter will be investigated in light of any new evidence, and the assault on you is the basis for that. When we dig deeper into the reasons for the attack, everything else will come out into the open.'

Úrsúla took a deep breath, winced, and allowed herself to sink back onto the pillow.

'Hell, my chest hurts,' she sighed, and Gunnar realised that he still had a headache. Both of them were pretty rough around the edges, he decided.

'I have something interesting for you,' Boris said to Úrsúla, clearing his throat. 'When we were going through the communications between Óðinn and Jónatan, I came across something else. Strictly speaking, we don't have clearance to look at this, but as I'm being transferred to Europol anyway, I don't really care one way or the other if there's any fallout. I just think you need to see it.' He took a folded sheet of paper from his breast pocket and handed it to her. 'It's an email to Óðinn from the prime minister.'

119

Úrsúla inhaled the outdoor smell of the children's hair. They had both practically thrown themselves onto the bed as soon as they had appeared in her hospital room.

'Isn't your dad with you?' she asked, and they shook their heads.

'No, he's waiting in the car,' Herdís said. 'He said he'd talk to you later in peace and quiet, and that you have some problems that you need to sort out.'

'Are you divorcing?' Ari asked.

Herdís jabbed him with an elbow. 'Don't ask things like that, idiot,' she hissed.

Úrsúla took a deep breath.

'No,' she said. 'I don't think so. At least, I'll do everything I can to put things right. It's been a bit difficult for us to talk to each other recently.' It was a cliché, but it wasn't easy to find the right words to explain the situation to the children. 'But whatever happens, we both still love you.'

'Yeah. Dad said that as well,' Ari said, getting up from the bed. There was a perplexed expression on his face, the one that always appeared when he didn't quite understand what was going on.

'You look better than you did yesterday,' Herdís said, clearly keen to direct the conversation elsewhere, and Úrsúla knew she was doing this to stop herself bursting into tears.

'Thank you, sweetheart,' Úrsúla said, and patted the back of her hand.

The previous evening had been a fog of confusion. She had slept and woken at intervals, and remembered seeing Nonni and the children at her side in the intensive-care unit. There had been so much that she would have liked to say to Nonni, but she'd drifted out of consciousness before she could say anything, and the next thing she knew, a woman in white appeared to take her blood pressure.

'Good morning,' the prime minister announced as he swept into the room with a vast box of chocolates in his hands.

Úrsúla kissed the children and felt a pang of guilt as she saw the disappointment on their faces as they disappeared sadly and silently through the door. They had probably become accustomed to being in second place. She promised herself she would deal with this: give them more of her time and make them a priority over meetings and assignments.

Úrsúla shook herself. Now she would need all the strength she had. She reached for the remote control and lifted the upper part of the bed as far as it would go, pulling herself into as much of a sitting position as the pain in her chest would allow. Then she reached for the sheet of paper Boris had given her and smoothed it out.

'I have a copy of an email,' she said. 'Sent by you to Óðinn, my permanent secretary, in which you ask him to be of assistance in preparing an announcement postponing the South Coast Highway initiative.'

Úrsúla straightened herself in the bed, winced at the wave of pain that shot through her, and read directly from the paper – the words that she had read again and again that morning.

"'...it would be perfect if you could arrange to leak some scandal or other so we can get rid of her well before elections, and so E can establish himself...'"

The hand holding the letter sank down onto the duvet and she glared at the prime minister.

He shuffled awkwardly.

'It seems I've been caught up in one of your famous prearranged series of events,' she said. 'I was supposed to do the shit job, cancel the South Coast Highway and make myself unpopular for doing that. Then Óðinn was going to leak something sensitive so I'd have to resign, and your golden boy Edvard would have a few months before the elections come around to make himself a popular minister.'

The prime minister sighed and sank onto a chair.

'It's politics, Úrsúla,' he said. 'It's nothing personal; just politics.'

'Thank you for this important lesson in the fundamentals of political science.'

The prime minister forced an embarrassed smile, and Úrsúla noticed how blue his eyes were, even though no daylight reached the ward, as dusk had fallen, leaving only the electric light with its yellow tint.

'It's a shame you bet on the wrong horse,' she added. 'Óðinn had everything planned in advance and then lost control of it. The journalist leaked the first juicy piece of information he pulled from the rubbish he had bought – the one about my father and Pétur. That took Óðinn by surprise and it was difficult for him to deal with.'

'What do you want, Úrsúla?' the prime minister asked. 'What was the job you applied for last year and didn't get? Head of the International Development Agency?'

Úrsúla snorted.

'I thought the normal way to do it was to try bribery first, and force next. You do it the other way around.' The prime minister muttered something unintelligible, and to her own amazement, Úrsúla felt some sympathy for him. 'I don't need to set conditions,' she said. 'I'll resign tomorrow for health reasons. That won't take anyone by surprise. It's already all over the news that the permanent secretary stabbed the minister.'

'In that case...' he began, and Úrsúla raised a finger, telling him to keep quiet.

'Yes,' she said. 'I'll blow off the South Coast Highway at the same time.'

120

Looking back, it had been the promise she made that first day in office that had been her downfall. If she hadn't pressured Óðinn to look into the rape charge against Jónatan, then everything would have worked out very differently. On the other hand, the promise she had made had also served to release her from the daze she had been in since coming home.

'The shortest ministerial career on record,' Eva said. 'Two and a half weeks.'

'True,' Úrsúla said. 'And I hadn't even made a start on all the things I was going to do. I haven't even touched immigration, and that was the first thing I had on my list.'

'Like I said, two and a half weeks. Considering everything that's gone on, it's probably no surprise that you don't have any towering achievements behind you.'

'Hmm.'

This was the only thing that Úrsúla regretted about leaving office; the loss of her opportunity to bring about changes to the treatment of those seeking asylum in Iceland.

'Are you sure you want to take responsibility for the South Coast Highway issue?' Eva asked yet again, as if repeating the same question in another guise might elicit a different answer.

'Yes, I want to do that,' Úrsúla said. 'Trust me. You can hold a press call here in the ward. I'll lie in bed and announce that I'm standing down for health reasons, and will let them know that my last act in office is to postpone the South Coast Highway initiative as there are serious failings in the preparatory stages.'

'People will go crazy,' Eva said. 'That's such an open way of putting it.'

'Yes, I know,' Úrsúla said. 'That's why I need you here to make sure the press people know in advance that I'm not answering questions, and this is just a short statement. With me lying here in a hospital bed, they'll have to behave themselves.'

'You're learning fast!' Eva said in delight. 'They'll be so excited to see you and take pictures of you in bed that they'll accept not getting to ask questions.' But the look of concern reappeared on her face. 'You're absolutely, completely sure about the road issue?' she asked. 'You could just leave it. Considering how the PM was planning to manipulate you, he deserves to handle this himself.'

'He would never do it himself,' Úrsúla said. 'Some unsuspecting victim would be persuaded to shoulder responsibility for it. But don't worry about it. The blame will end up where it belongs.'

Eva leaned over her and kissed Úrsúla's forehead.

'I hope it works out,' she muttered. 'I can see you're plotting something.'

'I'm not plotting anything. I'm just thinking of going in new directions. I'm considering applying to work at the homeless shelter.'

'What?'

'The shelter for homeless people. I reckon I owe my father that.'

'The papers will love that,' Eva sighed. '"The Minister and the Bums",' she said, drawing quote marks in the air with her fingers as she imagined the headline.

'That's fine. It raises awareness of the homelessness problem. I've been lying here wondering what kind of aid work I can do that would let me stay at home with Nonni and the children. I need to be there among the people who need help. I'd just wither away if I was doing an office job for the Red Cross. And going back to overseas aid work is more than I can ask Nonni to accept.'

'This is all news to me,' Eva said, shaking her head in disbelief. 'But I can see you're plotting something. This has to be an election stunt, or something.'

'You remember what you said to me when I took the job, Eva?' Úrsúla said. 'About the politics bug? That it's easy to catch but difficult to get rid of? Well, I think I've managed to get away with it.'

She winked at Eva, who looked at her with the same concerned expression on her face.

'The girl came, as I asked her to,' she said at last. 'Shall I show her in?' she asked.

Úrsúla nodded.

121

Stella came into the room shamefacedly, and hesitantly approached the bed, as if she expected Úrsúla to scream at her, or worse.

'Sorry I said that on TV about the journalist guy. Your assistant said that your marriage is wrecked because of it. I didn't even know you were married. I was just trying to help – make up for what I did. It's just wrong that you have to resign because of some shit that leaked because I sold the rubbish. I'm so sorry.'

Úrsúla put out a hand, and Stella hesitated before taking it.

'Your part in all this was quite small. Óðinn is the guilty one. He was manipulating Thorbjörn. He meant for Thorbjörn to pin some sort of scandal on me so I'd have to resign. Thorbjörn had his own methods to get close to me – he used … personal methods, and bought the ministry trash from you. But then he started digging into my father's death, and it all started to go wrong for Óðinn; all that coming to light again was disastrous for him. So your part in all this wasn't a big one. You were caught up in it, like so many others.'

The tears flooded from Stella's brown eyes, and she blinked quickly as if trying to hold them back. Instead they gathered on her long eyelashes and glittered like pearls.

'How are you feeling?' she asked and sniffed hard. 'Are you going to be all right?'

'I'm going to be fine,' Úrsúla said. 'Especially if you can help me with one last thing. That would easily make up for selling the ministry rubbish and blathering on TV.'

'Anything,' Stella said eagerly. 'Tell me what you want me to do.'

Úrsúla cleared her throat.

'I want you to go to your friend at the TV station,' she said.

'You mean Gréta?'

'That's right. Go to Gréta and tell her that you heard me mention that the reason behind the cancellation of the South Coast Highway is Ingimar Magnússon.'

'The government's pulling out of the South Coast Highway?'

'Yes. I'll be announcing it tomorrow, but your friend can be ahead with the news, and if she does her homework well, then she'll understand why I cancelled the initiative.'

'People are so excited about that road…' Stella began and Úrsúla held back a sigh.

'Don't worry about that,' she said sternly, sounding like a strict teacher. 'Just tell Gréta that you heard me say that the initiative was cancelled because of Ingimar Magnússon. She can find the rest of it out for herself. You remember the name?'

'Ingimar Magnússon. Who's that?'

'That doesn't matter. And tell her that you're giving her this as an anonymous source. Nobody else must know that this came from you. OK?'

Stella nodded.

'This is going to help you?' she asked, eyes wide and sincere. 'I don't really want to meet Gréta again. It's a bit awkward between us, but if you reckon it'll help you…'

'It would,' Úrsúla said. 'You've no idea how much this would help me. As the old saying goes: the truth sets you free. And this is the truth. Ingimar Magnússon is the reason I have to cancel the initiative.'

She closed her eyes and gave herself a mental pat on the back. Experienced politicians seemed mostly to weave their own realities, trying to manage facts only as they were presented, but the truth was a powerful weapon; maybe even the most powerful. She imagined how events would play out tomorrow.

The media would publish their pictures of her, injured in her hospital bed as her resignation was announced, and there would be a wave of sympathy that would soon enough turn into astonishment and even fury as the South Coast Highway was cancelled. But when Gréta came up with her scoop, leaked via Stella, people would understand why she had been forced to cancel the road. That way she would be recognised as having ended a venture backed by Ingimar the Terrorist and his friends, all of which stank of corruption.

The government parties would be slaughtered at the next election, and it would take the media and investigating committees months on end to get to the bottom of the road project's financing. It would be just as bad for the prime minister to be seen as corrupt as it would be if he was seen as having been taken for a ride, when it emerged that he hadn't known with whom he was dealing on such a critical matter. On top of which would be all the bitterness left by broken election promises.

It would be tough, but the social democrats would be reinvigorated over the next parliament, even if they were in opposition. To be fair, it would do them good to take something of a beating. It might breathe life into them and a new leader would probably emerge towards the end of the parliamentary term. Maybe what she had said to Eva earlier wasn't entirely true. Perhaps she hadn't got away from politics uninfected.

Stella took a black marker pen from her pocket and took hold of Úrsúla's arm.

'I'll draw you a rune,' she said. 'It's an old Icelandic one that will help you recover and give you power.'

'Yes, please,' Úrsúla said. 'That would be very welcome. I could do with some extra strength.'

She watched as Stella drew fine lines with the marker pen on the inside of her arm, first a cross and then two more lines that made it a star, a circle around the point where the lines all crossed, and then a whole forest of hooks, point and curves that crossed the lines at intervals, so that it soon looked like an ice crystal.

'You put your arm across your chest,' Stella said, demonstrating to Úrsúla. 'And then the magic goes all the way to your heart and it makes you brave and strong.'

'What's this rune called?' Úrsúla asked.

'It's a stave called the Power Giver,' Stella said, drawing the final line and blowing on the ink to dry it.

'Maybe I'll get it tattooed there,' Úrsúla said. 'I'm going to need all the strength I can find.'

She would talk to Nonni. She needed to tell him about Ebola, to explain how the plastic protection suit that had been in between her and suffering had become steadily thicker until it had become armour that nothing could penetrate, neither Syrian high explosives nor the love of her husband and children. She needed to tell him that she had had to face losing first him and then her own life to be able to find, deep in her heart, the truth of just how much she loved them all.

She would recover. She was certain of this now. As she thought of a way of working with homeless people – men such as Pétur and her father – she felt a surge of anticipation. The feeling was warm and unexpected, and she had not had such a sense of expectation for a long time.

The ink on her arm was dry and Stella let go of her wrist. Úrsúla laid her arm against her chest as Stella had told her to, and closed her eyes. Whether it was the rune's power or not, she felt a new energy swell inside her.

ACKNOWLEDGEMENTS

Many thanks to my translator, publisher, editor, designers and all the others who have made it possible for this book to be published in the English language. But first and foremost, thank you to all the women who enter politics with the vision to better our societies. Writing this book made me realise how much courage it takes to do your jobs.

—Lilja Sigurðardóttir